The F

KT-556-695

C334568436

The Flip Side

JAMES BAILEY

PENGUIN BOOKS

PENGUIN BOOKS

UK | USA | Canada | Ireland | Australia
India | New Zealand | South Africa

Penguin Books is part of the Penguin Random House group of companies
whose addresses can be found at global.penguinrandomhouse.com.

First published 2020
001

Copyright © James Bailey, 2020

The moral right of the author has been asserted

Set in 12.5/14.75 pt Garamond MT Std
Typeset by Jouve (UK), Milton Keynes
Printed and bound in Great Britain by Clays Ltd, Elcograf S.p.A.

A CIP catalogue record for this book is available from the British Library

ISBN: 978–1–405–94571–4

www.greenpenguin.co.uk

Penguin Random House is committed to a
sustainable future for our business, our readers
and our planet. This book is made from Forest
Stewardship Council® certified paper.

For Nan and Pap

Winter

I

One hundred and thirty-five metres above London, with one of the most spectacular city views in the world as your backdrop, who could say no?

I now know who could say no.

Jade Toogood.

The girl I had called my girlfriend for four years. The woman who, until just a few moments earlier, I planned on spending the rest of my life with. The person who I am now trapped inside a glass capsule with, 443 feet above ground.

She could say no.

Rather, she had said no.

New Year's Eve. The London Eye. The girl of my dreams. A ring. A future together.

What could possibly go wrong?

I planned everything so meticulously. It was all meant to be perfect. The perfect end to the year, the perfect start to the next. I spent months secretly scouring websites, magazines and shops, looking at rings, thinking of ways to ask, waiting for the right moment. It was only when Jade mentioned how much she wanted to go on the London Eye that I settled on it for the chosen place. The venue for the story we would repeat over and over again to our friends, family and future grandchildren.

The glossy brochure advertising the 'Proposal Package' certainly sold it – if you ignore the exorbitant cost, what could be more romantic than hiring a private capsule? The pages were full of joyous couples smiling, laughing, kissing. It featured beautiful-looking people shedding tears of happiness. There were high-definition images of the magnificent view. The word 'magical' was emphatically printed in bold type. 'Special', it said. 'The perfect romantic setting'. There was no disclaimer declaring that it might not always be perfect. There was no small print proffering the warning she may say no. There was no money-back guarantee if she did. After all, as the tagline declared, who could say no?

We are not even high enough to witness the promised iconic skyline when it all starts to go wrong. We have only just boarded our capsule. Our private capsule which, for the next thirty minutes, is reserved for just us, a box of luxury chocolate truffles and a bottle of champagne. I don't even like champagne. But what with the nerves, and the pressure of the situation, I down a glass before we even set off.

I pop both the bottle and the question too early.

If there is a playbook for London Eye proposals then I imagine it would instruct you to get down on one knee as you reach the highest point of the rotation, when you have the maximum impact of the spectacular 360-degree view. Not before you even leave the ground.

But I don't wait.

Maybe she would have said yes if she had been faced

with the wondrous sights of Big Ben, Wren's baroque architecture and the modern metropolis of the City. Instead, as I utter the fateful words 'Will you marry me?', we are face-to-face with the London Dungeon. The question scares her more than the blood-soaked billboards.

'No, Josh, no.' Jade stares straight into my eyes. A horribly blank expression. She looks at me like I'm a stranger she's never met, rather than the man she lives with. The man she is meant to love.

We met while working together in Bristol, the city in which I grew up and where we live. I took what was intended to be a temporary job at a hotel after studying History at King's College London, simply as a way to tide myself over until I decided what I wanted to do in life. Jade started a few years later, after her father, the owner, found her a job as a receptionist. It wasn't quite love at first sight, but just as we both fell into the career, we soon fell into a relationship. Four years later, after we'd been a couple for three and lived together for two, did she not think that I would ask soon?

'Marriage, Josh? Really? What are you thinking? I said I wanted you to take me on the London Eye, not for you to propose to me on it.'

It can't have come as too much of a surprise. Does she think you get champagne, truffles and a private capsule all for your standard £24 ticket?

'OK, I'm sorry. Obviously I've got the timing wrong. But why would you not even consider it? Why are you so adamant we're not ready? You know how much I love you, right? We want to spend our lives together? Isn't this the next step?'

'You can stand up now,' she says bluntly, ignoring my questions, as I realize I am still on one knee, ring in hand. For someone who is usually so touchy-feely, she moves as far away from me as is possible.

I get back on my feet and look out of the capsule in disbelief. Just as the perfect moment is annihilated, so too are all the happy times I have spent around this area. Forever ruined in my mind. The childhood memories of family trips to the capital, when everything seemed bigger and brighter and generally more impressive, to the student days and nights spent catching an art-house film at the BFI, pretentiously perusing the stalls of the booksellers underneath Waterloo Bridge, or getting a last-minute discounted ticket to a play at the National, which I wouldn't understand but I'd pretend to enjoy.

The South Bank has always been my favourite place in London. The paved street snaking alongside the river, encompassing so many of the city's sights, full of tourists pulling suitcases and mums pushing prams, joggers navigating flocks of schoolkids, skaters weaving in and out of pigeons, couples holding hands, cameras and coffee cups. I know the area well. So well that I could tell you that the roof of the National Theatre is home to around 60,000 bees, or that the Shell Mex House opposite has the largest clock face in the UK. I could tell you all these things but I couldn't have told you that my girlfriend doesn't love me the way I love her. I couldn't have told you she would say no. And that is now all I can think of. I now never want to see this place again. Most of all, I don't want to be here right now. I want to be somewhere else.

Except I can't. I can't be anywhere else, not for another twenty-eight minutes at least.

I pace lengthways across the capsule. Even though the transparent pod normally holds twenty-odd people, it suddenly starts to seem very small with just two. I feel claustrophobic. Her Dior perfume, a smell synonymous with happy times, consumes the capsule and now suffocates me. Can they not just let us out? Or put the system into reverse? Is there not a panic button somewhere? There must be a way to escape in an emergency. And this really is an emergency.

Her words continue to echo inside my head and reverberate around the capsule, getting louder and louder as they bounce off the windows.

No. No. No.

What does *no* even mean? Is that a *no* for now? Or a *no* for ever?

I check my watch. Twenty-seven minutes to go. What is wrong with this wheel? Is it broken?

Jade is silent. She runs her painted nails through her bleached hair. She has been blonde for as long as I've known her, but her dark eyes give away her natural colour. Her hands stop when they reach the back of her head. She looks at me, exasperated. I can tell she wants to say something. I've seen that face before, when she broke the news to me that she'd accidentally smashed my favourite Bristol City mug.

'I didn't want to tell you this. Not now. Not over Christmas. I'm sorry, Josh. I've actually been meaning to tell you . . . well . . . I'm just going to come out with it, I actually think we should . . . break up.'

What?

'I've met, I mean . . . I've been seeing someone else.'

Talk about sticking the knife in. I can barely breathe.

This can't be happening. Is this a wind-up? An elaborate prank? It must be one of those candid camera TV shows.

I look around, trying to spot the hidden cameras.

There are none.

'What do you mean, you've been seeing someone else?' I nervously take a sip from my glass.

Despite the champagne, my mouth has gone dry.

'I thought it was obvious we haven't been working well recently. It doesn't excuse my seeing someone else but –'

'Who is . . . ?' I struggle to speak.

'His name is . . . George,' she stutters hesitantly back.

Who the fuck is George? George Bush? George Clooney? They are the only Georges I know of, and as far as I am aware she has never met, let alone had an affair with, either. How could Jade know any more Georges than I do? We work together. We live together. We have the same social groups. What other George is there?

'Who is he?' I repeat, wanting to elicit more information than just a name. As I ask it, I realize I am not entirely sure I want to hear the answer. 'Do I know him?'

I'm surprised my voice doesn't crack as I ask.

'Umm . . .' She pauses before delivering the fatal blow. 'Yes, you've met him before, but you don't really know him. He's stayed at the hotel . . . Mr Henley?'

Oh God. George Henley. He is one of our regular customers. One of the businessmen who stay every week. The same routine, the same room. Smart, always in a suit, and I'm pretty sure married. Have they really been business trips? No wonder she has been getting such good TripAdvisor reviews. Those recently published comments race through my mind; the words *friendly, helpful* and *attentive* suddenly conjure up different connotations.

'Look, I'm really so sorry, Josh. Obviously I didn't want to hurt you.' She rubs her hands over her face, holding them in front of her mouth, before fiddling with the necklace I bought her last year.

I wonder if she takes it off when she sees George? I wonder if he's bought her a necklace too?

I try and shake these thoughts from my head.

'I'm just trying to be honest.'

'It's a bit late for that now.'

How did I not realize? Why didn't she tell me this before we spent Christmas Day together, cuddled up under the tree, kissing under the mistletoe, exchanging presents?

Oh crap.

Jeremy.

I got her a fucking rabbit for Christmas.

It was meant to be the start to our new modern

9

family. Pet, engagement, marriage, kids. That was the life plan.

'But what about Jeremy? How could you do this to him?' I ask indignantly, speaking as if the rabbit we've had for a week is our seven-year-old son.

'I guess we'll have to sort that out. And the flat.' She looks at the floor, not wanting to make any eye contact.

'What am I going to do about work? I can't carry on working with you now. Especially with *him* staying at the hotel every week.'

'I'll have a word with Dad and see what we can do,' she says apologetically. 'I'm sure he can pay you for your notice period,' she adds, as if she has already thought all of this through.

Living in a flat owned by your girlfriend's father and working in the hotel he owns is all fun and games until your girlfriend starts having fun with somebody else.

I want to be angry. I want to cry. But I can't do either. I am just in shock. Physically shaking. I can't look at her beautiful face. Instead I glance down below, at a London which now appears to be a toy set. Miniature boats float down the river as if they are remote-controlled, Hornbyesque trains shoot across the Hungerford Bridge. Black cabs and red buses play a game of Connect4 across the streets. Loved-up couples browse the German Christmas Market, sharing mulled wine and laughter. Young lovers hug and kiss. Terrys and Julies cross Waterloo Bridge. Why can't that be us?

London falls silent for a moment, as if out of respect for our fallen relationship. I can just make out the music playing from the speakers down at ground level. With *Now That's What I Call Christmas!* having been played on constant loop in the hotel foyer since September, I have heard nothing but festive songs for the last few months. Just from the few notes that penetrate the glass, I recognize it immediately.

'Lonely This Christmas'.

As I stand there eating the truffles, trying valiantly to get my money's worth, I can't help but laugh. It is as if a DJ is playing a soundtrack to accompany my life. Jade doesn't seem to find it as amusing. She, in what has been demarcated as her side of the capsule, sits down and begins to cry.

Why is she crying? It should be me crying. She has no right.

'Get ready to pose for your official London Eye photograph,' the tannoy announces with devilish timing. 'Smile!'

When they publish their updated marketing brochures, I think it is highly unlikely the team at the London Eye will use the photo of us, standing at opposite ends of the capsule, Jade in tears, me laughing manically and stuffing my face with chocolates, to promote their Proposal Package.

In contrast to the happy couples and families in the other pods, who I can see laughing and joking away, enjoying the experience together, we don't speak for the rest of the ride. There seems little point. Of course, there are more questions I could ask, more answers I want, but what would it change? I know it is over.

'There you go, take that,' I say to Jade, as I shove a

plastic card into her hands when we step back onto solid ground.

'What is it?'

'The room key to our suite at the Sea Containers. It was all meant to be part of the surprise. We were going to see in the New Year watching the fireworks together from our hotel room, as an engaged couple. But that's not what you want, apparently.'

I'd secretly checked in earlier while she was looking around the shops, but I don't want to stay there now, not alone.

She waits, and pauses, and looks as if she is going to say something big and meaningful.

'Josh, I can't. I can't stay there alone,' is all that follows.

'Why don't you ask George to stay with you?'

I know full well that George Henley doesn't even live in London. After three years, those are my parting words to the woman I wanted to marry.

She takes the key and turns left, walking away through the buskers and the human statues, past the vintage carousel carrying excited kids, through the various aromas of the Christmas market, past the repurposed double-decker bus selling frozen yoghurt and towards the hotel and our suite which was meant to be for the two of us, but now will sleep just one.

I watch her until she's out of sight, the truffles still in my hands, before I turn right.

As I cross Westminster Bridge, I don't take note of the iconic and illuminated buildings which line my peripheral vision. I don't want to look up. It feels like everyone is watching me, judging me. As if they all know what just happened. Even the fish sculptures entwined around the lamp posts appear to be staring. I am all alone in one of the world's busiest cities. Nine million people, and I have no one.

As I focus my gaze firmly on the ground, I notice a fifty-pence coin glinting in the descending darkness. I need all the money I can get to recuperate the cost of today so I bend down and pick it up. What was it Mum always used to say? 'Find a penny, pick it up, all the day, you'll have good luck.'

Does this mean I will get fifty times the amount of luck?

I have never been one for superstition like she is, but if I ever needed a change in fortune, now is the time. As I put it in my pocket, it jangles next to the ring box.

Why the fuck did I get the ring engraved? What am I going to do with that now?

I battle on against the hordes of partygoers walking in the opposite direction, bottles in hand, trying to secure the best vantage point for tonight's celebrations. As the clocks tick closer to midnight and to the New Year, the world's eyes turn to watch the London Eye. Images will be beamed across the planet of fireworks exploding from where we've just left. It will be a scene of jubilation, of triumphant celebration. Along the River Thames, hundreds of thousands of revellers will be singing and dancing merrily. Millions more will be snuggled up at home in front of the TV, all counting down. Counting down to sharing a kiss with their loved one. Ten, nine, eight . . .

That was meant to be me. I was meant to be mumbling along to 'Auld Lang Syne' and kissing my fiancée as we watched the spectacle from our perfectly positioned suite. Instead I spend the last few hours of the year squashed up next to an absurdly large man eating his Sainsbury's Meal Deal on the Megabus back to Bristol. Back to an empty flat I have to move out of. Back to a job I have to quit.

The realization hits me. I've lost my girlfriend, my home and my job all in one evening.

Happy New Year indeed.

2

'Well, Josh, at least you've learned that if something sounds *too good* to be true, then it probably is.'

I wondered just how long it would take someone to come up with that witty remark about Jade's surname. Eight minutes and thirty-seven seconds into the party was even quicker than I had predicted.

He has not even entered the house yet, but the honour goes to my uncle Peter. A man whose appearance suggests he has arrived not in a Mercedes 4x4 but a time machine straight from the summer of 1976. He looks like a member of Hall and Oates, the one with the dodgy moustache. His shirt, unbuttoned halfway down his chest, reveals a gaudy gold chain and a lawn of grey chest hair.

As he comes through the front door, he shakes my hand formally, and with a strong grip, as if we're at a business conference rather than a party. Twenty years working in the City gifted him not only a healthy pension, early retirement and a fancy car, but also a knack for shaking hands with everyone he meets: train ticket inspectors, supermarket cashiers, toilet attendants.

'Sorry we didn't have time to change it,' he says, showing no signs of regret or embarrassment as he bundles a gift into my hands. He gestures towards my cousins, Petula, Penelope and Percival, who are clambering out of the car and too busy with their new iPhones to look up.

I hate opening presents in front of people at the best of times. There's always that moment, as soon as you've opened it, when you have to pretend to smile. Today, I won't be smiling, or fake smiling, so as he stands in the doorway beckoning me to open it, I don't have the energy or inclination to argue. I tear off what appears to be recycled Christmas wrapping paper to reveal a book entitled *How to Plan the Perfect Wedding.*

Brilliant.

The £1.99 sticker is still plastered on the front. I am not sure what is more insulting.

'Sure it will come in handy one day!'

He chuckles and pats me on the back as he makes his way past me to shake hands with everyone else who has already gathered in the front room, and where the party is getting into full swing. Swing being the operative word. Think Sinatra and Martin, rather than Drum and Bass. Dad doesn't like modern music, and he considers anything post-1960s as modern.

I stuff the wrapping paper into my pocket. I am still wearing the same clothes I had on in London last night. I decided I didn't want to go back to *our* flat. Not alone. Not after everything. Fortunately, my parents live just outside of Bristol. And there's no place like home at a time like this. Or so I thought.

My cousins follow their father in through the door,

each greeting me with their own double-edged condolences, as if their entertainment for the drive was not listening to the radio but thinking up suitable comedic lines.

'Jade Toogood? More like Jade Up-to-no-good.'

'Clearly proposing wasn't *too good* an idea.'

'She was obviously *too good* for you.'

I do my best not to react.

Mum had got slightly over-excited when I told her I was going to propose and thought it would be a good idea to gather family, neighbours and seemingly a string of strangers together for a surprise engagement party. What could be worse than spending a day celebrating your engagement with people you barely know? The answer is spending the day mourning your failed engagement with them.

'The invitations have already gone out,' Mum said when I asked her if we could cancel. She looked at me as if well-wishers have been camped out in the street for weeks, and it wasn't as simple as phoning round and telling people not to worry about coming over.

The 'Happy Engagement' banner, hanging across the front of our brick-clad 1960s house, had been felt-tipped over, rather creatively I'll admit, with 'Happy Homecoming'. It is certainly a novel spin to put on why I have moved back with my parents so suddenly. Most people would have just bought a new banner. Then again, most people would have just cancelled the party. My parents are not most people.

Mum has been waiting for this day, and a chance to

show off to the neighbourhood, for ages. The last party she threw was when I became the first person in the family to get a place at university. She told everyone I turned down offers from Oxford and Bath, rather than Brookes and Spa. Showing off is the national pastime in this village. It is about all there is to do in Cadbury. While nearby Weston-super-Mare may have a pier, and donkeys you can ride on the beach, Cadbury has a fish and chip shop, a chemist's, which unofficially doubles as the meeting place for the Weight Watchers group, and the 'National Pub of the Year', as the sign proudly states. Only in small print does it mention this accolade was awarded in 1987, with the establishment having had five different landlords since then. No one ever graduates from the village. I wanted to escape, to see the world, to learn about art and literature, to fall in love, but thanks to a series of bad choices I've been sucked back with nothing to show for it. No girlfriend. No career. Nothing.

I step away from the front door and peek into the lounge. Dad, as he does with any gathering of people, is using the event as a money-making opportunity. Dressed in a tartan shirt, and desperately clinging on to his last few strands of hair, he's in the corner, conducting a sweepstake on which village resident will die next. If you select the person who kicks the bucket first, you take home the kitty (obviously after Dad's taken a sizeable percentage cut). I'm not sure if this is worse than when he cashed in on my graduation ceremony by buying extra tickets and touting them for extortionate prices outside the Barbican.

Mum, meanwhile, is in her element, swanning around the room with platefuls of canapés as if she is a grand society hostess in 1920s New York. Having recently retired from her job as an estate agent, she helps herself to a few too many of the chocolate bites so she can attend the Weight Watchers group, which she sees as more of a social gathering and an excuse to have a good gossip. The only outlet she has otherwise is Graham, her therapist, who she has started to see every week and who claims to predict the future. Presumably he didn't tell her this was coming.

Nan, who seems to be getting shorter and shorter every time I see her, is dancing and singing in the middle of the room, putting on a one-woman performance of *The Wizard of Oz* to anyone who will watch. She is the life and soul of any party.

Despite the gathering apparently being thrown in my honour, I don't recognize most of the other people who are crammed into our front room. In fact, I barely recognize the room. Mum has decorated it with an assortment of furniture, ornaments and knick-knacks, which Dad will return to the shops tomorrow. For one day only, it looks like we live in a *Good Housekeeping* show home. The sofa is new. There are throws and cushions and pouffes. There are little signs with inspirational quotes such as 'Everything Happens for a Reason', 'Keep Calm and Carry On', 'What Doesn't Kill You Makes You Stronger'. Even the drinks coasters are telling me to 'Live, love, laugh'.

Along the mantelpiece, there are a whole series of

pictures of me through my school years, albeit all covered with the copyright imprint stretched across my face. Dad thought he was getting a bargain, and, more importantly, one over on the system, by framing the proofs rather than purchasing the 'bloody rip-off' 10x8 prints.

Of those people I do recognize, there is Madeline, the self-elected village mayor, who is usually chief organizer of such events and who, no doubt, will be firmly assessing this one. She is with her husband, Geoff, who has an anxiety disorder, meaning he hates any awkward situations and has a phobia of eating in public. Wanting to avoid any awkwardness, he is too polite to refuse a canapé when they are passed around, so by the end of the day he'll have pockets full of cream cheese and smoked salmon vol-au-vents.

I turn around and spot our neighbour, Desmond, hitting on women half his age and telling awful jokes that never reach their punchline. Soon he will be snoring and choking on his false teeth. His wife, Beryl, is sitting in her wheelchair telling anyone who will listen that 'she doesn't want to talk about her health' before regaling them with her entire medical history. It is incredible that, whatever medical issue anyone else has in the street, Beryl soon also develops it, as if dementia were contagious and then curable within one month.

The doorbell rings again, and I rush back to my door duty.

'Oh, I'm really so sorry, Joshy,' Karen, my childhood babysitter, says as she enters. Mum really did invite everyone. Karen seemingly fails to realize two decades have passed since she used to tuck me into bed, and Josh would suffice these days. She hands me a tub of Celebrations, which I pile on top of the rapidly growing mountain of other boxes, tins and containers of chocolates I have already been given. We probably gave these people the very same tubs last week, and they are simply returning them with just the Milky Ways and Bountys remaining.

'Don't worry, I'm sure you will meet someone else soon.'

'Thank you,' I say through gritted teeth. 'If you just want to head that way.' I gesture towards the front room, where Geoff is now starting to sweat profusely.

I am not sure what is worse, the jokes or the sympathy. I am not ready for any of it yet. I want to be curled up in a ball somewhere, bawling my eyes out, stuffing my face with all this chocolate. It has only been twenty-four hours. I am not worrying about meeting someone else, sooner or later. I don't want that beautiful, alluring, currently enigmatic soulmate who everyone keeps promising me is somewhere out there in the big wide world waiting for me. I want Jade, I want the future we had planned, and I want my normal life back. And as if it isn't bad enough that I have moved back into my parents' house, it seems I'm now expected to be sharing it with the entire village.

Before I can welcome any other stranger from the past, I hear a shriek from the front room. As I rush to see what's happened, I spot Geoff, now shaking and unable to breathe, having a panic attack. Whose idea was it to invite the world's most anxious man to the world's most awkward party? He is told to sit down on the sofa, but he forgets about the volume of cream cheese in his back pockets, which explosively smears everywhere. Mum grabs a wet tea towel and runs around manically complaining that the stain won't come out. Dad's face drops when he realizes he won't be able to return the sofa to the shop and he may have to pay out on the sweepstake too. Madeline, far from being concerned about her husband's welfare, looks suspiciously happy that this party won't topple her summer soirée. Nan is insisting her one-woman show must go on. Beryl is feigning having a panic attack too. And Desmond is somehow sleeping through everything. With everyone else crowding around Geoff, there is nothing I can do to help, so I use this distraction as a decoy for my departure and escape to my bedroom. The last thing I see is Uncle Peter shaking hands with the paramedics as they arrive.

I haven't lived here for ten years, and I couldn't have been offered a more visual interpretation of going backwards in life. My room is surprisingly untouched. The teenage posters of David Beckham and Michael Owen still plaster the beige walls, there is a lava lamp on the shelf, and the Beanie Babies I collected as a kid are sitting on top of my cupboard. I half expected to find Dad had listed my room on Airbnb, but the only person in my room is my pap, who is sitting on my bed watching *It's a Wonderful Life* on the TV, oblivious to the catastrophe and panic ensuing downstairs.

'Sorry, Josh. Hope you don't mind. Bit noisy out there for me.'

Mum definitely didn't inherit her social gene from the paternal side of the family. Unlike Nan, who loves being the centre of attention, Pap's never been one for social gatherings. In fact, he's rarely seen in public. The only time he ventures out is to a weekly OAP dance class with Nan, and even then he is keen to leave as soon as the class finishes, while Nan likes to hang around, chatting to everyone. Aside from that, he spends all his time playing the organ they have in their cottage, or watching the TV. Yet, despite their differences, they've been married for almost sixty years and always look in love.

'What do you think about it all?' Pap always asks this question, and I'm never quite sure what he's referring to.

'The party? Put it this way, you're not missing anything by being in here.'

'Keep me company and watch the film with me, then.' He beckons me to take a seat next to him on my bed.

I've seen this movie almost every Christmas I've been alive. It's the only film that always makes me tear up.

We sit there in silence, watching the TV. Unlike everyone else, he knows I don't want to talk about Jade. As George Bailey and Mary are about to be reunited on screen, Pap realizes that maybe this isn't the best thing for me to watch either.

'We all know how this ends. Do you want to watch

something different?' He goes to give me the remote control.

'Don't trust me to make that decision, I can't get anything right at the moment,' I say.

I wonder if he's heard me, as he doesn't respond for a good thirty seconds.

'I think you're being very harsh on yourself. There's a girl somewhere in London right now who has made the wrong decision, not you,' he replies eventually.

We both continue staring at the TV as we converse, bouncing our words off the screen.

'Thanks, Pap, but seriously, look at all the choices I've made and where they've got me. I took the wrong job. I chose the wrong girl, certainly the wrong time to propose. Half the time, I don't know what I want, and then when I do make a choice, it seems to be the wrong one.'

I look over at him. 'Sorry to rant.' I've been wanting to get these thoughts off my chest; they have been whirring around inside my head for the last twenty-four hours.

He places his hand on my lap.

'You have to remember, when I was young, we didn't have as many choices as you have, we just got on with it. I left school at thirteen and started working. Did I want to be a builder? I never knew any different. I'd have loved to have been a pianist, but it's just what it was. Before my time, men would just go down the mine and marry the girl next door.'

'Maybe that was better,' I mutter, until I remember

I'm claustrophobic, and the girl next door is the eighty-three-year-old hypochondriac downstairs.

'Maybe it was, and I'm not saying it is better now or it was better then, but I look at your generation and think how lucky you are to have so many opportunities. You can do what you want with your lives. You just need to work out what you want and go for it.'

'But how do I know what I want?'

'When you find it, you will know, you're a smart lad.' He turns around for the first time, gives me a wink and ruffles my hair. 'You've got much more time than me to work that one out too.'

'I wanted Jade.'

'I know, and I know whatever I say won't change that. But there was a girl that I liked before I met your nan, and I was devastated when she went with one of my friends instead. It turned out it was the best thing that ever happened to me. A few weeks later I saw your nan for the first time. Just think, you wouldn't be here today if things had worked out differently.'

I've seen old black-and-white photos of Pap as a young man and struggle to believe any girl would have turned him down. He still has the same side parting, but his hair is now white rather than brown.

He starts to slowly navigate back to the menu page to see what else is on, and I avoid the temptation to snatch the remote off him to do it quicker.

'It looks like *The Grinch* and *Home Alone* are about to start?' he says curiously as he scrolls through the movie listings.

'I don't mind which we watch.'

'Why don't we toss a coin? You got one?' He checks his own pockets, forgetting that his coat and wallet are hanging up downstairs.

I rummage around in my pockets and pull out the contents. I stare down at the fifty-pence coin I picked up last night and the ring box. I notice Pap catches sight of the box but he pretends not to see.

'Come on, let's hurry up and flip that coin you have there.'

And then, just like that, as I flip the coin and watch it spiral into the air, the idea comes to me.

And it's fantastic.

3

Well, I thought it was a fantastic idea at least.

'You're doing what? Have you literally gone mad?'

If I'm being completely honest, it's not quite the reaction I'd hoped for after telling my friends about my new approach to life.

I hadn't even planned on telling them. In fact, I planned on quite the opposite. I was going to keep it hidden from them at least for a while. I knew what they would think. If I could just trial it first and then show them the benefits later, they would be more inclined to think it was a good idea. But as we stand beside the bar and I flip a coin to decide whether I want a Gem or a Thatchers, I'm forced to confess everything.

'So, let me get this straight. You're going to toss a coin for every decision you make for a whole year? Is that right?' Jake asks, looking perplexed as we pay for our drinks. He is tall and thin, in a gangly way, and looks down at me through his horn-rimmed glasses as he combs his fingers through his floppy strawberry-blond hair.

Standing behind the bar, Big D, the sixty-year-old landlord with a 1980s mullet, who always attempts to hijack conversations, is looking equally confused.

'Yes, that's what I said, didn't I?' I give my answer to

both of them as if I'm performing to a crowd. It feels like I'm on trial.

'What is this, like, some kind of weird New Year's resolution?' Big D chirps in.

'I suppose you could call it that.'

Even before I take the first sip of my pint, I realize I have made a mistake. I remember why I wasn't going to mention anything.

We make our way from the bar to a table in the corner of the room where Jessie is sitting. A converted former bank lobby, it's the same as all those fancy gastropubs where they serve pub food but at Michelin-star prices, where they have craft beer on tap and where the interior is dark, soulless and missing the sticky floors, wooden circular tables and a dartboard of yesteryear. Even the walls look confused, as if they've wandered into the wrong building. The century-long history of this Clifton building has been condemned and confined to a three-line blurb stolen from Wikipedia and printed on the food menu.

'You do know that most people's New Year's resolutions are usually something like lose weight, give up smoking, stop drinking, right? Jessie, what's yours this year?' Jake asks as we take our seats next to her. Her dark hair is down, and even though she is as tall as me, it flows almost to her waist. She's submerged in a padded orange fluorescent jacket and looks like she should be in St Moritz. She's always cold and she is never subtle with her outfit choices. While Jake tries desperately to be hipster, Jessie pulls it off without realizing.

'My resolution? I'm going to run the London marathon,' she says, far too keenly for someone committing to that kind of torture.

'OK, well that's still somewhat crazy, but it's a *lot* more normal than flipping a coin for every decision,' he replies.

'What's this about flipping a coin?'

And now Jessie knows too. Great.

'Haven't you heard yet about this mad idea Josh has to flip a coin for every decision he makes this year?'

'No, I haven't, have you gone crazy, Josh?'

This seems to be the stock reply.

'What I can't believe is, we don't see you for a few weeks, and in that time you manage to propose, break up, lose your job, move back home and decide to entrust your whole life to a coin. Is this what happens when I'm not here to advise you on everything?' Jake rolls his eyes dramatically. As he says this, I realize my Christmas does sound as cheerful as a character's on *EastEnders*.

'It worked OK for Hewlett Packard. Did you know they flipped a coin to see which way round their names should go?' I retort.

'That's true,' says Jessie. 'Packard Hewlett does sound more like an upmarket law firm than a tech company. But that was one decision, they didn't keep flipping the coin, their computers aren't designed by what the coin says.'

'So you're going to flip it for literally every decision? What socks to wear? What sandwich to eat? Flipping hell, that's mental. Excuse the pun,' Jake laughs.

'Yes,' I say, as I simultaneously realize I might not have thought all of this through properly. 'I guess I just feel I've clearly not made the best decisions so far, so why not let fate guide me for a bit? Maybe the coin might actually be able to help me find myself, and love. What have I got to lose?'

'Your dignity,' Jessie sniggers under her breath.

'No, no, Jessie, don't ridicule him. It all makes perfect sense now he has explained it to us.' Jake is being as sarcastic as ever.

'I read last night that the average human makes approximately 35,000 decisions a day, that's over one million a month, or twelve million a year. Think how long I deliberate about each of them, how much time I'm wasting and ultimately how many of them I'm getting wrong.' The other two sip their drinks politely while I rant.

We are waiting for the weekly pub quiz to start at the Cricketers' Arms; it is back on after the festive break. We all met when we started working at the hotel at the same time and use our weekly meet-up as an opportunity to catch up. Jake left the company a few months ago and is now managing another hotel in Bristol. It sounds good until you realize his hotel is ranked thirty-fifth of thirty-six in the city on TripAdvisor. Jessie left a couple of years ago and retrained as a primary-school teacher. Apparently even five-year-old kids are less annoying than hotel guests. They are both a year younger than me, which they never let me forget.

'This coin flipping is all to do with Jade, isn't it?' Jessie has been stirring the straw in her drink for a while before she suddenly looks up as if she has just solved a great mystery.

Why does it have to become a therapy session? It's got nothing to do with Jade. It's about me wanting to do something different. Something better with my life.

'It's not about Jade,' I tell them firmly.

It's clear they don't believe me.

'Sorry, who is Jade?' asks Jake's new boyfriend as he takes a seat at our table.

This is the first time we've met. He is short, with light-blond scruffy hair, and works in social media marketing. He looks like someone who would go to a festival and wear the wristband for the rest of the year.

My break-up with Jade has had wider repercussions. Not only have I lost my girlfriend, but we have lost our fourth quiz team member. Josh, Jade, Jessie and Jake. We had been 'the All-Jays'.

She gets to keep the flat, I get to keep the quiz team. Great.

It turns out that replacing her in the quiz team is much easier and quicker than replacing her in my life. Just like that, we've managed to find someone else whose name begins with J.

Jake.

Yes, Jake's new boyfriend is also called Jake. It's very confusing. I had been perplexed for the last few weeks as to why (original) Jake had started referring to himself in the third person. I would ask what he was doing over the weekend, to which he'd reply something like: 'Jake has got a play on, so will go to that,' or 'Jake has to work, so nothing much.' I presumed he had just developed a habit of talking about himself in the third person, and I began to mimic him in reply: 'Oh, that's a shame, because Josh was wondering if you fancied meeting up.' It is only now, as he is introduced and leans across the table to shake hands, that the realization dawns on me.

'So because you think you made the wrong decision with Jade, you're going to flip a coin from now on for every choice?' Jake's Jake offers.

No, no, no. It's not about Jade.

I don't like Jake's Jake already. I'm not sure why he, or the other two, are having such a tough time process-ing what I have told them. It surely isn't that difficult to understand.

I'm going to flip a coin for every decision I make in life. What is strange about that?

'Welcome back, guys, presume you're all quizzing tonight?' Little D asks as he goes table-to-table collect-ing entry fees. Little D is Big D's son and the quizmaster. Ironically, he is two foot taller than his father and has lost all of his hair.

'Here you go,' I say, passing over our pound coins.

'You've changed your team line-up?' he asks.

'Yep, something like that.'

Do I have to explain my break-up to everyone?

As Little D hands over the picture round, three bespectacled men in their twenties saunter past us, smirking.

'I was hoping they'd still be on holiday,' Jessie whispers.

'They're always here. They've literally never missed a quiz night in the last three years,' I reply as they take their usual table by the bar.

'Who are they?' Jake's Jake asks inquisitively.

'Our main rivals. The Quizlamic Extremists. Three Bristol University astrophysics PhD students who win the quiz every single week, and I mean every single week. In the three years we've been competing, we have only ever managed to come second,' Jake explains.

Our combined knowledge of Disney (Jessie has never grown up), Beyoncé (Jake goes to Beyoncé dance classes every Thursday) and my specialist subject of Bristol City Football Club *circa* 2001 to the present day is never enough to topple the Quizlamic Extremists' all-conquering trivia skills.

'Is this a fierce rivalry? What have you got me into?'

'No, they barely ever acknowledge us. That's the worst part. Clearly they don't think we're even rivals.'

'Are you guys any good?' Jake's Jake continues.

'I don't think we're bad, I just think they're unbeatable,' Jessie replies.

'Like, I mean, if we went elsewhere, we'd probably win,' Jake says.

'Definitely,' I concur.

I look over at their table as they hurriedly jot down all the answers to the picture round, while we struggle to put a name to any of the faces.

'I reckon this is their main source of income. They

just go round different pub quizzes each night of the week and rake in the winnings.'

'It's not very fair for everyone else,' Jessie bemoans.

'Let's just hope they actually graduate soon and move somewhere else,' Jake says hopefully. 'Although it is funny each week how annoyed Josh gets that we don't win.'

'Jake, have you heard the story about Josh getting kicked out of a children's party for being a bad loser?' Jessie loves to repeat this tale to everyone.

What Jessie neglects to mention every time she tells this anecdote is that I was a child when I was kicked out of a children's party. I am not an adult who still attends kids' birthday parties and is asked to leave when I lose Pin the Tail on the Donkey. It is a somewhat subtle but extremely crucial difference that I have to pick her up on every time.

'OK, guys, we are going to get started. Everyone ready? Question 1 . . .' Little D stops Jessie from embarrassing me any more.

'In reverse order, we have Big Fact Hunt with forty-seven points' – Little D is careful with his pronunciation of that one – 'Universally Challenged with fifty-two, Trivia Newton John with fifty-four . . .'

Has he forgotten to mention us? Surely we dropped significant points on the music round. Little D performed the songs on a kazoo, and we couldn't tell if he was playing Jim Morrison or Van Morrison.

'And we have a tie for first place!'

We're leading? Surely not.

'The All-Jays and the Quizlamic Extremists are level on fifty-nine.'

He must have miscounted!

The Quizlamic Extremists look across at us, most perturbed.

'OK, give me two seconds. There's going to be a tie-break question to see who wins this week's jackpot.'

Little D clearly hasn't come prepared for such an outcome and is frantically trying to find a tie-break question on his phone. An awkward silence descends on the room, with the only noise coming from the kitchen. Despite the smell of the cooking drifting across the pub, I've yet to get my appetite back after the shock of the break-up. Jessie, meanwhile, has been nibbling away at her fries all night, and Jake's Jake has devoured his quinoa burger.

Of course, he is vegan.

'OK, so . . . Please can you write down your answer on a scrap of paper and remember it's the team who gets the closest wins . . . On average, how many euros are collected from the basin of the Trevi Fountain in Rome every year?'

Tricky.

We look at each other, nonplussed. I think we are all still slightly shocked that we are even in contention to win. After a year of attending week in, week out, this is our chance to bask in the glory we witness the Quizlamic Extremists enjoying every Wednesday.

'What do you think?' Jessie whispers, leaning across

the table which is now covered with empty pint glasses and plates.

We discuss our thoughts in hushed tones, not that it really matters, as we have no idea what the actual answer is and are struggling to even think of a ballpark figure. Jessie suddenly picks up the pen and starts scribbling some numbers down.

'What are you adding up?' I ask

'I'm just working out how many euros I think would be left each day and then multiplying that by 365.'

'Such a schoolteacher.'

'So a thousand euros a day would be 365,000 euros a year. Do you think that sounds about right?'

'Did you need to write that sum down?' I joke to her.

'I don't know, I think it might be more,' Jake's Jake chimes in. 'Think how many tourists must go there every night and throw a coin in. It's the thing to do in Rome, isn't it?'

'But do they throw a euro in each time, or just a few cents?'

'Not everyone is as tight-fisted as you,' Jake fires back at me, with a cheeky grin.

I look across the room at the Quizlamic Extremists, trying to lip-read what they are saying.

'OK, so let's go slightly higher, then?' Jessie gets to work on a new sum. 'Shall we say half a million?'

'I'm happy to go with that,' I nod.

'No, I think it's more like 1.5 million. I feel as if I've read this somewhere before.' The two Jakes look at each other in agreement.

'Surely it can't be that much? Shall we go for something in the middle?' Jessie hovers with the pen.

'I will give you ten more seconds, guys. Ten, nine . . .' Little D bellows.

We all look helplessly at each other.

'Seeing as the question is about coins, why don't we try flipping your coin, Josh?' Jake suggests.

Finally, they're coming around to my plan.

'OK. Heads we go with 500,000 euros and tails 1.5 million. Everyone happy?' I say hurriedly.

'Four, three . . .'

This is it, the coin's first big decision. Its chance to prove to all its doubters that it is right for me to follow its decisions. To win us £100.

'Write down your final answer.'

'Maybe we weren't meant to win,' I say sombrely as we trudge out of the pub, gutted to have come so close to finally beating the Quizlamic Extremists. If Jake, Jake and Jessie weren't sceptical of the coin's power before, they certainly are now.

'If you'd just listened to me, we would have won,' Jake says as he and Jake hug Jessie goodbye. 'Either way, you definitely weren't meant to tell Little D where to shove his kazoo. You're such a bad loser.'

'I'm not a bad loser!' I reply.

'He's still just venting his anger about Jade.'

'It's not about Jade!' I shout into the distance as Jake and Jake head off home into the night's darkness, waving goodbye.

'What do you think of Jake, then?' Jessie asks me as soon as they are out of earshot. I get a sudden flashback to when we used to work together on reception and would gossip about couples staying at the hotel. We started working at the hotel on the same day and bonded over idle chatter and mutual apathy for the job. Despite having Jade there, it was never as fun after Jessie left.

'Of Jake's Jake?'

'It's going to be so confusing, isn't it?'

'Tell me about it. He seemed nice, though, and knew quite a bit of trivia, which is key. Although it's hard to judge after just a few hours. Look at me. I couldn't tell after a few years.'

Jessie loiters beside me as we reach the bus stop; no one else is around apart from a couple of students stumbling home on the other side of the road. My lack of a driving licence has never been a concern before – having lived in London and then central Bristol – but I'm now stranded in the back of beyond with a very unreliable bus service to rely on. I took my driving test when I was seventeen and managed to fail three times. I had the same examiner each time, and on the third occasion he told me, 'I don't fail people, they fail themselves.' I couldn't bear to look him in the eye or try again after that.

'You know you don't have to wait with me,' I say, as Jessie shivers in her bright padded jacket, with the warmth of her flat only a few minutes' walk away.

'It's all right, I'm happy to. It's not that long until it comes,' Jessie says as she looks up at the electronic board. It never seems to be accurate and has currently been stuck on *eight minutes* for at least four minutes.

'So, have you seen her yet after the incident?' Jessie asks. The London Eye debacle is now just being referred to as 'the incident'. Jade is 'her', or 'she'.

'No, I haven't. She doesn't want to see me, apparently. She's going to drop my stuff to the hotel so I can collect it. And my P45.'

'I suppose that is the problem when you live in a flat owned by your girlfriend's dad.'

'And also the problem when he owns the hotel you work in.'

'I know it's rubbish, but come on, you can now find a job you actually enjoy. You were wasted there. You should have left when I did.'

'But I still don't know what I want to do. At least you knew you wanted to go into teaching.'

'You'll figure it out, I promise. Just think, you won't have to work those horrendous back-to-back late/early shifts again. Have you got enough money saved up in the meantime?'

'I spent most of my savings on the ring! Fortunately, I get a few weeks' pay from the hotel, so that should keep me going for a while until I can find something else, I hope.'

'That's good, at least, and I'm sure you will find something soon. Having a bit of a break in the meantime isn't a bad thing. You've been working there solidly for – what? – seven years? It will be good for you to have some time to find yourself.'

'But if I don't know what I'm looking for, how will I find it?'

'You'll know when you find it. Trust me, everything will work out.'

'Thanks, Jessie. I really hope so. I just can't believe how everything has turned out. If asking the girl you love to marry you and finding out she's been cheating isn't bad enough, then it's not made any better by having to move out of your flat and losing your job.'

'The girl you love or *loved*? Don't tell me you still love her? Not after what she's done to you?'

'I know I should be hating her, but all I can think of is: where did it go wrong? What did I do? Why did she go off with someone else?'

'You did nothing wrong, I promise. I know we're all friends and I like Jade, but come on, Josh, what she did was brutal. There's no coming back from that. You deserve so much better. Just think that you swerved a bullet before it was too late.'

It is nice to know she is on my side. But no matter what Jessie says, I can't pretend I'm not wishing I was heading back to Jade's flat right now. I can't bear to think of her being there with *him* instead.

We're soon interrupted by the bus, which, completely out of sync with the electronic board, pulls up next to us and nearly mounts the pavement. I wonder how this driver passed his test.

'I know it doesn't feel like it now, but it will all work out for you, Josh, I'm sure. I'm here whenever you want to talk about it, or not talk about it.' Jessie smiles.

'Thank you, and sorry we didn't win the money tonight.'

'I know, we were so close. Maybe next time?'

As the bus driver passive-aggressively coughs and attempts to shut the doors, I wave goodbye and board the bus back to the middle of nowhere.

4

It is not even 9 a.m., and I've already flipped the coin seventeen times since waking up.

Heads. Get up, rather than stay in bed longer. *Ugh.*

Tails. Shower instead of a bath.

Tails. Jeans beat chinos.

Tails. Frosties over porridge.

Heads. Orange juice not apple.

I'm quickly getting the hang of this, but I am not getting used to being back at home and living with my parents.

'If you're just going to flip that coin rather than spend it, I'll take it off you,' Dad jokingly remarks as he joins me and Mum at the breakfast table and opens his newspaper. Apart from our brand-new, cream-cheese-stained sofa, the house is back to normal after the show-home decorations were returned.

'Can you ask the coin if City are going to win tonight?' He looks up at me from the sports pages.

'You know it's not a magic coin, Dad. It doesn't predict the future.'

I scroll hopelessly through endless job adverts on my phone, none of which are suitable. It seems that even for the most basic role you have to go through about seven application stages. Entry-level jobs impossibly require you to have a minimum of five years' experience in that field. And anything that seems interesting turns out to be an unpaid internship.

'Neither of you are being very helpful,' Mum sighs as she jabs at the iPad attempting to do the online food shop. 'Can one of you tell me what you'd like for dinners this week?'

During my first few days at home I was treated to roast meals and steak dinners. Now we've had beans on toast three nights in a row, and I can't tell if this is Dad limiting the grocery budget or whether they want rid of me already.

Before I can answer, I'm distracted by my phone vibrating. I glance down and see the message is from Jade.

She has been texting me non-stop. Not apologizing or begging for us to get back together. Rather, she wants to sort out what's happening with Jeremy. Everyone always bangs on about how dogs are not just for Christmas, but no one ever warns you about rabbits. There are no bumper stickers, no charity TV appeals. There is no twenty-eight-day return policy. I had planned on starting the New Year with my fiancée, and our new, very modern family. Instead I'm in a custody dispute over a pet rabbit.

'What's Jade saying now?' Mum leans over, looking over the top of her iPad.

Not only does moving home mean baked beans for dinner every night, but it also means losing any sense of privacy. While Mum reads my messages, Dad thinks he works in the Royal Mail sorting office, opening all my post before passing it on to me. Bank statements are scrutinized, personal letters are read, and invitations to events are pinned to the calendar.

'She wants to know if I'm going to take Jeremy,' I reply, knowing there is no point in hiding it from her. 'Apparently George is allergic to rabbits.' My heart feels like it's being stabbed every time she mentions his name.

Mum puts the iPad down and Dad puts his paper down simultaneously. Dad speaks first.

'If we have the rabbit, you're going to have to pay for his upkeep. And look after him. I'm not going to be cleaning up after him.'

'Yes, that's fine. I will look after everything.'

My only childhood pet was a goldfish who mysteriously died after the local shop increased the price of fish food. I'm not saying Dad definitely killed him, but looking back, it does seem a bit suspicious.

'How do you feel about her mentioning . . . *George*?' Mum mouths.

My wallowing has quickly evolved into vividly fantasizing about George dying, and meticulously planning the most intricate details of his murder.

'I don't know. I didn't realize they were that serious already,' I reply.

What troubles me the most is that I just don't understand what he has that I don't. Sure, he is rich and handsome, and I am now unemployed, and living with my parents, but still . . .

'I could make an appointment with Graham, if you'd like? It might help you to talk to someone?'

Just when I think things can't get any worse, Mum is offering to pay for me to go and see her therapist. The same man who tells her that her problems date back to her seventeenth-century self. The last time she took me to see one of her healers was when I was stressed during my school exams and she convinced me acupuncture would help. I thought she'd booked me in for a session with an actual Chinese medical therapist, not Sue Lee from the village who learned online.

'No, thanks. I don't really want to see Graham.'

'OK, then, why don't we see what your horoscope says today instead?' Mum grabs one of the newspaper supplements from Dad.

'Mum, stop. I don't want to see any therapists or read my horoscopes. Please?'

Dad, who is incapable of discussing feelings, looks up from his newspaper.

'You're better off without her, son,' he says as he chews his marmalade-smothered toast.

I nod back, unsure of what to say in response.

'So are we taking Jeremy in, then?' Mums asks, as Dad returns to the sports pages.

'I guess we'll see what the coin says.'

I flip it for the eighteenth time today.

'What is it? Heads is always yes, tails no?' Mums asks as she awaits the result.

'Yep, and it's heads. Looks like we have a new family member.' I show her the coin in the palm of my hand.

Dad groans, whether about Jeremy or the football news I'm not sure.

'Do you want me to give you a lift to collect him?' Mum offers.

'No, I will be fine, thanks,' I say, as I stand up. 'And anything but baked beans, please . . .'

I take the bus into town, listening to music to pass the time as we journey through every countryside village en route. It is only when I get off that I realize the headphone jack isn't connected properly to my phone and everyone else on the packed bus could hear me listen to 'Unbreak My Heart' on repeat for the entire journey.

Why did no one say anything?

Eventually I let myself into the modern block of flats that towers above Bristol and was famously besieged by scandal when Cherie Blair bought a couple of apartments as an investment. Jade said she wouldn't be in, so I buzz the tradesmen button on the intercom in order to bypass the main doors to the building and board the lift up to the top floor. As I reach the top, I remember the first time she invited me back here after we'd been on a date to Bristol Zoo. We'd spent the day laughing and fooling around, discussing what animals we'd be, holding hands as we braved the dark creepy-crawly section and feeding the penguins together. As I dropped her back, she asked if I wanted to watch a film, but we only saw the opening titles before we were all over each other on the sofa. It wasn't until the next morning that I saw the view. The most wonderful panoramic views stretching across Bristol that no other flat could match.

I wonder if Jade and George have done the same here.

On the sofa, in the bedroom, in the kitchen, in the bathroom.

I try to get rid of these images from my head as I unlock the door and push it open.

The flat is only small – one bedroom with a neat kitchen, a lounge and bathroom – but I don't have to head further than the entrance hall before I spot Jeremy's cage. He, the innocent bystander in this messy situation, is asleep inside. The pet shop told me he is a Mini Lop, but there's nothing mini about this big boy. He's more of an Obese Lop. Considering I no longer have a job to support myself, I fear how I'm going to look after him.

Beside the cage there is a cardboard box, with no note. I prise the Sellotape open to see what's inside. Some more of my belongings that she's found. Some kitchen utensils, a few books and a tiny metallic tin with sentimental items that she has decided would mean more to me than her. It's amazing how three years of your life can fit into a box. A whole relationship, all those moments and memories confined to no more than a biscuit tin. I flick through a heap of Polaroid photos we took on holiday in Majorca, ticket stubs, birthday cards, Christmas cards, Valentine's Day cards, 'just because' cards. I realize how few photos there are of me: I was always the photographer, Jade the model.

I turn around and notice that, despite being asleep,

unnervingly Jeremy's eyes are wide open. Maybe Jade has asked him to keep watch. I should just pick up my things and go, but I flip the coin for permission to move past the cage and into the lounge. It feels strange sneaking around a flat I know so well, but I want to look for clues that George has already moved in.

There is only one toothbrush standing by the sink, no man's coat hanging up, no extra pair of shoes. In fact, now I look around, despite the cardboard box of possessions, my departure hasn't changed the landscape of the flat in the slightest. A game of 'spot the difference' would be challenging, given that all the decorative items and furniture were Jade's. I never considered it before, nor had an issue, but now it seems like I was only a guest. I made less of a mark on the flat than the smudges of raindrops on the window.

I stand there and look out of the wall-to-wall window, remembering the times Jade would hang out of it smoking like a French film star in a black-and-white photo, both irritating me with her bad habit and scaring me that she'd fall. Or when we'd just sit on top of the desk, kissing, drinking and watching the world go by. The rain spitting at the windows quickly turns into an avalanche of water and interrupts my reminiscing, attacking the glass and drumming down on the roof above. Park Street below, which is normally full of students grabbing coffees, is almost vacant as the rain cascades down the hill like a water slide. A woman fighting with an umbrella races for cover under the scaffolding at St George's. A man dressed head-to-toe in an orange high-vis suit watches on as the leaves he has just brushed from the road rebel and naughtily scuttle back into the path of oncoming cars, which employ their headlights even in the middle of the day. The wind rasps and harrows as it hurls past the flats, and trees dance vigorously in the breeze. Seagulls and construction workers in white hats scuttle off building tops as swimming pools form on flat roofs. The picturesque image of Cabot Tower, surrounded by gorgeous green parkland, and rows of Bath-stone Georgian homes looks like a Seurat pointillist painting through the drops of rain stuck to the windows. A dense mist masks the Mendip Hills on the horizon, the masts of the SS *Great Britain* and the towers of Bristol Cathedral are no more than silhouettes.

I swing around at the sound of a strong knock at the door. Who is it? Not Jade. She has her own key. Who else would be visiting? Maybe a neighbour? I got to know a couple of them after we attended a very awkward event next door, when the conversation fizzled out after we had each covered how long we'd lived in the flats, described our flat's layout and realized they were all identical.

Could it be George?

My heart spikes, as I consider what I'd say to him after weeks of planning to kill him.

Should I answer it?

I take the fifty-pence out of my pocket and flip it into the air to decide, the coin now an accessory to anything that happens.

I hold my breath as I peek through the peephole on

the door, expecting to see my nemesis on the other side.

I let out a sigh of relief when I realize it's just the regular postwoman delivering a signed-for parcel. Working split shifts, I've been home plenty of times when she's needed a signature in the past, typically for Jade's clothes orders.

'Hi, how are you?' she says casually, not realizing she won't be seeing me here again.

I sign the machine that she thrusts into my hands and give it back, not that the electronic squiggle bears any relation to my actual signature.

As she leaves, I take one last look around the flat, saying goodbye to my former home, and my former life. I briefly consider smearing rabbit fur around the flat to induce George's allergies but instead I simply pick up the box and the cage and shut the door on the flat for the last time, leaving my key behind.

'It's just you and me now, boy,' I say to Jeremy.

He doesn't say anything back.

5

Does anyone ever run a marathon without feeling the need to tell everyone they are running it?

A month has passed since our near triumph, and ultimate disappointment, at the pub quiz. What with Jessie constantly at the gym, Jake rehearsing his latest dance routine and me bawling my eyes out, it's our first quiz since. Jake has been caught up in the hotel and is having to stay on late to deal with a guest who is attempting to blackmail the receptionist for a free night's stay. I am sitting with Jessie, and she is talking about her marathon preparations – again.

This is the first time she's run the London marathon, or any marathon, for that matter. I have already sponsored her but have made it abundantly clear I want the money back if she fails to complete it. These online giving pages accepting your money before the actual event seem a bit of a con if you ask me.

'Why don't you start running too? Or join the gym at least? Trust me, it will help you. The endorphins will make you feel great, and you can focus on getting in good shape, rather than thinking about Jade.'

I excuse the dig at me not being in good shape and imagine the torture of running. I am actually secretly impressed at her for even attempting the marathon.

'Especially at your age. It's good to keep fit.'

'Jessie, I'm one year older than you.'

I toss the coin nonchalantly.

'I suppose it can't hurt to give it a go,' I say, grimacing, hating the coin's decision.

'What? Are you still doing that flipping the coin thing?'

'What do you mean am I still doing it? I only started a few weeks ago, it's meant to last for the whole year. Don't you remember?'

'Well, yes, obviously I remember, but you're already three weeks further into this than I thought you'd be. Normally these fads of yours last two days, max.'

'What are you talking about? I don't have fads.'

'OK, remember last summer when you told me you were going to become a magician?'

'I don't think I quite said I'd become a magician per se . . .'

'OK, you were going to learn some magic tricks.'

'I wanted to learn one magic trick that I could use as my party piece, as I realized I didn't have any party pieces.'

This was after everyone went round in a circle performing their party tricks at Jake's birthday, at which point I realized I had no discernible talent whatsoever. At least Jake can act, Jessie can run. I can't play an instrument, I can't sing, I can't even juggle. I decided I wanted to learn to play the piano and one magic trick.

'OK, so did you learn that one magic trick?'

'Well, it depends.' I sip my drink, a new craft beer they are stocking, which Big D recommended to me.

'It depends on what? I'm not asking if you're Harry Houdini. It's a yes or no. Can you perform a trick for me right now? And before you make excuses, I know they have a pack of cards behind the bar.'

'If you put it like that, probably not without risking injuring you, no.'

'And how long did you try and learn your trick for?'

'Fine, it lasted about one day, but you can't stereotype me for ever because of one thing.'

'Can you play the piano? Have you written that novel? Have you set up that new candle business – what was it called, Wicks and Mix . . . Pick and Wicks?'

I still have 2,000 unused candles in storage. I thought it would be the next big thing.

'We're not talking about any of those things. This isn't a fad. It's a way of life.'

I am quite happy with that line. It sounds like something well-paid ad executives at Saatchi & Saatchi would think up during a brainstorming session.

'If you're still following this "way of life" in a month's time, I'll start to take note.' There is no need for her to make speech marks with her fingers. That is uncalled for.

'So, do you want to hear how it's been going so far, then?' I ask Jessie, who is now spreading out over the comfy, cushioned leather inbuilt seats while I'm stuck on the wooden chair. She looks more interested in singing along to the Rihanna song that is playing through the speakers.

'I'm guessing you're going to tell me whether I want to or not. And I'm presuming from what you're wearing it's certainly having an impact on your style.' She laughs as she looks me up and down.

I am sitting in bright-red trousers and an old green top that the coin selected from my wardrobe this morning. It is a daring combination, and this must be the only time Jessie's not been wearing a more outlandish outfit than me.

'It made its first big decision over the weekend. Did you not notice I've had my hair cut?'

'Umm, not really, it looks the same as normal. Maybe a bit shorter on the sides?'

The coin's decision for me to cheat on my usual barber hasn't paid off. That was a waste of time, going to a new hairdresser, paying triple the price and meaning my journey time anywhere across Bristol is ten minutes longer, because of the diversion I have to take to avoid walking past my normal barber's.

Jake strolls in. He has to pull down his glasses and squint to see where we are. He's obviously had a long day. His Jake is either away or has had enough of our team already. Probably the latter.

'You've missed hearing all about Josh's new way of life.'

She says it again with air quotes.

'Is this the whole coin thing still?' Jake asks.

'Yes, it's the whole coin thing still,' I say back.

'OK, I've got a decision for you to make – would you like to buy me a drink?'

Even having had time to ruminate about my new way of life, he clearly still doesn't understand it.

'That's not really what this is about, you see.'

'Come on, let's see what the coin says.'

I cave in.

'Ah, it's tails. Sorry, you've got to buy your own. You know I'd normally buy you a pint, but I can't go against the coin. Those are the rules.'

'You know you've never bought me a pint, and we've been coming here every week for over three years.'

'It's just not meant to be.'

'OK, so do you want to buy Jessie a drink?'

'This isn't fair. You're abusing the system now. It's not a game. It's only to be used for real decisions. I was never contemplating buying Jessie a drink.'

'Oh, thank you very much.'

Maybe it was better when they weren't interested.

'Anyway, before I forget, Josh. I've decided I'm going to help set up a Tinder account for you,' Jake says as he places his jacket over the back of the chair.

'I am not sure Josh is ready for that. It's only been a few weeks.'

'No, it will be good for him to move on. He can't just sit and mope around for the rest of his life.'

I listen as Jake and Jessie discuss me as if I've become invisible.

'Hello, guys, I am here. I'm not sitting and moping around but I agree with Jessie, I don't really feel like going on a date right now, to be honest.'

'Nonsense, it will be good for you. I thought the whole point of the coin was to help you find love.'

'Yes, I'd like to find love, but Tinder wasn't quite what I had in mind.'

'You can just have some fun, then. Isn't that the benefit of being single again? I know you're old, but you were not really old enough to be getting married yet, anyway.'

I let the inevitable *old* joke go.

'But Tinder? Really?' I reply.

'That's how everyone meets these days. Either on a dating app or at work. Seeing as you don't have a job, you only have one option. Plus, it's not up to you . . .'

'How come it's up to you?' I interrupt, starting to get fed up with Jake's interference.

'It's not up to me either. It's up to the coin, isn't it?'

'I suppose so,' I say begrudgingly.

Jake performs a victory dance as it lands heads. The coin that saved me buying a round of drinks has now turned its back on me.

Traitor.

'Why do you have to help me with my account? Can I not just do it myself?'

'No, you can't be trusted. You need both of our expertise.' Jessie sticks the knife in.

'Give me your phone, and I'll find the best photos we can use. Now, weren't you meant to be getting us all a drink?'

6

As I stand in the kitchen getting a glass of water, Mum hands me a pink envelope with my name and address printed on the front.

'I just found this out in the porch for you. It was under the mat. The postman must have delivered it earlier.'

I look down at it, confused, mainly wondering how it evaded Dad's postal inspection. I presume it's another wedding invite from a university friend. I am starting to receive wedding invites as often as bills these days, and the requests that I buy a happy couple some new crockery are worse than the impersonal charges from EE.

'Are you OK to turn all the lights off before you head up? Dad and I are going to bed,' Mum says.

'Yep, that's fine. Night, Mum.'

I wait until she has reached the top of the staircase before opening the envelope.

It is not a wedding invite. Or a bill. It is a red card decorated with a cartoon bear holding a heart-shaped balloon. The flowery text reads 'Happy Valentine's Day'.

Who is sending me a Valentine's Card?
It must be from Jade?
She must be apologizing for everything?

Wanting me back?

My heart beats rapidly.

I anxiously open it, expecting to see a long, hand-written message inside explaining everything.

'Dear Josh, Happy Valentine's Day, from your secret admirer xx.'

I read it again. I know the handwriting. It's not Jade's. It's not even a secret admirer's. It's Mum's.

If there is anything more tragic than not receiving a Valentine's Card, it is receiving one from your mum. At the age of twenty-eight.

I grab a whole tub of Ben & Jerry's ice cream from the freezer and head to my room. As I reach the landing, I hear Mum and Dad lock their bedroom door and I immediately grab the remote, to switch the TV on and turn the volume right up. At least when I lived here before I was oblivious to what the sound of their bedroom door shutting meant.

I decide there and then that Valentine's Day is the worst day ever invented in the history of mankind. If single life isn't bad enough for the rest of the year – when you must eat two meals by yourself to take advantage of offers, or you have to take a homeless person to the cinema to use your 2-4-1 code – then February 14th truly takes the biscuit. The heart-shaped, candy-coated biscuit.

This time last year, Jade and I were spending Valentine's Day at the Bristol Lido, snuggling up in the hot tub, enjoying a couples' massage. Now, I lie on my single bed, in my parents' house, crying while watching a

1990s rom-com next to Jeremy the Rabbit, who is defecating all over my teenage Bristol City duvet set. The coin loves Phish Food and Hugh Grant and doesn't care that I feel sick immediately afterwards.

It is ironic that I'm spending Valentine's with a rampant rabbit when I'm not getting any. The most action I've had since Jade leaving me was at the optician's, when I struggled to decide whether the image was clearer using my right or left eye, and the optometrist wouldn't let me use my coin to decide. He then leaned in too close, lingered and whispered sweet nothings (or instructions) into my ear.

It's just as well that he said I have twenty-twenty vision, as the box television at the foot of my bed is vintage now, with its small screen the size of a mobile phone screen. As the film draws to an end and Hugh Grant inevitably gets the girl, I flick through the channels to see what else can upset me. A series of Valentine's-themed reality shows. Skip. More rom-coms. Skip. After rejecting hundreds of stations, I land on one of the adult channels, where some semi-naked, overly tanned woman is writhing around and inviting me to call her. She's wearing matching red underwear, with the tiniest tartan skirt worn around her waist, barely covering her tiny thong. Her ensemble is completed by thigh-high stockings and high heels. Her straight, dark hair flows down her back.

I've not sunk to this level, have I?

'Hi, guys, so the phone line has just become available. Select option number one to get horny with me, guys. Why don't you be my next caller?' the model asks with a suggestive wink.

I twist the coin through my fingers before launching it into the air.

Heads.

I tentatively reach for the phone and dial in the number.

'Press one to speak to the sexy girl on screen, or press the hash key if you just want to listen in,' a pre-recorded voice says.

What am I doing?

'Unfortunately, that girl is currently busy with another caller. Remember, you can press the hash key to return to the main menu or press the star key to switch to another girl.'

I look at the screen of my phone. I've already been on the call for over ninety seconds. All of a sudden, I hear a man's voice.

'Oh yes, baby, I would fuck you so hard, I would destroy you.'

Is this what women want?

'Yes, I love it rough, baby.'

Apparently so.

'I'd grab your throat and choke you while I'm fucking you.'

Is this what George does with Jade?

'Yes and I'd love you to spit on my face,' the woman instructs him.

Should I have been spitting on her? Is that where I went wrong?

'Yeah. I want to turn you over and fuck you,' he grunts, sounding like he's going to have a heart attack. He coughs and splutters so much down the phone, I can almost feel the phlegm landing on my face.

Jeremy looks at me disapprovingly. I think he preferred watching Hugh Grant.

There's a lengthy delay between the call and the screen, so her actions don't match with her words. It's like watching a film with subtitles where you know everything that's about to happen. Fifteen seconds after announcing it, she removes her bra, climbs onto the office table, crouches down on all fours, and spanks her bum.

The phone line goes silent.

'It is your lucky day. In just a moment you will be talking live with one of our sexy babes . . .'

Crap. What do I say? How do I follow that?

'Hello, baby, what's your name?'

'Jo . . . hn.' I decide to give a fake name just in case someone else I know is listening.

'What did you say, baby?'

'John,' I reply hesitantly.

She sits back down on the table and makes an exasperated face as she throws her arms into the air. I think she's taken an instant dislike to me, but then I realize with the delay she's just unhappy with the last caller for hanging up so abruptly.

'Oh hey, John, have we spoken before?' she speaks in a strong Essex accent, but it's hard to hear what she's saying. For a premium phone line the connection is very poor.

'Nope.' My voice cracks up. This feels wrong.

'What can I do for you this evening, then?'

'Umm, I just fancied a chat,' I say quietly so that my parents can't hear, not that they are concerned about me hearing their own antics.

'Oh yeah, you want a naughty chat. Are you nice and hard for me there?'

'Ummm.'

'Am I turning you on?'

'Ummmm.'

She begins to mime lewd actions with her hands as she tells me what she would do. I cover Jeremy's ears.

'Oh John, fuck me, John. Yes, just like that.' She moans in a most exaggerated fashion, which sounds more like she is having her leg amputated than pleasuring herself.

The phone line breaks up, and the call is disconnected. I see her huff, annoyed at someone else cutting her off in mid-flow. I don't want to think how much my next phone bill is going to be.

I decide I will stick to talking to Jeremy instead.

I take a tissue out of the pack of Kleenex in my drawer and use it to wipe away my tears.

Spring

7

The Uber driver clearly doesn't know what to think when he picks us up from outside Jake's house. He must be used to seeing plenty of unusual sights driving around Bristol on a Saturday night, but he does a double take when he sees us two.

I'm dressed as James Bond, wearing a tuxedo and toting a toy gun, while Jake is dressed in a dog onesie complete with floppy ears.

'You're going to Woodfield Road?' he asks very hesitantly as we clamber into the back seats.

'Yes, that's right, thank you,' I reply, avoiding the temptation to impersonate Roger Moore.

We certainly don't look as if we should be going to the same event.

'Why are they holding it at Dan's house this year?' Jake asks as we drive across town.

'Apparently his place is a bit bigger, and presumably it's his turn to host. It's been at Jessie's the last two times, hasn't it?'

This is Jessie's third fancy-dress birthday party in a row, and it's always a joint party with Dan, one of her university friends, who shares the same birthday. It's become something of a tradition. Following on from Disney and Harry Potter, the theme for this evening is the London Underground. The coin chose for me to go as Bond Street rather than Oxford Circus, and me having to dress up like a clown.

'Drop off Josh,' the automated voice of the sat-nav instructs the driver as we pull up on the side of the road. He's not spoken to us during the ten-minute ride, presumably worried that we are complete psychos.

'I bet you he's going to give you a bad rating,' Jake says as we walk along the pavement, looking for where we're meant to be going. We're somewhere in Redland, but I'm not familiar with this area.

'My rating is already bad from when I took Jade to Longleat Safari that time. I had to get an Uber, as neither of us could drive.'

'Oh yeah, I remember that. Didn't the car get damaged or something?'

'Yeah. One of the monkeys pulled the wing mirror off. The driver went mad. I thought he was going to kick us out in the lion enclosure.'

'Oh God.' Jake looks around to find where Dan's house is, as the driver has seemingly taken us too far. 'Do we know what number his house is?'

'Number three, wasn't it?'

Jake trails behind me, adjusting his dog costume as I ring the doorbell. I get into character and point my gun at the door, waiting for Jessie or Dan to answer.

As the door opens I realize it's not Jessie. Or Dan. Rather, I'm pointing a gun in the face of a horrified old lady, who starts to scream.

'Oh no, Josh, it's number five,' Jake, looking down at his phone, calls out from around the corner.

Thanks, Jake, thirty seconds earlier would have been lovely.

To my right, I see a group of nuns filing into a house a few doors down. There are one, two, three . . .

Seven Sisters. That's the house.

I realize I'm still pointing the gun towards the woman, who is now cowering.

'I'm very sorry, madam, I believe we have the wrong house. Sorry to disturb you.' I put the gun back into the inside pocket of my dinner jacket and leave the grey-haired lady rooted to the spot.

She looks out into the street in horror as I walk away.

After we eventually arrive at the right house, we make our way inside and are immediately swarmed by bakers and bankers.

'Told you everyone would come as Baker Street or Bank – so obvious.'

'I don't see any other dogs.'

We head through the crowded house to find Jessie, aware that the other guests are judging our costumes. The place is smaller than I was expecting and messier. The unwashed plates are stacked up beside the sink, and in the lounge there are so many shoes left lying around that it looks like Clarks during sale season. We spot Jessie standing next to a couple of members of ABBA. She's dressed as Paddington Bear, complete with a luggage tag and marmalade sandwiches. Her long, straight dark hair escapes from underneath her red hat.

'Are you going to hold on to that all night?' I say, pointing to the sandwich, which is already the worse for wear.

'They're getting a bit soggy actually,' she says as she gives us both hugs. I try and avoid her rubbing marmalade over my tux. 'You both look great – Bond Street, I presume, and . . . what are you this year, Jake?'

'Isn't it obvious?'

'Well, I can see you're a dog again. I'm trying to think what station that is. Dog, doggy, puppy . . . oh, is there an Isle of Dogs?'

Jake shakes his head and woofs.

'Woofing Broadway? Woofing Bec?'

'No, I'm Barking.'

'You certainly are barking. Are you going to wear the same outfit every year?'

Jake came as Fluffy from Harry Potter last year and Tramp from *Lady and the Tramp* the year before.

'Anyway, happy birthday! Are you enjoying your party?' Jake says, dejected.

'Yes, I'm having a great time, thanks. Nice to see everyone has made so much effort. Or at least most people.'

Right on cue, a girl walks past wearing jeans and a T-shirt with a coat hanger draped round her neck.

'Hanger Lane,' Jessie whispers, looking highly unimpressed.

'Oh, of course.'

'Twenty-seven, then? You're getting on. How does it feel?' I can't help ribbing her after all the abuse she gives me for my age.

'Pretty much the same as twenty-six so far. Strangely enough.'

'Twenty-seven is a good age.'

'I'm surprised you can remember, it was quite a while ago for you.'

'I don't think you can make any more jokes, now you're in your late twenties.'

'Twenty-seven isn't late twenties. It's still mid twenties, surely?' She looks genuinely concerned.

'Won't be long 'til thirty,' I joke.

'But you will always be older than me.'

I can't win this one.

Jessie turns around as Björn Borg (Wimbledon) approaches with a birthday card for her. Jake and I retreat to the corner, trying to work out who everyone is dressed as.

'Presumably the couple in cabin crew outfits are Heathrow terminals? What's the person wearing the crown meant to be?'

'Umm, King's Cross?'

'Yes, good shout, I was wondering why he looked so grumpy. What about the guy in the astronaut outfit?'

'What station could that link to?'

'Is there something moon-related? Space . . . ?'

'Or star something? What about Eurostar?'

'No, I've got it. I think it's Euston.'

'Euston?'

'Yes, as in "Euston, we have a problem!"'

'Oh God, that's so tenuous.'

'How about the guy holding the snooker cue?'

'I have no idea. Jess, what's the guy with the snooker cue meant to be?' I catch her as she's going to get another drink.

She looks around to see who we mean. He's standing next to two guys wearing Arsenal and Tottenham football shirts.

'Oh, apparently he's meant to be Kew Gardens, I think they all left their outfit choices to the very last minute.'

'Really? After all the effort we put in?' Jake says.

Jessie rolls her eyes.

'He's probably wondering why you've come as a dog, to be fair.'

'It's Barking! Zone 4. Hammersmith and City, and District lines. It's actually a very clever costume.' Jessie has gone before Jake has even finished his defence.

'Wasn't that girl here last year?' I discreetly point to a girl standing across the room. She has also managed to repurpose her previous outfit and is again wearing a toilet seat around her neck. Perhaps I should start recycling my costumes, as my wardrobe is full of outfits worn once that I need to stick on eBay.

'Yeah, I remember we chatted with her last time. Why don't you go and say hi?'

'Why can't we both go?'

'Well, you're single, and she's clearly here on her own and is very good-looking. Do I need to say more?'

'She's dressed as a toilet!'

'Go on, it will be good practice for you!'

'I don't know. I'm not sure if I'm ready.'

'You don't have to propose to her, just have a chat . . . Hang on, I've got to take this. It's the hotel.' Jake follows Jessie into the kitchen to take the phone call. He's on duty all weekend, meaning he has to be prepared for any emergency. At the thirty-fifth of thirty-six hotels in the city, there tends to be a major problem every week.

'Very convenient timing,' I say to him as he walks away, which makes it look like I'm talking to myself.

I flip the coin to decide. It tells me to go and talk to her, rather than standing on my own and playing on my phone. I take the long route round the room to give me time to build up my confidence. This is a bad idea, as I am now approaching her from behind. I weigh up whether I should tap her on the back to get her attention until I decide against this and instead spring around, looking like a maniac.

'Oh, hi,' she says, almost jumping. 'I didn't see you there.'

'Sorry . . . hi . . . I think we met last year?'

'Yes, I have some hazy memory of that,' she says with an Irish lilt.

She is pretty, with shoulder-length ginger hair and bright blue eyes.

'I like the outfit, again,' I say, looking down before jerking my head back up quickly so it doesn't look like I'm staring at her chest.

'Yes, I had to get my money's worth for this toilet seat. Moaning Myrtle . . . Waterloo. I'm hoping next year is a music theme so I can come as Lou Reed.'

'Or Lou Bega. Both musical geniuses, really.'

'Very true. I am just annoyed that those guys dressed up as ABBA stole my idea and came as Waterloo. Thought I'd be unique.' She looks across the room, before turning back to me. 'What are you?'

I take my gun out.

'Bond Street, James Bond Street.'

Did I really just do that?

'Of course, looking very suave. Especially compared to everyone else.'

'Yes, that's not too hard when that guy's carrying a can of beer and has got a dildo on his head, dressed as Cockfosters.'

'So have you had a good year?' she says, laughing as she looks at the guy I'm referring to.

'Yeah, not bad, thanks. You?'

'Yep. It's gone quickly, hasn't it?'

What else do you say to someone you only see on an annual basis?

Think of something, Josh.

I try to recall anything I can remember about her from last year.

Fortunately, Jessie joins us on her way back from the kitchen, holding a couple of drinks.

'Did you want one?'

'Only if it's shaken, not stirred.'

Really, Josh?

'What were you two chatting about? Can I join?' Jessie asks Waterloo.

'I was just asking how . . . sorry, what's your name?'

'It's Josh.'

'How Josh's year has been.'

'Oh, he's not started telling you about his coin, has he?'

I swing round to look at Jessie.

'No, what's this about a coin?'

I watch on as Jessie recaps everything to this random girl dressed as a toilet.

'Wow, that's very brave. So how does it work? Would you have to flip a coin if I ask whether you're coming out with us afterwards?'

'Yes, that's about right.'

'This sounds like it could be fun,' she smiles.

After too many drinks at the party, we walk from the house towards the Clifton Triangle. The motliest crew you've ever seen. To my left I have an Angel, to my right someone dressed as a Victoria sandwich. Four guys dressed as ABBA, a handful of Bakers in white chef's hats, two of the Seven Sisters, the guy with his snooker cue, Waterloo and Jessie, still holding her marmalade sandwiches, make up our entourage, with others following further behind us. I don't know where Jake has got to.

'Did you see they've changed their name back to Lizard Lounge again?' Waterloo asks me as she takes a puff of a cigarette. She's left the toilet seat behind, so looks the most normal of us all.

'Are we really going there? Surely there's a better club we could go to. The music is so cheesy.'

'Yes, that's why it's great, duh.'

'Why don't we go to La Rocca?' one of the nuns suggests.

'Josh, flip your coin to see if we should go to Lizard Lounge or La Rocca,' Waterloo demands.

'OK, everyone, heads is Lizard Lounge, tails is La Rocca. Agreed?'

Everyone huddles around as we pause on the pavement to make the big decision.

I toss the coin into the night's sky.

'Heads. Lizard Lounge it is!'

Benny, Björn and the Bakers all celebrate wildly.

'Yay. Let's go.' Waterloo grabs my arm, excitedly, and drags me down the road.

I haven't been to Lizard Lounge since school. It is predictably full of students and schoolkids pretending to be over eighteen, and the music is as cheesy as I remember. By the time we're in the club, our entire group has heard about the coin. Jessie is trying her best to discourage everyone, but it's no use. Before I know it, everyone is chanting 'toss the coin' as a row of shots are lined up for me to down.

The room starts to spin as Waterloo puts her arms around me, and we dance to a medley of nineties hits, getting closer and closer with each song. Our hands all over each other. She leans in right next to my face to be heard over the Spice Girls.

'So, Mr Bond Street, let's see if the coin thinks you should kiss me.'

We spend the next twenty minutes interchanging

between coin flipping and sloppy, tobacco-tasting snogging.

The next thing I know, I'm waking up the following morning. I don't know what time it is. I don't even know where I am. I struggle to open my eyes. My head kills. Light streams in through the translucent grey curtains.

Is this the house where the party was? I don't recognize it, if so. It's not Jessie's. It's not Jake's. Is it Waterloo's? Did I sleep here? Did we sleep together? How did we get back?

I look down. I'm still dressed in my tuxedo, although judging by the state of it, no one's going to want to buy it on eBay. I frisk myself for my phone and wallet. Fortunately, I still have them, but I seem to have lost my gun. It's not in any of my pockets. I turn over in the bed to look for it and, to my surprise, I'm lying next to an Elephant. She is still wearing her trunk.

I decide to get out of bed and out of this mystery flat, before Castle turns up.

8

I'm waiting at the bus stop, half-asleep, when my phone rings. I squint at my mobile. Even looking at the bright screen hurts my eyes.

It's Jessie.

'Hey, Josh, I'm just checking you're still on for meeting me at the gym?'

Oh. Crap.

'Josh, are you there?' she shouts.

I quickly move the phone away from my ear.

'Yes,' I say reluctantly.

'So, I'll see you there in an hour, then?'

'Maybe we could do another day instead?' I plead.

'Come on, you can't cancel on me. I've got you a one-day trial membership for today.'

'I'm not cancelling, I'm just postponing.' A moped revs loudly past.

Why is everything so loud?

'You've already been postponing for ages. You promised the coin you'd come with me. You can't cancel on the coin.'

'But I feel so ill.'

'Well, that's your own fault. You should have stopped drinking when I did.'

'And I haven't got anything to wear,' I say, looking

76

down at my outfit, which is dirty, smelly and wholly impractical.

'What are you wearing now?'

'I'm still in the tuxedo.'

'You haven't been home yet?'

'No, I'm just waiting to catch the bus.' I don't try and explain where I've been all morning.

I hear talking in the background.

'Jessie?'

'Sorry, just give me a second.'

She is talking with someone else. From the muffled noises, it sounds like her housemate. She lives with two girls, whom she works with.

'What size shoe are you?'

'Are you talking to me now?'

'Yes, you.'

'Ten, I'm a ten.'

'OK, eleven will do. Izzi said you can borrow some of her boyfriend's gym gear.'

'But . . .'

'No arguments. Be there.'

I feel self-conscious as soon as I walk into the changing room. It doesn't help that everyone is staring at me as I get changed out of my tuxedo. Izzi's boyfriend is a gym freak and he has all the clothing to match. I'm wary as I slide on his bright-orange trainers that I look too much like a regular. I know I'm not very fit, and I don't want my outfit to miscommunicate that. I'm only here because of Jessie and the coin. Sometimes I hate them both.

'OK, let's start with some push-ups. Show me how many you can do.'

Crap.

I'm sweating from my hangover even before I've started.

'Come on, Josh, show me what you've got, mate.'

I lie flat on my face on the ground, attempting to do one push-up. This is embarrassing. There are people all around watching.

I don't need a day pass to see if I like the place. I decide after one minute that I don't.

Come on, I must be able to do one.

'No, you have to keep your back straight, mate. Come on. We'll stop once you get to ten.'

Ten?

'I'll give you one and a half stars for that. Let's go and jump on the treadmill.'

I didn't realize the free consultation involved a rating system. I don't think I'm going to get five stars for anything.

He tries to motivate me in his strong northern accent.

'We'll just start off at a gentle jog, try and keep at this pace for five minutes, and then we'll change it up. Let's just get your muscles and heart working. Come on, you can do it.'

There are only a few things I would run for. A bus. A train. An ice-cream van. But running for the sake of it? No, thank you.

'Go easy on him.' Jessie walks over from another

treadmill. Adam the PT puts his arm around her shoulder as she joins us.

Brilliant. Now I have two spectators to laugh at me.

'How did you get on?' I realize that Adam has now forgotten about me and has started a conversation with Jessie instead. They are enjoying a friendly chat while I'm dying.

'Not too bad, thanks. Just ran for an hour. Did eight miles, which was OK.'

An hour on the treadmill? I'm bored already.

'When is your next long run?'

'I think I'm going to do a sixteen-mile one this weekend.'

I don't know why I sponsored her so much now. The marathon doesn't seem to be a challenge for her.

'Josh, when you've finished with Adam, you can come to Boxercise with me and see if you like that.'

When I finish with Adam, I will probably need an ambulance.

'Hang on, the coin only decided that I come to the gym, not that I took classes too.'

'Don't try and get out of it now.'

'I've got to flip again,' I say as I reach into the zipped pocket on my sweaty shorts before struggling to flip and jog simultaneously. For a second I think I'm going to fall off the back of the treadmill.

Why does this coin hate me so much?

My pained facial expression says everything.

'There you go. Now hurry up and finish your running and meet me over in that studio,' Jessie says, pointing to a room with a transparent glass wall so everyone can watch my suffering. This gym is like a gladiatorial arena.

It turns out that I am the only man in the Boxercise class, and I am hoping it's not too energetic, as I can barely stand up. I envisioned it to be full of young, muscly wannabe boxers, but aside from Jessie, everyone else is over forty, so at least I won't be too humiliated.

'Do you know what happened to Jake?' I ask Jessie as we stretch to warm up.

'Just as we thought. There was a problem at the hotel, so he had to go and help sort it out.'

'What was it this week? Not another fight?' A couple of weeks ago Jake was called at 4 a.m. by the night porter when a man on a stag party discovered that another guy in the group had slept with his girlfriend. All hell broke loose, with a mass brawl erupting in the reception area. We all wondered why the porter called Jake rather than the police . . .

'No. Apparently there was some guy who started running around the hotel naked, and then he started smearing his own faeces on the walls of his room.'

'Lovely.'

'It got worse when the cleaner came in, saw what had happened and threw up everywhere. Aren't you glad we're not working in the hotel industry any more?'

I didn't really leave by choice.

'Poor Jake. Do you think other hotels have guests like this?'

'Goodness knows. Anyway, enough about Jake,

what happened to you is the bigger question,' she says seriously.

'Come on, guys, split into pairs. One of you pick up the pads, and the other the gloves. There should be enough,' the coach interrupts.

'What do you mean, what happened to me?' I say, as I punch Jessie's pads.

'I'm worried about you, Josh. It's not like you to act like that. You were absolutely wasted. And then hooking up with Louise, whom you barely know.'

'Louise?'

'Waterloo.'

'Oh, Lou, wearing a loo seat. I should have remembered that ... I can't really remember much, if I'm honest.'

I try and recall last night, but most of it is blank.

'You don't remember rolling around on the floor of the club, humming the James Bond theme tune, pretending to shoot everyone?'

'Oh, God, did I do that?'

'You don't remember Louise getting upset when you tried to kiss someone else?'

I'm glad I can't remember anything now.

'Do you know how I ended up in the same bed as the Elephant? Did we ... ?'

'You mean Sara. And no, you didn't.'

'That trunk would have probably got in the way,' I say.

'Josh, this isn't a joke. You really don't remember anything? She let you sleep it off at hers after you got us all kicked out of the club.'

'Oh no, really?'

'Yes, really. That's what I mean. Jake thinks it's good you're letting off steam, but I'm worried about you. You never go crazy like that. I don't think this coin thing is a good idea, if it's encouraging you to make choices like you did last night.' Jessie sounds like my mum.

We switch pads and gloves, which I'm not sure is a good idea, with Jessie in this mood.

'Am I not allowed to have some fun? It was the first time since Jade I've had a good time.'

'Obviously you can have fun, but I thought flipping the coin was meant to help you get your life on track, not make things worse?'

The throbbing pain inside my head concurs with her.

'You have a point.'

'I mean, do you really need to flip a coin to decide if you want another drink? Everyone was just taking advantage of you last night. I thought you were trying to be careful with your money until you get a new job.'

'But I made a pact.'

She pauses for a second as she thinks.

'Why don't you switch to only flipping it for big decisions? Or just a few times a day? I don't think that's cheating.'

'Isn't it?'

'No, it's not.' I'm sure she punches my pads harder as she says it.

I try to think things through, but my head is too sore, which answers my query.

'Maybe you're right. I probably shouldn't flip a coin

to see whether I should drink shots, and to be honest I probably don't need it to pick what socks I wear either. I'll just use it for big choices, or when I'm stuck and I can't make a decision.'

'I'm always right!' Jessie smiles, finishing off with a one-two combo.

'OK, everyone switch partners,' the trainer barks.

As we all rotate around the room, I'm separated from Jessie before she can confiscate my coin. I find myself opposite a tiny, middle-aged woman wearing librarian-style glasses. She holds her pads up first while I gently punch them as if she was a little child, wary of not hitting her too hard and hurting her.

'If you haven't done so already, swap roles now.'

I take off the gloves and switch them with the woman.

With her first punch she sends me tumbling to the ground.

9

If Russian roulette is dangerous, tossing a coin to decide who to match with on Tinder is deadly. I'm only one flip of the coin away from being tied up in someone's basement and used as a sex slave. Given it is Jake's idea for me to get back into the dating game, I decide it is all his fault if I end up in a dungeon.

There are only about seven women under the age of sixty living in a five-mile radius of our house, so the coin doesn't have a wide pool to choose from. One describes herself as a 'learner of witchcraft and lover of Satan'. Fortunately, the coin rejects her.

Instead, at exactly 7.28 p.m., I'm standing in the village precinct waiting to meet the coin's choice: *Emma, dark hair, 24 years old, 5 ft 9, hairdresser. Loves Taylor Swift, prosecco, and pineapple on pizza.*

I scroll through our chat on Tinder as I wait for her. All of our correspondence has been perfunctory – 'How was your weekend?', 'Sorry for the slow response', 'Are you doing much this week?' I'm hoping in real life the conversation springs into life.

The precinct is empty, with the chemist and newsagent already closed. I look around to see if Emma is approaching, but I only spot a couple of solitary dog-walkers on this cold evening. I shiver due to both the cold and the nerves. I haven't had a date for years, and I've spent the last few hours worrying about what to wear, what to say, what to do.

'Hey, is it Josh?' she says, appearing out of nowhere.

'Yes, it must be Emma? How are you?'

She reaches her arms out to give me a hug, and I almost head-butt her in the process.

Don't do that for a start, Josh.

'Actually everyone just calls me Em for short,' she smiles as we let go.

'Better than "ugh",' I joke.

'What do you mean?'

'You know, your name. Em-ugh. Better to be called Em than "ugh".'

She stares back at me.

'Don't worry, it was just a bad joke.'

Can I start again?

'Oh, I get it now.'

As she laughs belatedly, which sounds more like snorting, I check her out. She is almost as tall as me. Her hair is long and layered, and darker than in her photos. She is good-looking, and seems sweet. But it is clear there is no immediate spark.

Give it a chance, Josh.

'So anyway, pub or chippy, then? I'll let you choose!' I say, beginning to freeze in the cold.

'What a choice. That's the problem with Cadbury, right? It's always one of the two.' As well as a lack of suitable dates, there are even fewer date options in the village: the pub, which will be full of nosy villagers, or the less-than-romantic chip shop.

'I know, sorry. Maybe next time we could go into Bristol instead.'

'Do you know what, I'm actually pretty hungry, so I don't mind going for fish and chips, if you're happy?' she suggests, saving me from having to pull out my coin.

'Sounds good to me ... I should have made a reservation.'

'I don't think you can reserve a table.'

'No, I know. Just another joke. I'll stop now.'

Fuck. I forgot how awkward dating is.

I slide open the glass door to the chip shop and let Emma in first.

There are only two tables, and one is occupied by two men who are wearing paint-splattered overalls and discussing horse racing.

'What would you like? I'll get it,' I say to Emma as we stare up at the menu.

'Thank you. Can I get a fishcake and chips, and a Coke?'

I order while Emma takes a seat at the vacant table.

'We're all out of Coke, I'm afraid, love. We have Sprite or Tango?' the woman behind the counter says to me in a thick West Country accent.

I act as an intermediary, relaying the message to Emma and back again.

'Sprite, please,' Emma tells me.

'Sprite, please,' I tell the woman.

'Salt and vinegar on them, love?'

'Do you want salt and vinegar, Em?'

'Just salt.'

'Salt and vinegar on one, and just salt on the other, thanks.'

'Taking away, love?'

'Umm, no, we're sitting in.' I look around at the lacklustre setting, not the best place to create sparks on a first date.

'OK, there you go. Enjoy, love.'

I pick us up a couple of miniature wooden forks, and embarrassingly struggle to open the sauce sachets as I join Emma on the metallic chairs. The table is decorated with graffiti and ketchup stains.

Well, this is romantic.

The draft from outside blows in through the gap in the door. It's freezing.

'Would you like to take it away, actually? I'm not trying to be forward here, but we could eat it at mine. Might be a bit warmer,' I say hesitantly, unsure if that's a good idea. I haven't told her yet I'm still living with my parents.

She looks equally hesitant.

'It's OK, don't worry, I'm not going to kill you or anything,' I try to reassure her.

Josh, just shut up.

'OK, yes, why not?' She stands up, and we ask for a bag to take our order away with us, leaving the two men to continue discussing the afternoon's races.

Mum and Dad are away for the week on a cheap getaway that Dad found in the papers. I wouldn't consider inviting Emma over otherwise. Mum would be horrified to think that I've met someone on Tinder. She is still concerned about paedophiles grooming me. I think I'm past my sell-by date as far as they are concerned.

As we walk back across the small village precinct, I realize that, if this evening goes well, I am going to have to invent some extensive and elaborate backstory to explain how we met just so that Mum never finds out. We will then have to maintain this pretence for the remainder of our lives, tell the fictitious tale at our wedding and take it to our graves with us. It almost seems more work than it is worth.

'Here we are!' I say as we approach home and I unlock the door. Even if it's as innocent as eating fish and chips, I feel a strange sensation bringing a girl back home with me. It almost feels like I'm cheating on Jade, which is ironic.

'This looks a lovely house,' Emma beams enthusiastically as we enter.

She takes her high heels off and leaves them by the door as she walks into the hallway, revealing her red-painted toenails.

'Is it OK just to leave my coat here?' she asks politely, revealing the tight leather trousers and grey T-shirt she was hiding underneath.

'Yep, of course, just hang it up there.' I point to the bannister. 'Can I get you any other sauces?'

'Some more ketchup, please.'

'Cool, I'll just get us some plates too. Do you want to take the food into there and have a seat?' I direct her into the lounge and I head into the kitchen.

I try to dig the ketchup out from the back of the fridge. We had a food delivery a few days ago, although with three of us now living here, Dad has decided to cut costs and switch from Waitrose to Tesco. Not wanting to lose face, Mum asked the Tesco delivery van to park around the corner, where she met him armed with Waitrose bags in her pockets.

'You have lots of photos of yourself,' she shouts out to me, as I carefully balance the bottle of ketchup, two plates and some cutlery in my hands.

Shit. I forgot Mum decided to leave them up on the mantelpiece.

'I know. Most of them are very embarrassing too,' I say, as I rejoin Emma, who is standing inspecting each of the photos.

'No, you were a cute kid.' She thanks me as she takes one of the plates and starts to empty the chips out of the paper wrapping. The chips overflow off the plate.

'I think we could have probably gone for small portions. That's ridiculous.'

'I know, so many.'

'I hope they're not too cold now?'

'No, they're all good, thanks,' she says, tucking into them.

The conversation might still be stilted, but at least it's more comfortable here than in the chip shop.

'You must have done well to be able to afford to buy already,' she says, looking up.

'What do you mean?'

'Buying a house. I'm still trying to save up.'

Fuck.

I realize she thinks that this is my house, not my parents'. And worse, that I have decorated my house with photos of just me. She must think I'm an egomaniac.

'Oh no, it's –'

I'm interrupted by the doorbell.

'Give me a minute, I'll just see who that is.' I put my glass down on the table and head to the door. It's too dark outside to make out who it is through the glass panels.

No. No. No.

'What are you doing here?' I whisper in disbelief and panic, as I unlock the door and open it slightly, blocking them from entering.

'What do you mean, what are we doing here? We live here, Josh. Are you going to let us in?' Dad says as he and Mum barge past me into the hallway, dropping their suitcases down by the phone cabinet. I try and kick Emma's shoes out of sight.

'But I didn't think you were coming back until Sunday.'

'Why are you whispering? Your mum had a bad premonition about our hotel and needed a therapy appointment with Graham to discuss it, so we had to cut the trip short.' He rolls his eyes.

'What's that smell? Have you had fish and chips?' Mum asks.

'Yes, I got a takeaway earlier. How about you take your bags upstairs and unpack? You will probably want to get straight to bed after your journey. I can bring you some food up, if you'd like?' I say, panicking.

'It's only eight o'clock, Josh. I know we're getting on but we don't need to go to bed just yet.' Mum edges further and further down the hall despite my protestations.

How do I get out of this one?

'So actually . . .' I go to explain the situation.

'Oh, sorry, we didn't realize you've got company.' Mum spots Emma, who has wandered into the hall to see what all the commotion is about.

'Hello, is it Jessie?' Mum asks as she greets her.

'No, I'm Emma.' She looks confused.

'Hello, Emma, I'm Josh's mum.'

'Oh, hi, ummm . . . how are you? I didn't realize . . . Josh didn't tell me that his parents would be joining us this evening.' She looks at me, puzzled.

'I didn't know that they would be joining us either,' I try to explain.

'Do you live nearby?'

'No, darling, we live here.'

'Oh, I thought this was Josh's house?'

'Yes, Josh lives here with us.'

'It's certainly not his house, though. He doesn't even pay any rent,' Dad unhelpfully chips in.

I can feel Emma looking at me, but I keep my head down, avoiding her gaze.

'Ah, you do have fish and chips. Have you got any left over for us? We're starving.' Dad breaks past me and heads straight into the lounge.

I chase after him.

'Could you go into the dining room, perhaps? You can take the rest of the chips with you.' I try to shepherd him back out.

'The more the merrier, right? I'm sure Emma doesn't mind me and your dad joining you,' Mum calls out.

Emma stands rooted to the spot, still baffled by what is happening.

Mum and Dad head into the kitchen, and I think they've finally got the idea that we'd like to be left alone, until they return with plates, cutlery and glasses of their own.

Before I can stop it, the four of us are all in the lounge sharing the remaining chips, Mum and Emma squashed next to each other on one sofa, Dad and I on the other.

'So how do you two know each other?' Mum asks.

'We met on . . .' Emma begins

'Emma lives in Cadbury too,' I interrupt.

'You've never mentioned an Emma before. So is this a date, then? You didn't tell us you were seeing anyone,' she excitedly whispers across the room.

'You know everyone can hear you, Mum.' I want the world to swallow me up.

'You're so secretive now, not like when you were at school and you'd happily tell us about your day. I remember when you would come home and tell us about who you spoke to at break times −'

'I'm not seeing anyone.' I can feel my face blushing.

'Well, I for one think it's great you're moving on from Jade.'

Emma is now wondering who both Jessie and Jade are.

'Mum, can you stop?'

'Sorry about him, Emma, I'm not sure why he's in such a bad mood tonight. Tell us about yourself. What do you do?'

'I'm a hairdresser, or a trainee one. I work on the high street,' she says, looking completely bewildered by what is happening.

At least I'm learning something about my date, even if I'm not the one asking the questions. Dad, meanwhile, is oblivious to everything, scoffing down half my fish, which he's stolen.

'And where do you live?'

'Just the other side of the village. Do you know the houses behind the church?'

'Yes, I know where you mean. I actually go to yoga with a woman who lives near there – Susan?'

'Yes, that's my mum.'

'How funny! What a small world. So you're not embarrassed to be living with your parents, then, unlike somebody?' She points her fork and winks at me.

'No, we get on really well.'

The fact that we are both twenty-somethings still living with our parents seems to be the only thing we have in common.

'Can I ask what star sign you are?'

Oh God, she's not going to start giving her a horoscope.

'Mum, I think that's enough questions now.'

'Emma doesn't mind, do you?'

Emma smiles back helplessly.

'Actually, just wait there. I'll go and get my tarot cards and I can do a reading for you . . .'

Surely not?

'Oh, that's very kind of you . . . But I have to . . . I have to start work early tomorrow, so I should probably be going,' Emma timidly says.

'Do you not want to finish your dinner first?' Mum pats her on the lap. Emma has barely touched any of her chips since Mum and Dad joined us.

'No, I'm not really hungry. Thank you, though.' She springs to her feet and heads out into the corridor to reclaim her coat.

'We do have a spare room you can stay in, if you don't want to walk back in the dark,' Mum, following behind her, offers, without any consultation.

'It's only forty-nine pounds a night for a room,' Dad butts in, with his mouth full. I'm not sure he's joking. Next, he will be giving her a price list for towel hire and late check-out.

'Oh, Gary, don't be rude. You can give Emma a lift back actually.' She turns to Emma. 'I don't want you walking back by yourself.'

'I'm honestly OK –'

'I'm not going to take no for an answer. Hurry up, Gary.'

Dad disappointedly puts his plate of chips down

94

and grabs the car keys again, having only just driven back.

'Hopefully we will see you again,' Mum says as she gives Emma a hug goodbye.

Emma, already halfway out the door, decides against giving me a hug.

Mum and I stand in the porch waving my Tinder date off as Dad drives her home. She sits in the front seat looking petrified.

I didn't need to worry about Emma being the weirdo. That was me. Poor girl.

'What's that?' Jake says as he walks into the pub, pointing to the pram next to our table.

'A pram, a pushchair, a stroller, a buggy, a perambulator . . .'

It's always ironic that I am the first to arrive despite living the furthest away. I am sitting at our normal table and put my phone away as Jake arrives.

'Very funny, yes, I can see that, but whose baby is it? That's not your next surprise, is it?'

'It is indeed mine, but it's not a baby, don't worry. I'd have to have sex to have a baby, and, trust me, that definitely hasn't been happening.'

'I take it your Tinder date didn't go too well, then?'

'Don't even go there.'

Jake walks around the table and peers over the bonnet.

'Flipping hell, what's he doing in a pram?'

'Jeremy's been playing up at home, and Mum and Dad are out tonight, so I borrowed a pram from one of our neighbours and brought him with me.'

'You do make me laugh sometimes, Josh,' Jake says as he takes a seat. 'So have you got any other Tinder dates lined up?'

'No, I got banned.'

'What? Banned from Tinder? How did you manage that? What did you do?'

'I actually have no idea. It just says I'm banned.'

'Did you send some inappropriate messages?'

'No, of course not. I can only presume people reported my photos as they didn't believe I could be that good-looking.'

I'm pretty sure Emma reported me immediately after leaving our house.

'OK, so Plan B, then. Bumble? What do you think?'

The coin lands tails up.

'I'm not sure dating apps are for me.'

'Hinge?'

'It's tails again.'

'OK, then how about I set you up with one of my friends?'

'What is this now, Plan D? I'm really OK, thanks, Jake. I think I can manage on my own.'

He looks at me and then looks down at the coin, raising his eyebrows.

'Fine, then, you're just going to keep going until it agrees. There we go, heads. Happy now?'

'It's not about me being happy, it's about making you happy. What's your type?'

'I don't know. I don't think I have a type. Just some-one who won't cheat on me would be nice.'

'Hmmm, there might be a girl who comes to the Beyoncé dance class with me ... Oh no, actually, I know the perfect girl, Miss England.'

'What? She's a model?'

'No, stupid. Do you think Miss England would want to go out with you? That's just her name. Olivia England.'

Makes more sense.

'OK, do you think we'll get on?'

'Yep, she's really nice. Just make sure to be a proper gentleman, she likes that. And don't go on about your coin-tossing. Leave it with me, and I'll set you both up on a date.'

'Cheers . . . I think. How are things with you and Jake?'

'Can I be honest?' he says, still faffing around taking off his coat and scarf.

'Yes, of course you can.'

'Everything is going so well. Like, really well.'

'Why didn't you want to tell me that?'

'I don't know, Jessie would say not to rub it in.'

'Don't be daft. Just because my love life is a train wreck right now – or scratch that, my whole life is a train wreck – that doesn't mean I don't want you to be happy. I'm very pleased for you.'

'Thank you. Yes, I can't quite believe how good everything is. We just really click, we have a great laugh, sex is great . . .'

'OK, well, I don't need to hear everything.'

'Sorry,' he laughs.

'So do you think he's the one?'

'Oh, I don't know. I think it's too early to say, but there are only two things that I don't like so far.'

'The fact he's still wearing that festival wristband from two years ago?'

'Not that, actually. The first thing is our names being the same.'

'You've just realized how confusing that is?'

'Yes, I never know who people are talking to when they call our names. I've almost stopped responding to my own name now because I think they're talking to him.'

'Shall we start calling you Jakey to differentiate?'

'No, thanks!'

'Big Jake?'

'I'm OK,' he laughs. 'Anyway, the other, bigger issue is the vegan thing. I'm sorry but I just can't. I am so fed up of having to eat lentils all the time. I like proper sausages, what can I say?' He grins.

'I think if these are your only problems then you're doing very well,' I smile.

As we take a sip of our drinks, a couple of attractive girls walk past our table and catch sight of Jeremy.

'OH MY GOD, that's so cute. What's his name?'

'Can we hold him?' they ask simultaneously.

'Yes, feel free, his name is Jeremy. Be careful, he's quite heavy.' I lift Jeremy out of the pram and into the brunette's hands.

'He's so cute.'

'Like his owner!' The blonde girl giggles.

'I didn't realize rabbits were such babe magnets,' Jake whispers to me as the two take it in turns to cuddle Jeremy.

'Nor did I. It didn't work with Jade. She never even requested weekend visitation rights.'

'Why don't you ask one of them out? Or both! They're totally into you.'

I flip the coin. It's tails.

I shake my head.

'Oh, go on, ignore what the coin says. This could be the start of a beautiful romance, and Jeremy would have a mum.'

I can't say I'm not tempted as the blonde girl smiles at me. She is attractive. Her vintage crop top reveals a large sprawling tattoo which stretches around her back. Her forearm is punctured with a microdermal piercing. I don't know what the point of this is, but I know it means she is too cool for me.

'No, I can't go against the coin,' I say reluctantly.

'If you ever want someone to look after him then let us know. We only live around the corner.' She smiles and waves me and Jeremy goodbye.

'If things don't work out with Jake, maybe I'll have to get a rabbit too,' Jake says, looking on.

As the girls head out of the pub, they're replaced by the three usual suspects – the Quizlamic Extremists. They don't acknowledge us, which feels worse than if they goaded us as they walked past. Jessie follows them in, making a face behind their backs. She's dressed in a garish yellow ski-jacket.

'Bit cold?'

'No, I'm OK, thanks. How are you two?' she asks as she takes a seat, deciding to leave her jacket on, and putting Jake's coat on over the top too.

'Yeah I'm g –'

'Actually, now you're both here,' Jake interrupts me in typically exaggerated and dramatic fashion, 'I've got some news to tell you.'

'You've won the lottery?'

'You've quit your job?'

'Your hotel is now the thirty-fourth best in the city?'

'Nope, nope, nope. We're going to be on TV!'

'What do you mean? Why are we going to be on TV? All of us?'

'A few months ago I signed us up to go on a new quiz show that they're filming in Bristol and this morning I got a phone call to say they want us to be on! So exciting, right?'

'You signed us up for a TV quiz show? But we can't even win this quiz!'

'What were you thinking?'

'Well, maybe we will win when we don't have to face the Extremists.'

'Or maybe we'll completely humiliate ourselves in front of millions?'

'Don't worry, it's only daytime TV, so no one will actually be watching. It will just be a load of unemployed and retired people sleeping through it. Actually, Josh, you should be good, as that's all you do all day, watch these kind of shows.'

'Yeah, yeah, very funny. Actually, I don't just watch daytime TV, I'll have you know, I spend most of my days doing stupid job applications. It's just not that easy to get a job.'

'Well, there you go, you could do with the prize money, then.'

This is true. My hotel pay-off money is nearly all gone, not helped by having to buy rabbit food constantly and spending far too much on drinks at Jessie's party. I can't bring myself to pawn the engagement ring, not yet. And worse, it seems that I'm never going to get a job. Having applied for literally hundreds of vacancies, yesterday I mucked up an automated video interview by not realizing the video had started to record.

'Don't we have to audition or something first?' I ask.

'I've already done that too. One of their researchers gave me a call, and I had three minutes to answer as many questions as possible. They were quite easy. And then I just had to send photos of us all and tell them a bit about us.'

'And get our permission, presumably? Thanks for checking first that we actually want to do it!' I say.

'Well, I knew you wouldn't have a problem with it and I didn't want to get you excited before it was confirmed.'

'I'm not sure I want to go on TV,' Jessie says apologetically.

'What do you mean? Come on, it will be fun!'

'When is it?'

'Not for a few months, so we have time to revise. Are you guys in?'

I fling the coin into the air. The movement has become second nature.

'I suppose so,' I agree begrudgingly.

'Great, and Jessie?' Jake asks as we both look expectantly at her.

'Oh, go on, then, if I have to. Although I've got to survive the marathon first before I can think about this quiz, anyway.'

These marathon runners love to keep bringing it up.

'You haven't actually got long to go now – how are you feeling about it?'

'I think I'm feeling about as positive as I can be at this point. Although I haven't told you guys yet that I'm going to run it dressed as a unicorn.'

'I think you've both lost the plot,' I say, baffled. 'Isn't running the marathon hard enough without being dressed as a unicorn?'

'It's just I need to raise some more sponsorship, so I'm hoping fancy dress might help, and, well, you know I love unicorns, so it seemed the best choice.'

'Have you got your outfit yet?'

'Yes, I bought it online. Her name is Ruby.'

'Ruby? You've named your unicorn outfit? I don't think I can appear on TV with you two!' I say, as I rock Jeremy back and forth in his pram.

I've never been on a blind date before but I decide that I need to make a good first impression. As I step off the bus, checking my appearance using my iPhone camera, I opt to buy some flowers.

The florist is closed, so I pop into Sainsbury's instead. I have no idea about flowers, or what Olivia England is going to like, not helped by the fact Jake has remained tight-lipped and kept her an enigma. I debate about which ones to buy before using the coin to flip between the multicoloured gerberas and the pink tulips. The tulips win. As I pay at one of the automated checkouts I try to remove the labels from the cellophane to make them look slightly more upmarket.

I arrive at the restaurant early. This branch of the high-street pizza chain is located inside an old lead works building, but its interior is as generic as every other one up and down the country. Dozens of dark mahogany wooden tables matched with beige chairs are already laid-out with cutlery and wine glasses. It's immediately clear that I didn't need to reserve a table; the large venue, which probably seats a couple of hundred people, is all but empty this evening. One solitary thirty-something man, sitting at the far side perusing the menu, looks up at me, seemingly pleased that he will not be completely alone any more.

A smiley waitress comes over to greet me.

'Hey, how are you doing this evening? Table for one?'

'No, two actually,' I say almost defensively. 'I did reserve a table . . .'

Before I can finish, she is leading me to the far side of the restaurant, grabbing two menus en route. Despite having the entire restaurant available, she seats me right next to the man, who has to move his backpack, and gives me an awkward nod as I sit down on the leather seating which stretches the length of the restaurant wall.

We're literally sharing the same seat. What is wrong with every other chair?

'Would you like some drinks to go on with?'

'Just some tap water, please . . . and also I have this voucher, do you want me to show it to you now?' I retrieve and unfold a voucher from my coat pocket and show it to the waitress.

I wasn't hesitant about this date because of Jade, or how badly my Tinder date went, but more so as I have no money. Given I blew my savings listening to an old man loudly orgasming down the phone, I'm stuck with £17 in my account and an engagement ring worth hundreds sitting in my drawer. Fortunately, I spotted this restaurant is running an offer on 2-4-1 meals if it's your birthday, and I figured if the Queen is allowed two birthdays a year, then why shouldn't I?

I worry the waitress is going to ask for some proof but she doesn't even look at the voucher as she takes it.

'Thank you, I'll just go and scan it into the till.'

I'm glad that Olivia isn't here yet. She doesn't need to know I will only be paying half the price for our meal.

I pull out my phone and open Facebook to double-check what she looks like. Jake refused to show me any photos, but I managed to find her profile via his. The problem is, the only photo I can see is a group picture from three years ago. I carry on flicking through Facebook, Instagram and Twitter to kill time before refreshing each one again in case there are any new posts.

Fortunately, it's not long before Olivia arrives. She utters something to the waitress and starts walking towards me. It's quite a long walk, giving me plenty of time to decide how I'm going to greet her. I smile enthusiastically, and then realize I can't keep smiling for the entire thirty seconds it's going to take her to reach the table in heels. I then wave, really awkwardly, before finally deciding to stand up.

'Sorry I'm late.'

'That's OK, Lisa, I haven't ordered yet,' the man next to me says as she takes a seat at his table.

No. Please no.

She smiles at me sympathetically.

As I sit back down and hold my head in my hands, I hear another woman's voice.

'Josh?'

'Yes, oh, hi, is it Olivia?'

I smash my knees on the underside of the table as I stand up again to greet her.

I'm having an absolute nightmare.

'How are you doing? You look very nice,' I say, trying to mask the pain.

She genuinely does look very nice. She may not be Miss England, but she is certainly attractive. Jake has done well. She has long blonde hair cascading down past her shoulders and green eyes, albeit she also has enough teeth for three people. She presumably bankrupted the tooth fairy as a child.

'Thank you, you look really good too – I like your shirt,' she says kindly.

Another choice made by the coin, given I was stuck between which shirt to wear.

'Thanks very much. Oh, I got you these.' I nearly forget to hand over the flowers.

'They're lovely. You know you didn't have to, but that's very sweet,' she says taking them.

The coin is on a roll.

'So, how has your birthday been so far?' the waitress asks as she delivers our jug of water.

'Yes, it's been great, thanks,' I respond immediately, hoping Olivia won't ask how the waitress knows it's my birthday.

'Did you do anything fun?' the waitress continues, in a thick Spanish accent.

What did I do for my birthday? Crap.

I am sure at least fifteen minutes have now passed since she asked the question. I am starting to sweat profusely. My blue shirt, which Olivia just complimented, is quickly changing colour. Pools of wet patches forming under my armpits are cascading into a sea of sweat. I have to wipe my forehead with my napkin.

Just say something, Josh. Anything.

'I went to Laser Quest,' I stutter, to the surprise of the waitress, Olivia and, most of all, myself.

Where did that come from? What twenty-eight-year-old goes to Laser Quest for their birthday? Does Laser Quest still exist?

'Ah, cool, did you get any nice presents?'

What is with all the questions? Is she going to start waterboarding me next?

I suddenly realize what she's doing. She is on to me. She can see straight through my story. She has probably alerted the authorities that I've defrauded the restaurant. I will be frogmarched out and arrested. If I can't deal with these questions, I have no chance on the stand opposite a crackpot barrister. I'll be admitting to all sorts of charges. I'll be locked up for years. I am about to faint.

'I got a yo-yo.'

A yo-yo? What on earth am I saying?

She looks confused. I hope it is because yo-yos aren't big in Europe and she presumes a yo-yo is a new games console or name of a new mobile phone, which would make far more sense for a twenty-eight-year-old to have received. Why didn't I say that? What is wrong with me?

'OK, well, happy birthday from me!' She's trying to be friendly, but I am not falling for it. I have seen enough reruns of police dramas to know this routine. Good cop, bad cop. She isn't tricking me that easily.

'Let me know when you're ready to order.' She leaves us, presumably going to ponder her next move.

Just when I think I am about to get a break from the inquisition, Olivia starts.

'Jake didn't mention it was your birthday. I am very flattered that you've decided to spend it with me.'

'Oh, no, it's . . . Yes, don't worry, it's my pleasure,' I say clumsily.

I realize I have just told my attractive, sophisticated date that I spent the day running around in a dark room pretending to shoot people. I've got no chance with her.

'I will have to give you a present later,' she smiles, before realizing how flirtatious it sounds and then starts to giggle. I start laughing too.

I knew following the coin's decisions would work out well.

'So, what do you fancy, then?' I try and divert the conversation away from my fake birthday. The coin has already pre-picked my choice, but given my interrogation from the waitress, I feel too nervous to eat anything.

'It's on me, by the way. I'd love to treat you, it's not every day I get to take such a beautiful woman out for dinner.'

That actually sounded all right, didn't it?

'Oh, no, that's very kind but . . .'

'I insist. It's . . . well, it's my birthday, so you can't argue with me.'

'Well, that's very nice of you, thank you.' She smiles.

'What would you like?'

'I quite like the look of the sea bass'.

Hang on. At that price, I'm not surprised you like it.

'What about the spaghetti? I've had that before here, and it was really good,' I say, trying to convince her to pick a cheaper option. Even at 2-4-1, I can't afford the sea bass.

'Umm, OK, yes, that sounds nice,' she says, trusting my recommendation without reading the description. 'It's very quiet, isn't it?' she says, looking around the deserted restaurant.

'You see, I decided to hire the whole restaurant just for you,' I joke. I'm going to make a comment about the couple next to us not getting the memo until I realize they can hear me. Even the chef can hear every word we say. Couldn't they put some music on?

As the waitress approaches again, I worry she is going to grab the dangling light bulb, shine it into my face and launch into the next round of interrogation.

'Have you both decided yet?'

'Yes, I think we're going to have one margherita pizza, and one spaghetti,' I say, pointing to the menu.

'Great. Any drinks?'

'I think we'll be fine with the tap water,' I say before Olivia can order anything else.

'OK, that will be with you soon. If there's anything else you need, just give me a shout.'

'Thank you very much,' Olivia says to the waitress enthusiastically.

'So how do you know Jake?' I ask.

'I actually know Jake's boyfriend, Jake.'

'It's confusing, isn't it?'

'Yes, just a little,' she giggles. 'So I've been friends with him since school and got to know your Jake recently. You worked with him, right?'

'Yep, we used to work together in the hotel.'

'But not any more?'

'Um, no . . . I'm in between things at the moment, really. What about you?'

'I'm doing my PhD . . .'

I'm too distracted by the couple next to us to properly listen. They are passionately making out across their table, inches away from us, taking the *Lady and the Tramp* spaghetti routine to new levels.

'So . . . Jake was telling me you broke up with your ex quite recently?' I lean over to ask, trying to divert my eyes from their spaghetti antics.

Why did I ask her that?

I am not sure that both suffering bad break-ups means you're destined for each other, and it doesn't necessarily make great conversation either. It's not the most optimistic subject to discuss over dinner on a first date.

'Yes, I found out that Hamish was cheating on me.' She says it in exasperated fashion, as if she still can't believe it. 'He was a lecturer, very intelligent, really good-looking, much older than me, and we'd been together since I was nineteen. Then we went for dinner at my best friend's new house. It was the first time we'd been to her house, and he struggled to explain to me how his phone automatically connected to her home Wi-Fi.'

He wasn't that intelligent, then.

'It turns out that they'd been seeing each other behind my back.'

What kind of person would lie to her?

'The most annoying thing about the whole incident is that we had just bought a house together, so I'm now living there on my own.'

Buying a house? I can't afford a full-priced meal.

Before she starts talking about other grown-up things like credit cards, pensions and babies, she asks me to recite my own tale of woe. It is like playing top trumps with break-ups, and I feel thankful I haven't lost my best friend too. To give him credit, Jake has actually done well here, setting me up with Olivia.

Just don't fuck this up, Josh.

Given the lack of other customers, our food is quick to arrive. The waitress has put a candle in the pizza, and starts singing 'Happy Birthday' to me. For the first time this evening, I'm glad that no one else is in the restaurant. I couldn't have coped with a packed restaurant joining in. I sit there awkwardly until the rendition concludes, and Olivia starts clapping.

Knowing I don't have Mum here to carry the conversation this time around, I looked up some good dating conversation topics, but I don't need them, as we pleasantly traipse through the standard questions about family, hobbies and holidays. Olivia twirls her hair around her fingers, and her spaghetti around her fork. My margherita tastes better in the knowledge that I'm only paying half the price. I worry that I am morphing into Dad.

The couple next to us, who have spent more time eating each other's faces than their food, settle up and leave. This finally prompts someone to turn the stereo system on, but they appear to have picked a love songs playlist, which makes everything even more awkward, as we sit now in a completely empty restaurant to a soundtrack of Whitney Houston.

'Can I get you any desserts?' the waitress asks as she clears away our plates.

'I think we're good, thank you. Can we just get the bill, please?' I say regretfully, wishing I had enough money to pay for a second course so we could carry on chatting.

Olivia looks equally disappointed that I cut our dinner short.

I pretend to go to the toilet so I can stop at the till to check the bill is right. £31.85. That seems expensive. After buying the flowers, I've only got £14 in my account.

Has the waitress busted me?

'Sorry, I don't think you've taken off the birthday discount,' I say, nervously.

'Ah, sorry about that, I will change that now. There you go. That should be right now.'

£16.90. Still too much.

I scan down the bill, sure that I added everything up correctly. As I reach the bottom, I notice the discretionary service charge.

I gulp.

'Sorry, is the service charge optional? Can I get it removed, please?' I say, wishing the world would swallow me up. The waitress looks shell-shocked, as if she has spent ages genuinely taking an interest in my birthday all evening.

'And what is this extra £1.50 charge?'

'That is a charity donation. We're supporting Fight For Life, a children's cancer charity, this month.' She starts printing off a new bill.

I can't.

'Um, can I get that taken off too, please?'

'Really? It's for charity.'

'Sorry, yes, please would you mind removing it?' I look at the floor.

'OK. I'll bring the bill to you, sir,' she says passive-aggressively.

She has certainly stopped any pleasantries as she follows me back to the table and slams the bill down.

She's just annoyed she didn't catch me out.

'Are you sure you're happy to get this? I'm happy to pay for mine,' Olivia says, as I take the bill, relieved that the meal has only come to £13.70.

'Of course I am, I've really enjoyed my evening,' I say chivalrously as the waitress rolls her eyes.

She's certainly not getting a tip now.

I pull out my wallet from my pocket and go to take my debit card out, and then I panic. It's not there.

Oh fuck.

I mean to say this to myself, but I say it aloud, as both Olivia and the waitress stare at me.

I frantically frisk myself, checking if I put it back in another pocket. No. Nowhere. I take out all the other cards from my wallet – railcard, provisional driving licence, a bunch of store cards I've accumulated – in case it's hiding behind them and scatter them all on the table. It's definitely not there.

She's going to think I've done this deliberately.

'Are you OK?' Olivia asks, as I start sweating again. The waitress is tapping her foot impatiently.

'I know this is incredibly awkward, but I think I've actually left my card somewhere. Is there any chance you would mind paying? I'm so sorry. I can transfer you the money straightaway.' I empty the rest of the contents of my pockets onto the table – the coin, my mobile, my keys and a tissue – to prove that my card isn't there.

The waitress looks at Olivia sympathetically, thinking that she deserves much better.

'OK, sure, that is no problem.' She looks a bit confused as she reaches for her purse again. 'How much do we owe?' She has a look at the bill. 'That seems very reasonable. Do you get to keep the tips, or do they just go to the restaurant?' Olivia asks as she hands over her credit card.

'There is normally a discretionary service charge added to the bill, but I was asked to remove that.' She looks at me unimpressed. 'Tips on card go to the restaurant first, but cash tips come directly to us.'

'We'll leave you a cash tip, then. Thanks very much for making it such a lovely evening.' The waitress smiles back at Olivia, before blanking me as she walks away.

'I'm very sorry about this, I must have left it in the shop when I bought you the flowers . . . I had to put my card into the machine . . . and I'm so used to just using contactless now . . . so I guess I left it there,' I try to explain.

'Honestly, it's fine, don't worry. You should probably cancel your card, though,' she says, helping me collect all my other cards from the table.

She picks up my provisional driver's licence, which I still carry around as ID.

'Oh God, look at you here, this photo is hilarious . . . you look much more handsome now,' she smiles.

Despite my faux pax, remarkably she doesn't seem put off.

'Why does it say your birthday is in September?'

Fuck.

Fuck.

Fuck.

What do I say?

I can't lie any more.

'This is slightly embarrassing, but I actually don't have much money right now, so I may have pretended it was my birthday so we could get fifty per cent off.'

'Oh, OK.' She pauses. 'I'm not quite sure whether I should be offended or impressed with your savviness . . . Although, as it's not your birthday, there won't be any present for you today.' She smiles, more half-heartedly this time. Honestly, I can't believe she's not walked out yet.

I start putting everything back in my pockets, embarrassed.

'I think the least you can do, though, is leave a tip.

You can put that fifty-pence coin in, and I'll see what other loose change I have.' Olivia points at the coin lying on the table.

Fuck.

'Actually . . . Sorry, I . . . I can't.'

Oh Josh. You idiot.

I can't make out what Jake is carrying until he gets closer to the bus station.

'Apparently we missed your big day,' he says, unable to hide his big grin as he joins me in the queue for the coach to London.

It's a miniature birthday cake.

Hilarious.

Olivia obviously told him everything.

'Why would you want another birthday – aren't you old enough already? How old are you now?'

'You ask me every week how old I am. I'm only one year older than you!'

'I thought I told you to be a gentleman, not to be a complete cheapskate. That's the last time I set you up with a friend,' he says, shaking his head jokingly. 'Apparently she also thought your coin-tossing was a bit weird. Didn't I say not to mention that?'

'Well, I had no choice. I had to explain, as she wanted me to give the coin for a tip and she was getting upset thinking I was too tight-fisted to leave fifty pence.'

'Well, that does sound like you. Are you sure you just didn't want to leave a tip?'

'Shut up!'

'Well, anyway, I think you blew this one, but it's been

a good learning curve for you. Next time, remember to bring your card, listen to my advice and don't ever mention your coin-tossing to another girl again, as it does make you seem slightly mental. OK?'

'Don't worry, there won't be a next time. I'm done,' I reply.

It is my first time back in London since New Year's Eve. I'm pleased that I'm not going alone, even if Jake is the most annoying person to share a two-and-a-half-hour coach journey with. Not only has he packed a compendium of trivia so we can practise our general knowledge ahead of our TV appearance, but he fidgets non-stop. We've only been on the road for twenty minutes when he clambers back over me, less than gracefully, retaking his window seat.

'How are you meant to use coach toilets?' he asks rhetorically. I am trying to listen to music but have to keep removing my headphones every two minutes to hear what he is saying.

'Firstly, you have to somehow bend backwards to even get in, as they're only built for people under five feet, and then you have to somehow try and balance while the floor is moving all over the place.' He demonstrates, shaking and waving his arms wildly, elbowing me as he does so.

As soon as I think his charade is over and I put my headphones back on, he starts talking again.

'Also, why is it either absolutely freezing or completely boiling on coaches? Can they not just have it at a normal temperature?'

He starts to undress, elbowing me again as he removes his jumper. I look around, hoping there's a spare seat somewhere.

'I bet Jessie would still be cold.'

'Do you think she will like it?' He points to the jumper that is now on his lap. We made ourselves unicorn jumpers, complete with 'Run, Jessie, Run' written across in permanent marker. We also both have unicorn headbands with protruding horns, and a poster that looks more like something her Year 2 class has made rather than two so-called adults.

What the hell are we going to look like?

'Yes, I think she'll love them,' I say, as I check my watch. 'She will be heading for Greenwich right about now. I wonder how she's feeling. Have you messaged her?'

Today is the day all of Jessie's training has been building up to: 26.2 miles of absolute agony. With the help of Ruby the unicorn, she has managed to smash her fundraising target and followed her training plan to the letter. While she's raised thousands of pounds for charity, I've had to negotiate an overdraft with my bank just to be able to afford to come and watch. I was sure I'd have found a job by now, yet most companies don't even acknowledge my application, let alone invite me for an interview. My aspirations are sinking by the day, and I'm now applying for anything and everything. What was the point in getting a degree if all it gives me is a mountain of student debt?

After almost three hours we arrive at Victoria Coach Station. It then takes us another hour to cross

London to get to our first viewing point by the *Cutty Sark*. The city is swamped with family, friends and well-wishers trying to find a spot to cheer on the runners. Our unicorn horns keep prodding into people, and I spend most of the time apologizing. By the time we arrive we've already missed the competitive runners, and the first lot of amateurs are breezing past us, making marathon-running look easy.

'Have you got the sign ready?' Jake asks as we try our best to ignore the smell of sweat and human waste from the Portaloos nearby.

'Yes, here you go, but we are not going to see when she's coming from back here.' I pass the sign to Jake.

There are so many spectators that we are five people deep on the pavement, and it's difficult to see any of the action with everyone holding up their own signs: 'Pain is just the French word for bread', 'If Britney Spears can survive 2007, you can survive 26.2 miles', 'Why do all the cute ones run away?'

'Do you guys want to squeeze on through?' one middle-aged man asks us. He is holding a sign saying 'Go Random Stranger!' 'Who are you here to watch?'

'Just our friend Jessie. She should be coming past soon, according to the app.'

'We'll all cheer for her when she comes past,' another woman declares.

'There's Jessie!' One of our new fan-club members shouts out excitedly, prompting Jake to lift his sign aloft over his head.

'Oh no, that's not *our* Jessie. Our one is dressed as a

unicorn,' I reveal, as I spot the runner in question approaching us, her name emblazoned on her chest. There's a deflated atmosphere as imposter Jessie runs past, probably wondering why no one is cheering for her.

'Here she comes!' It is impossible to miss her, given her outfit and luminescent running shoes.

This time, Jake panics and forgets to lift the sign up. She runs past, glancing over as we all go crazy. I'm not sure she even realizes it's us.

'She was looking composed,' I say, trying to sound like I know what I am talking about.

'Yeah, and she's not ditched the outfit yet.'

We thank our fellow supporters and decide to split up to see her at the next interval. We flip the coin to see who goes where. Both Jake and Jessie have become so used to the coin now that it's part of our decision-making process without thinking. Maybe they're not yet supportive, but at least they're understanding. It decides that Jake will go to St Paul's, and I will head to the Strand. It takes me ages to get to the tube station, as I'm penned in, and everything is operating on a one-way basis. As I make my way up out of Charing Cross Station, it seems crazy to think Jessie will be running this entire way. I catch sight of the National Gallery standing proudly across Trafalgar Square and I decide to pop in to use the free museum toilets before standing on the pavement for another hour.

As I approach the gallery, the queue is stretching around the front of the building. As with every London tourist attraction, there are now bag checks in operation, and the gallery seems to have a particularly over-vigilant guard on duty today. I join the queue and bend down to tie my shoelaces, accidentally nudging the person in front with my unicorn headband.

'Oh, I'm sorry, that was just my horn,' I say, as I straighten up, and she turns around.

That doesn't sound right.

I do a double take as I look up at her face, freezing awkwardly halfway between crouching down and standing up.

Wow.

When Jake asked me what is my type, this girl is my type.

I look completely gormless as a huge smile takes over my face.

She's beautiful. Naturally beautiful, with minimal make-up, thick eyebrows and gorgeous dark eyes. Her brown hair is tied up scruffily in a bun, and she's wearing large, fashionable silver hoop earrings.

Stand up straight, Josh.

For a couple of seconds neither of us speak. I can't help but stare, and she seems to be looking at me as deeply. We look into each other's eyes as if we are transfixed. Whilst we've definitely not met before, there is something so familiar about her.

'No worries. Nice top,' she says eventually, breaking the silence. 'How's Jessie getting on? Has she finished yet?' She reads the message across my chest.

I can feel my face going red, embarrassed about my outfit.

'Not yet, she's still going. I'm just taking a break before I go back and watch . . . *my friend*.' I say vehemently, emphasizing the *friend* part so that she doesn't think Jessie is anything more.

I might as well shout I'm single, and I fancy you.

I realize I have been staring at her without so much as blinking. I divert my gaze down and notice that she's dressed in jeans, trainers and a yellow jacket, carrying a paperback and a handbag. The queue edges forward. A minute ago, I wanted it to hurry up, but now I want the guard to inspect every single item in everyone's bag so I have more time talking to her.

'Are you here to watch the marathon too?' I desperately try to keep the conversation going before she turns around again, not wanting this moment to end.

'No. Surprisingly, I'm going to see some art,' she says sarcastically, smiling. 'I thought it might be quiet in the gallery while everyone else is watching the race but I'm not so sure now. Are you wanting to see any paintings in particular?'

She asks the question as we reach the front of the queue. The guard waves her in, not worrying about checking her little handbag, which is decorated with pin badges. She hovers in the foyer, waiting for me to join her and answer.

'Sorry, sir, can we have a look inside your bag, please?' The tall, strict guard is annoyed that I'm not prepared.

I'm sorry I didn't have my bag ready. I've been talking to the most perfect girl.

'Everyone have your bags open to be checked, it will

make it a lot quicker for you,' he shouts at the line of people behind me.

I'm not sure why I'm being picked on. I open my bag, and he takes a suspiciously long time to look, pulling out my bottle of water.

'Can you just step over there a minute, please, sir?'

As the girl looks back to check if I'm following, I smile and then roll my eyes at being held up. She rocks back and forth on her feet, unsure whether she should wait for me.

The guard mutters some code into his walkie-talkie device, and I'm left to stand in the corner while he allows everyone else into the gallery. I notice a sign tucked away which says 'No Bag Checks Today'. Do they put that out on the days when the terrorists aren't working? Another security guard, presumably more senior, comes over and mutters something to the original guard. They point at me.

Another wave of tourists scurries in, blocking my view of her as she completely vanishes into the crowds.

'Sorry, sir, I just had to check whether the horn on your head counts as being an offensive item or weapon. I've been informed that it is OK and you are allowed in, but please can you remove it from your head and carry it. Sorry for the delay.'

You should be sorry.

I have forgotten that I desperately need the toilet and I hurriedly bypass a young red-headed man poised with a card reader. I'm already halfway up the large stone staircase, taking two at a time, by the time he's asked me to donate to the gallery.

As I reach the top, I see two signposts.

Left: 1200–1500 Bellini, Van Eyck, Piero, Raphael, Uccello

Right: 1500–1600 Titian, Holbein, Bronzino, Massys, Veronese

Which way did she go? I flip the coin to decide.
Right it is.

I stride straight past priceless works, not giving them a second glance. Instead I frantically look around the rooms, focusing on the people – those sitting on the leather furniture, those admiring the paintings, those milling around the rooms – trying to spot her. My heart beats rapidly and spikes every time I catch sight of someone wearing a yellow jacket. Every girl I see looks like it could be her. The dark floorboards become light, the wallpaper evolves from redcurrant to cranberry to ruby to salsa as I cross the thresholds between rooms. My heavy strides cause the wooden floor to squeal and squeak.

Where is she?

I reach the central staircase and wonder whether I should go further into the gallery or head back and take another turn. Surely she can't have gone this far already? The coin tells me to go back. My heart sinks for a moment as I contemplate that maybe she's meeting someone here. Maybe she has a boyfriend.

A husband even. I didn't check to see if she was wearing a ring. I reach another fork in the road and am ordered by the coin to turn left. The room in front of me is packed with crowds gathering around one painting.

Hans Holbein's *The Ambassadors*.

I studied this painting at university during lectures on the Tudors, although I can't remember anything about it apart from the optical illusion of the skull painted on the floor. It can only be seen if you look at it from one side of the painting and not the other. A group of tourists swarm around me, trying to examine the painting more closely. I try to reverse my way out of the crowd and as I do so, I bump into someone trying to take a photo.

'Sorry,' we both say, before I realize who I've just knocked into.

It's her.

'Hello again. They let you in, then?' the girl jokes.

'Yes, eventually. Apparently my unicorn horn is a weapon. All the terrorists are using them these days.' I laugh nervously at my own joke.

'Sorry, I would have waited for you . . .'

'No worries.' I smile back at her.

I look at her, bewitched, trying to think of something to say, but my mouth is dry, and I'm nearly knocked over by another tourist clambering to see the painting.

She giggles to fill the silence as we do nothing but smile at each other.

'I'm not here to see anything in particular, just generally browsing . . . to answer your question . . . you know, from before, in the queue,' I eventually stutter.

'There are so many paintings to see, aren't there? I have no idea which way to go, or where to start.'

'I know, it's a bit of a maze,' I reply. 'I remember when I was a kid, my grandad would always take me to the gift shop first when we went to a gallery. He'd buy a few postcards of the paintings, and then we'd have to go and find them. It was like a treasure hunt.'

'Wow. That's such a good idea,' she replies. 'Maybe we should do the same?'

I'm still smiling like a gormless fool.

'Only if you want to, though?' she adds.

'Yes, yes. I'd love to. Let's do it.'

We head to the gift shop together and start looking through the postcards.

'How many shall we pick?' she asks.

You can pick every single one if you'd like. I'm happy to be here for ever.

'Shall we get a few each?'

I pick a few from the left side of the shelves, and she picks a few from the right, before we make our way to the till.

'Are you paying separately? Or are you together?'

'I'll get them,' I jump in quickly.

'Are you sure?'

'Yes, of course.'

'OK, thank you very much.'

We exit the shop and head back into the gallery.

'OK, so what are we looking for, then?' I ask, glancing at the cards she's selected.

'I've picked this one by Canaletto, one by Renoir, a Degas . . .' We stand in the corner of the room while she shuffles through them, showing me the postcards. 'And *Sunflowers* by Van Gogh. I know it's a really obvious one, but I want to see it. It's really the reason I've come today.'

'Are you a big Van Gogh fan, then?' I ask.

'I wouldn't say I'm a huge fan but I've just been reading an anthology of the letters he wrote to his brother. They're quite interesting.'

'I didn't realize he was a writer too, I only know the basics . . . the cutting-off of his ear, the suicide, all the upbeat stuff.'

She laughs loudly, and we start walking slowly on, consumed in conversation.

'I didn't know much before, to be fair. I'm working abroad at the moment in an English bookshop and saw his *Sunflowers* painting at the gallery nearby. I realized how bad it is that I've never seen this version, given I'm from London. So that's why I thought I would come and check it out while I'm back here.'

'Where . . .' I start to ask her where she's working, but before I can she continues talking.

'It's quite . . . Sorry, what were you going to ask?'

'No, after you, carry on.'

'Sorry, I was just going to say it's quite sad reading about his life. He suffered so much heartbreak. Did you know he proposed to three different women, and they all rejected him?'

'Poor guy,' I say, keeping a poker face about my own situation. I look down at her left hand to see if she's wearing a ring. Thankfully her ring finger is happily unadorned.

'After the third woman said no, he kept sending her letters and travelled to Amsterdam to look for her, but she didn't want to see him.'

'He didn't play that one that cool, then,' I joke, knowing how he felt.

'No, he most definitely didn't, but do you know what, I quite like that. Admittedly there's a line, and OK, the woman was his cousin, which is also a bit odd, but no one wears their heart on their sleeve for love any more. What's the equivalent now? Super-liking someone on Tinder?'

'Sliding into someone's DMs?'

'Exactly, how sad is that? No wonder they say romance is dead.'

'Would you like someone to cut off their ear for you, then?'

'OK, maybe that's a step too far.'

'What do you mean? I was about to cut mine off and give to you.'

What am I doing? Am I flirting about cutting my ear off?

'Sorry,' she laughs and pats my upper arm as we pause and look into each other's eyes again.

'We've missed one already,' I say, pointing to the landscape of Venice we've just walked past.

'We've got to stop chatting and concentrate,' she jokes.

We move closer to the painting.

'I really like Canaletto,' she says, admiring the brushwork.

'So do I. The detail is amazing, isn't it?' I realize I'd agree with her right now even if I hated the painting. 'Have you ever been to Venice?'

'No, I haven't, actually. I'd love to go, but I'd love to go everywhere. That's the problem.'

Before I know it, I am planning our first date, imagining our first kiss, envisaging the first time we tell each other 'I love you'. I'm thinking about our romantic getaways to France or Italy or Spain, where we will spend blissful evenings walking hand in hand, stopping at quaint bookshops. I'm planning my wedding speech. I'm picking our kids' names.

'OK, we've found one painting. What's next?' I ask.

'We're looking for Renoir and Degas.'

'I think they're through here.' I lead her into the next room. 'So you sound like you know lots about art?'

'No, I really don't know much at all. I'm more of a book girl, but I do like these types of paintings.' She points to the Impressionist works as we slowly stroll past, stopping intermittently at pieces that catch our eyes and the ones replicated in our postcards. 'I went to the Tate Modern yesterday and I'm not too sure about modern art.'

'What, you mean the canvases with just a dot of paint on them?'

'Yes, or the single piece of string.'

'Did you hear that story about the person who left a pair of shoes in the corner of the Museum of Modern Art in New York, and everyone walked around them thinking they were an exhibit?'

Her dark eyes squint when she laughs, almost disappearing into the happiness.

'I always want to know whether the artist genuinely believes their work is good, or if they're just having a laugh.' She smiles.

'I know. It's so funny to read some of the descriptions. They're so pretentious.'

We both laugh, and as we do, we catch each other's eyes again, forgetting that we're surrounded by hundreds of others. For a second, it's just us.

As I get swept away, I suddenly remember the real reason I'm in London and quickly pull out my phone.

'Oh, is it time for you to go and watch Jessie?' she asks as I check my phone, hoping Jessie has slowed down and I can spend some more time exploring the gallery with my new friend.

'Oh, wow, yes, it looks like she's almost here. I'm really sorry, but I'd better head out and fight my way to the front of the crowds.'

'Don't apologize. I wouldn't forgive myself if I kept you from watching her big moment.'

'But we haven't seen *Sunflowers* yet,' I say.

We look at each other, trying to decide what to do about the situation.

'Maybe I could come and watch with you? . . . And I don't know what you're planning to do after, but maybe we could come back and see *Sunflowers* later together? You're probably wanting to spend the evening with your friends, so no worries if not . . .' she rambles.

'No, I think that sounds like a very good idea. I'd love to do that. Maybe it could be . . . like a date?' I bite the bullet.

'Yes, *like a date* sounds perfect.' She smiles.

As we make our way to the exit, we pass by some of history's best portraits. Even amongst all the paintings of beautiful women, I can't help but think she is by far the best-looking woman in the gallery.

13

'Did you see the woman dressed as the Mona Lisa? That was quite good, and Mr Potato Head?' Jake admires the medal hanging around Jessie's neck. 'You should have invited them to your next fancy-dress party.'

'Yeah, people who actually make an effort.' Jessie's dig goes over his head. 'Mr Potato Head was annoying, actually. He ran next to me for a while, but all the crowds were just cheering for him instead of me. I kept trying to lose him.'

'I couldn't believe there were so many people watching,' Jake says as he accidentally stands on one of the hundreds of Lucozade bottles littered across the ground.

He looks up and notices me standing behind Jessie. I eventually found the two of them amongst the crowd beyond the finish line.

'Why have you been running?' Jessie, wrapped in silver foil and looking through her goody bag, asks me as she turns around. I'm not quite sure a free keyring would convince me to run 26.2 miles, but she seems happy enough.

'It looks like you're the one who has just run a marathon, not Jessie,' Jake jokes as I stand there, sweaty and breathless.

'I know, I know, but I've got big news. Massive news. And I need your help.'

'Go on then, spit it out.'

'So this may seem stupid, but, I think I've just found the one. You know, the one I've been looking for. The girl of my dreams,' I say excitedly, stumbling over my words, still short of breath having just sprinted across St James's Park, looking like a marathon runner who'd gone the wrong way.

'Wow! That's great, Josh. Where is she?' Jessie drops the keyring back into the bag and looks up.

'That's the problem. That's why I need your help.'

'Why do you need our help? Give her a call and tell her to meet us here. We can all go for a drink together.'

'I can't call her.'

'You know you're not making much sense right now, Josh?' Jessie takes a big gulp of water.

'So while I was waiting for you, I popped into the National Gallery, and I started talking to this girl who was in front of me in the queue. I bumped into her inside, and we explored the gallery together, but when we came out to watch you we got separated in the crowd, and I've spent the last twenty minutes running around looking for her.'

I'm waiting for Jessie to realize I missed her run past.

'What was her name? I'm sure we can find her on Facebook. I've got pretty good stalking powers,' Jake brags as if it's a skill he should list on his LinkedIn profile.

'That's the thing, I don't even know her name.'

'What do you mean, you don't know her name? Is this person real?'

'Yes, of course she's real,' I snap.

'So let's go through this again. You didn't at any point say, "Hi, my name is Josh, what's yours?" You didn't think to do that?'

'No, we just got talking, and then I was planning on getting her details later, but before I knew it I lost her in the crowds.'

'Are you sure she wasn't trying to lose you at the first opportunity?' Jake jokes.

'Stop it,' Jessie scolds Jake.

'No, definitely not. It was her idea for us to come and cheer Jessie on together. She started talking to me, or maybe I did, I can't remember. But no, definitely not. It was definitely mutual. She wouldn't have run off.'

Would she?

I start doubting myself.

'Did you say anything to her before this that may have put her off? You didn't mention, I don't know, the coin, proposing to your ex . . . ?'

'No, I didn't say anything bad. We were having a really nice time. She definitely liked me too.'

Didn't she?

'I know it sounds crazy, but I really liked her. Like, really. Since Jade, I've not been interested in anyone, and well, we just had this spark, you know what I mean? How am I going to find her?'

'Let's go and look for her. She can't have got too far,' Jessie says, throwing off her foil blanket.

'Surely you want to go and lie down?'

'No, I'll be fine. It's not every day you meet the one. Come on, let's go and find her. I'll just text my parents that I will meet them a bit later,' Jessie says as she hobbles along.

We head down The Mall, past the Duke of York column.

'Where were you when you got separated?'

'Just by Embankment Station. The police were trying to control the crowds, and I presume she got stuck on the other side of the road.'

'So chances are she will still be around there? No one can get anywhere very quickly with all this congestion.'

'She might be, but I have a feeling she might have gone back to the gallery. She suggested that we go back there to see Van Gogh's *Sunflowers* after we saw you.'

'OK, how about we head to Embankment, and if we can't find her there we'll go to the gallery?' Jessie suggests. 'What does she look like?'

As we trudge along the streets behind all the other tired runners, I try and picture her in my head.

'So she's probably in her early to mid twenties. Dark hair, up in a bun. About five foot five.'

'And what was she wearing?'

'She has a yellow jacket on, with denim jeans ... And a handbag with different-colour badges on.' I try to recall as much as I can.

We walk along the bottom edge of Trafalgar Square, the National Gallery looming at the other end.

'Should we split up so we can cover more ground?'

Jake suggests. 'One of us could walk around Embankment and the other two go straight to the gallery?'

'Yes, that sounds sensible.' I consider where she is most likely to be, before flipping the coin to decide where I should go.

'What's the verdict?' Jake asks, as we're separated by a stream of people.

'Me and Jessie will go to the gallery. Are you happy to try Embankment?'

'Yes, I will accost anyone who matches her description.'

'Thanks very much, Jake.' We head in the opposite direction and approach the same security guard who stopped me before. This time he lets both of us in without any hold-up despite our unicorn costumes.

I think to myself that in London, with an additional 650,000 marathon spectators, the odds of finding her are about as good as seeing a real-life unicorn.

'I'm sorry, I haven't even said congratulations yet,' I apologize to Jessie as we head up the stone steps. In all my excitement, I realize I've hijacked her big moment.

'That's OK, you've listened to me talking about the marathon enough for the last few months anyway. This is much more important.'

'Excuse me, where is Van Gogh's *Sunflowers*?' I ask one of the volunteers patrolling the room.

'In Room 44, so just straight on and head right.'

As we head through the gallery looking out for her, it feels like déjà vu. This time, though, I know where she's going to be.

She's going to be by *Sunflowers*, waiting for me.

I walk across the laminated flooring and, as the crowd thins, I spot the painting. The shades of glowing yellow paint captivate me before I look around the room.

Where is she?

We pace from room to room looking for her.

She must be here.

'Shall we just take a seat and wait?' Jessie suggests, almost unable to walk now.

We sit down on the leather seating, watching an end-less stream of people coming to admire the painting. We wait and we wait. But she doesn't appear. Jake messages to say he's had no luck either.

'I'm sure even if we don't find her today, you can find her online. Did she say anything that might help iden-tify her?' Jessie tries to lift my mood.

I replay everything in my head, but it's all a blur. I keep seeing her smile, and her twinkling brown eyes, but nothing that will help identify her.

'Was she English? What accent did she have?' Jessie tries to prompt my memory.

'Yes, she was English, but she didn't really have any particular accent. Hang on, no, she said she was from London.'

'Did she say what she does for a job?'

'Oh yes, of course, so she mentioned she was work-ing abroad right now in a bookshop near to where Van Gogh's other painting of *Sunflowers* is.'

'Perfect. So we know where she lives, then. That's a big clue. Where is the other version of *Sunflowers*?'

We look at each other, thinking this is something a semi-decent pub-quiz team should know.

We really are going to embarrass ourselves on TV.

Jessie reaches for her phone, dismisses the flood of congratulatory texts, and googles *Sunflowers*.

'You do realize he painted more than just one other version of *Sunflowers*, right?' Jessie breaks my heart as she reads this.

It was never going to be that simple.

'How many are there?' I say, fearing the answer.

'Twelve.'

Twelve! What? Really?

'No, hang on, there are two different sets.' She starts to read aloud. 'The first series, executed in Paris in 1887, depicts the flowers lying on the ground, while the second set, executed a year later in Arles, shows a bouquet of sunflowers in a vase. So it's the second set we're interested in, they're the same as the painting here.'

I look at Jessie, trying to process the information.

'In the second set, there were seven paintings.'

Slightly better than twelve at least.

'Wait a second.' Jessie carries on reading, almost to herself now. 'One was destroyed during the Second World War, and one is in a private collection, so we're down to five.'

Even better.

'And I don't suppose these other four are all in the same gallery by any chance?' I ask hopefully.

'No, unfortunately not. In fact, they're not even in the same country. So there's the one here in London . . .

and then there are other versions in Amsterdam, Munich, Philadelphia and Tokyo.'

Philadelphia? Tokyo?

'But at least you've narrowed it down to four cities.'

'Yeah, but they're not exactly the smallest cities in the world. Goodness knows how many bookshops there must be in Tokyo!'

'It's OK, at least it's something to work with. I think I'm going to need to lie down soon, if that's OK. You can stay if you want, though,' Jessie apologizes as she checks her watch. She must be shattered.

'No, let's go. She's not coming. Thanks very much for waiting with me.'

'I'm sure we will find her somehow,' Jessie says optimistically.

I take one last look around the room and at *Sunflowers*.

'I really hope so.'

14

When I left school I imagined my return would be an event of momentous and unparalleled fanfare. Baying crowds screaming my name, a limousine dropping me at the entrance. Instead, I'm heading to my ten-year reunion in the passenger seat of Mum's Ford Fiesta.

I've been dreading this day for weeks. Not because I hated school. Quite the opposite, I enjoyed it, so much so that I sometimes question whether my best years are behind me. Life was so much easier when all decisions were made for you and everything was mapped out. My biggest worry was getting to lunch first or whose football team I'd be on at break. I'm dreading it because I have absolutely nothing to show for the last decade.

As soon as Dad opened the invitation and pinned it to the calendar, I had no chance of getting out of it. Especially when the coin sided with Mum and Dad.

Judas.

I spend the next twenty minutes sulking, sitting silently in the car next to Mum as she drives me to school.

'It will be nice to see everyone again, see what they're up to. I'd like to see my old school friends,' Mum says as we drive along the dual carriageway. She went to a thirtieth anniversary reunion at her school a few years ago and insisted that she'd keep in touch with everyone, but they've not seen each other since.

'Come on, Josh, talk to me . . . what is going on? I thought today, seeing all your old friends, might cheer you up.' Mum always saves serious conversations for the car, when I have no way of escaping them. I half expect her to have put the child lock on to guarantee I can't jump out.

'I know you must be heartbroken about Jade, but it's been a few months now, and I'm worried about you. As much as we love having you at home, I don't think sitting around doing nothing is helping you move on.'

I'm not sure it's completely true that they love having me at home. After the water bill arrived for the last quarter, Dad put an egg timer in the shower to tell us how long we're allowed to wash for.

I finally break my silence. 'Firstly, I'm not doing nothing, I'm trying my best to get a job. I've sent off about five hundred applications. It's not my fault that it's literally impossible to get anything. And secondly, believe it or not, it's actually not about Jade. I've just had a crap few months and then I think my luck is changing, I meet someone amazing, and that turns out to be a lost cause too. Sorry, but I'm just not in the best mood.'

'You've met someone else? Why didn't you tell me? That's very exciting. When was this?' In her excitement she takes her eyes off the road and nearly crashes the car.

'It doesn't matter.'

'I know you're going back to school today, but please can you act your age, Josh? You can talk to me about these things.'

We sit at the traffic lights. The Audi next to us is blaring Radio 1 at top volume. I flick through Mum's CDs in the glove pocket, and go to put on Simply Red, hoping that might silence her questioning, but all the discs are in the wrong cases.

'It was when I was in London. I met a girl but I didn't get her details, so the chances of ever seeing her again are virtually zero.'

'You never know. The other day, I was thinking about Annabelle, who I used to work with, completely randomly, and then that afternoon I drove past her. Graham says that's called synchronicity.'

'I don't think seeing a woman who lives five minutes away and is always out walking her dog is quite the same, but I will keep thinking about her and see if she magically appears. Does it also work with money? And a job?'

The car jerks and screeches as Mum attempts to change gears, struggling to get up the steep hill.

'Can you drop me round the corner?' I ask, so no one can see her dropping me off.

'OK, well, I hope you will be smiling tonight, and you have a better time than you think, Gary, sorry, Josh . . .' she calls as I jump out of the car before she's even pulled over. I never understand how she mixes up me and my dad. She was the person who chose my name.

'Look who it is! Josh, how are you doing, mate?'

It's just my luck that Luke-fucking-Piercy walks past as I get out. He holds his hand out to shake mine.

'Not the best, Luke. You see, my car had to go in for its MOT this morning, very annoying.' I am impressed at my quick thinking and reckon I've got away with it until I remember my mum is not a trained improv actor.

'Darling, just text when you want me to pick you up later . . . and remember to let me know if you're going to want any dinner,' she yells out of the window.

Luke clicks the fob to lock his brand-new Mercedes, and we walk together towards the school gates.

'Oh and Josh, you need to let me know when you want me to book your dentist's appointment for you. Bysey-bye,' she shouts out as she drives off.

It's going to be a long afternoon.

Ten years after leaving school, each year group is invited back for a special reunion, which culminates with the digging up of a time capsule containing the hopes and dreams of our eighteen-year-old selves. It's essentially the school's gimmick to get you back into the building, to start giving them money and to collect our new contact details at a time when most people are moving into new houses, not old ones.

We follow the signs towards the dining hall, where everyone is gathered. Everything seems smaller than I remember, but very little seems to have changed. I pause to look at the photos of the staff on the notice-board, and even most of the teachers are still the same.

Entering the newly painted dining hall, I survey the crowd as I'm offered a glass of Prosecco by a sixth-former. The current pupils look so young, and the staff look so old. I spot the ancient rugby coach who ignored me for three years after I switched from playing rugby to football, and my English teacher, who used to set off the school fire alarm by smoking in the toilets. I look around at all these teachers, who fed us a narrative that we could be whatever we wanted to be, that we could achieve whatever we dreamed of. That was a load of nonsense. Why didn't they teach us how to cope with heartbreak and disillusionment rather than Pythagoras and the periodic table?

I sip my drink and browse the copies of the school magazine which have been laid out on the tables. I flick through the pages about alumni who have returned to speak to and inspire the current students. Maybe my invitations were lost in Dad's sorting office.

As I look up and around the room, memories come flooding back.

'Josh!'

I recognize the voice in spite of not having heard it for years. Will Stevens, an obnoxious kid who always thought he was the best at everything, bounds over to me.

'How are you doing?'

He pats me on the back strongly.

'What have you been up to, mate? You were in London, weren't you? And then working in hotels? Is that right?'

School reunions have been ruined by the internet. All the fun and suspense has been spoiled by the ability to keep tabs on everyone. It means there is very little to discuss, as everyone knows everyone's business already, and in some cases every single meal they've eaten in the last few years.

'Yes. I'm not working there any more, I'm actually in between things currently.'

'To be honest, if anyone was going to be doing something with their life, I'd have bet my house on it being you.'

Good thing you didn't have a bet then.

I catch sight of my name engraved into the prefects' board on the wall, beneath an illustrious roll call of people who have achieved great things with their lives – scientists, charity campaigners, TV stars.

'What are you doing now?' I ask him, not that I really want to hear the answer.

'So I'm working in the City for a headhunting company.'

Everyone seems to be working in banking or HR. When there are recruitment companies recruiting recruiters, then you know it has gone overboard.

'Are you enjoying that?'

'Yeah, it's not bad, I make a shedload so can't complain. What about your girlfriend? She not here? You must be getting hitched soon, you've been with her for a few years now, haven't you?'

'Actually, we broke up a few months ago now, so back to being single. What about you?'

On cue, a beautiful, tall, blonde woman walks over and takes him by the arm. She looks like a Victoria's

Secret model. I remember why I didn't like him at school.

'So me and Erin got married last year in the Maldives and, well, as you can see, we've got a new addition to the family on the way.'

I am so taken by the beauty of this woman, I hadn't even noticed the blossoming baby bump which Will is now patting. Considering I struggle to look after a rabbit, let alone a human, when a friend tells me they are pregnant I'm not sure whether to say congratulations or sorry. I think in this instance, as she proudly cradles her baby bump, I'm meant to be pleased for them both.

We look around the room as Will updates me on what everyone is doing. Eddie is a dentist, Alex is in politics, Greg is running a tour company, Louis is an accountant. There don't seem to be any of my old friends in attendance, just those who want to come back and show off about something. The people who were annoying at school and are even more annoying now.

'Can you believe that Tommy is now a doctor? He's just finished medical school. I hope he's not delivering our baby!'

This is the kid who ran an illegal tuck shop out of his locker for his entire school career, and would visit the school nurse most days due to smashing his head while playing excessively violent games of bulldog.

In contrast, my school reports were rapturous with praise. I was destined to do something great. I wonder what went wrong. Yesterday I woke up at 2 p.m., felt a sense of accomplishment that I'd cut my fingernails, but didn't want to over-exert myself by cutting my toe-nails, binge-watched a series on Netflix and got rejected for a job stacking shelves.

What happened?

'It's a shame we've not met up before this, really. How has time gone so quickly?' Will asks Hugo, another rugby jock, who has joined us.

'You know, I've just been too fucking busy, and vice versa, if you get what I'm saying.' He snorts as he downs his glass of Prosecco and elbows me in a jovial manner.

Twat.

'Miss Williams is still looking hot, I see.'

This was an all-boys school, so any female teacher under the age of forty was considered attractive, but there was one in particular whom all the boys fancied so much that some would collect her chewed pencils and water bottles she'd drunk out of.

'Sorry, guys, do excuse me, I'm going to go and work my magic.' He strides over to her confidently, and I am excited to watch him fail miserably, but he is replaced immediately by the school's development director, who has spotted the opportunity to swoop with his paper-work and pitch.

'Hi guys, just wondering if you would be interested in giving money to support the school and bursaries? Ten per cent of the pupils receive financial assistance, and as ever we really do rely on the generous support of our Old Boys.'

I know full well. I only attended the school because I was on a scholarship – there was no way Dad was going to pay to send me here. The man passes around direct debit and Gift Aid forms.

I can barely afford to support myself or Jeremy, but everyone else is agreeing, and I don't want to look bad, so I sign up to a regular giving scheme.

I'm never going to move out of home. Maybe I can just tell my bank to cancel the direct debit before they take the first instalment.

The bang of a gong rings out through the hall, silencing the conversation.

'Can everyone make their way downstairs?' the headmaster announces, holding a mallet.

We all follow him down the main staircase, out to the front lawn, where the school's gardener has already started digging up the soil to reclaim the time capsule. I never quite understood why they needed a full-time gardener to maintain the tiny plot of grass in front of the building. As the capsule is hauled out, I'm hoping that the contents have been ruined, but miraculously all our letters are perfectly preserved, and the headmaster distributes them. I glance over at Will's aims – to bleach his hair and to go to IKEA.

I hesitantly take mine out of the manilla envelope which has my name scrawled across the front. My handwriting was a lot neater then.

By 28:

I will be married to a supermodel.
I will be a successful entrepreneur.
I will own a house in Los Angeles.

I will drive a Lamborghini.
I will have travelled the world.
I will be world-famous.

I am twenty-eight, single, unemployed, living with my parents, unable to drive, never been further afield than Spain, and even my own mother can't remember my name.

Fuck.

15

'He could have put the quiz team first, really. He's the one who signed us up for the show.'

'Josh, it's his anniversary. I think he's allowed to go out with Jake tonight.'

'He could have celebrated his anniversary on another night, surely?'

'But that wouldn't have been his anniversary, then, would it?'

'Who celebrates their seven-month anniversary anyway?'

'I remember you and Jade did! In fact I remember you missing the quiz for it!'

It's a Wednesday night, but Jake has abandoned me and Jessie for a date night with Jake. We decide against quizzing. If we struggle to beat the Quizlamic Extremists with three, or four, team members, entering with just two would be challenging to say the least. Instead, we are sitting in Pinkman's, a modern bakery-cum-café, with a pot of tea and a deck of trivia cards, revising for our TV appearance. Situated a couple of minutes' walk from Bristol University's Wills Memorial Building, by day it is packed with students, but in the evening the long wooden communal tables are sparsely occupied, and there is just one other man working away on his laptop.

'So have you recovered yet from the marathon?' It's been two weeks, and it's the first time I've seen Jessie since the race.

'I'm not sure I'll ever recover. Think it will cost me a fortune going to a chiropractor for years. The day after was horrendous, and my legs are still pretty achy.'

'Would you do it again?'

'I don't know, despite the pain it was pretty amazing. Maybe. But it's your turn next, anyway. I'll come and cheer you on, and miss you running past.' She raises her eyebrows.

She knew all along.

'Yes, I'm really sorry about that, although they were exceptional circumstances.'

'Are you still hoping to find her?'

'I'd love to.'

'OK, then. How are we going to do it?'

'We?'

'Well, I'm as invested in this as you are. I had to walk around London for hours after running a marathon, so yes, *we're* going to find her.'

'I don't know, I've watched the entire TV coverage of the marathon back to see if I can spot her in the crowd somewhere, but no luck. I didn't see you either, but I did see someone else wearing the same costume as you, though.'

'I know, I meant to tell you. He had his photo printed in the *Daily Mail*. Why didn't they take a photo of me instead?'

'Ridiculous. I think he just copied you.'

'What outfit are you going to do it in next year?' Jessie asks.

'There's no chance I'm doing it next year, OK?' I say as I tuck into a slice of carrot cake, picked by the coin over an equally tempting Bakewell tart. Close to Jade's flat, the cakes here were always a dangerous temptation on our doorstep. I realize, as I take a bite, that I haven't thought about Jade at all since the marathon.

'So let's go through what we know about her?' Jessie says as she pulls a notepad and pen out of her handbag. She flicks through to a blank page and writes SUN-FLOWER GIRL at the top before underlining it.

'Well, not that much, really. Just what I told you after the marathon. I'm guessing she is in her twenties, she's got dark hair . . .' I worry that her image is already being distorted in my mind. I don't want to lose it for ever.

She notes down my comments in bullet-point form, and I half-expect her to draw a sketch from my description.

'That doesn't really narrow it down much.'

'No, I know.'

'And we think she lives in either Munich, Amsterdam, Tokyo or Philadelphia?'

'Yep, that's right.'

'So what's the combined population of those cities? Many millions, I'm guessing?'

'Thirteen million, roughly. I looked it up.'

Jessie notes down everything as if she's putting this all into an algebraic equation.

'So even if what she told you was correct and she lives in one of those places, then you have a one in thirteen million chance of finding her?'

'But we know she works in a bookshop, so that narrows it down.'

'I wonder how many English bookstores there are, though? You could look them up and email to ask if they have anyone matching that description working there?'

'No, that just sounds creepy, and I doubt any of them would reply. They'd probably just think it was a scam.'

'OK, how about you go and visit the cities and see if you can find her working in one of them?'

'Like Van Gogh?'

'What do you mean, like Van Gogh?'

'Oh, it was just something she said about Van Gogh chasing after a woman he was in love with. His cousin, I think she said.'

'Bit weird.'

'I know.'

'There's your inspiration, then.' Jessie sips her tea. 'Not to chase your cousin, but to go and find her.'

'Yes, but you're forgetting that I had to go further into my overdraft to pay for a slice of cake here, let alone travel around the world.'

I'm distracted by the smell of the sourdough pizza

wafting past me, as a couple on the other side of the café are served their food.

'Do we have any other way of tracking her down?'

'It's pretty hard without a name. I reckon if we had either a first or last name we might have been able to find her on Facebook, but what do we google – dark-haired girl from Philadelphia?' I don't tell Jessie I've already tried that and trawled through many pages of search results just in case. I've also googled every English bookstore and their employees but have had no luck. And I've created a new Tinder account to search through thousands of single women in Munich, Amsterdam, Tokyo and Philadelphia. I'm out of ideas.

Jessie pauses and reads her notes.

'What about if we started some kind of online campaign to track her down? That might work.'

'No, definitely not. That's even more creepy than emailing.'

'Is it? It might be kind of romantic?'

'I don't know. I am just so annoyed that I didn't get any details. I can't believe how stupid I was. I meet the girl of my dreams and I don't even get her name.'

'I think you have to be careful not to over-romanticize everything. I'm sure she's nice, but you spoke to her for – what? – thirty minutes max? I'm sure Jack the Ripper might have been nice for the first half an hour.'

The quiz round on serial killers from a few weeks back has clearly stuck in Jessie's head.

'Even if you do find her, I don't want you to go in

with massive expectations. Let's think of it in a different way . . .'

'You're going to give me one of your analogies now, aren't you?'

'Yes. Imagine you're in a furniture shop . . .'

'Are you just making this up as you go along?'

'Concentrate. You're in a furniture shop and you want a new table. Right?'

'Right, I'm looking for a new table. I've not even got a flat, let alone any money, but I want a table for some reason.'

'Stop being annoying, I'm trying to help you.'

'OK, sorry, carry on.'

'As you walk around the shop there are quite a few different styles, some you like the look of, others that won't suit your flat. And then you spot one which you think is perfect. It looks great.'

'OK, sounds good. What's the problem?'

'The problem is you didn't come to the shop prepared. You don't know the measurements of the table you really need. So this one looks great but you're not sure if it will fit when you get it home, or even look good. You've also not really properly checked it out. The legs might not be stable, there may be some nails sticking out underneath . . .'

I nod along.

'And while you're so fixated on this table, you're not looking around at the rest of the store to see if there may be one which actually suits your flat better.'

'So what are you saying? That I should get a receipt?'

'I'm saying that while this girl – sorry, table – may look great on first impressions, it may not be as good as you think and you may miss out on something better.'

'But what if this is the perfect table, and it *is* as good as it looks, and if I walk around the shop looking at others, someone else might quickly buy the perfect table?'

'Fair enough. I guess we're just going to have to think of another way to find this table, then.'

The man sitting next to us is no longer engrossed in his laptop but is looking at us like we're completely mental.

'To be honest, Jessie, I think you're just *objectifying* women,' I joke, and pick up one of the cards. 'Shall we start practising our general knowledge?'

Summer

16

'Following the end of their relationship, they were so devastated, so heartbroken, that in a state of despair they rushed up here to the bridge and decided to commit suicide. They jumped off the bridge . . .'

I've not reached that level. Not yet.

I've finally got a new job working as a walking-tour guide in Bristol and I'm telling the remarkable story of Sarah Ann Henley to my group of tourists as we stand beside the Clifton Suspension Bridge. The one good thing to come from the school reunion was Greg mentioning that he was looking for new tour guides to work for his company over the summer. The coin jumped at the chance to get out of the house, and finally my experience working in hospitality and even my history degree has come in handy.

'However, this was when women used to wear those large crinoline skirts, and it was a very windy day. Somehow, the wind managed to catch her skirt, and it acted like a parachute, breaking her fall. She landed in the mud at the bottom of the gorge some 245 feet below without suffering any major injuries . . .' After just a few tours, I have learned that tourists are far more interested in morbid details about suicides than hearing about Isambard Kingdom Brunel's engineering ability.

If I'm being honest, this isn't the job I dreamed of doing as a five-year-old. I didn't expect to spend nineteen years in education to end up wearing a luminous green T-shirt, leading a brigade of tourists around Bristol, only to be paid 'what they think it's worth' at the end. But right now I need any job to get me out of my overdraft and pay for Jeremy's food. Dad also wants to start charging me rent as Mr and Mrs Dawson four doors down have a lodger who pays for board and breakfast. I thought the one advantage of living at home was the ability to save money.

Apparently not.

We walk down from the Observatory, past the beautiful houses of Sion Hill and stop by the now defunct Clifton Rocks Railway. I rack my brain to remember everything I'm meant to tell them, adding in the usual jokes. Today's group is made up of three teenage French au pairs, a middle-aged German couple, an Australian backpacker, a group of friends from Spain and the most annoying American woman ever.

'Bath is obviously famous for having a spa, but Bristol tried to compete, and the water here was said to have healing qualities too . . .'

'Does Jane Austen still live in Bath?' It's the fifteenth question this American woman has asked me in the last twenty minutes.

'Unfortunately, she's been priced out of the city centre now, and has had to move away,' I'm tempted to answer. Instead I politely explain that Jane Austen has been dead for over two hundred years.

'As I was saying, Bristol and Bath started a rivalry, and the water here tastes much better. If you visit the Roman Baths in Bath, don't drink the water there, as it's disgusting.' The Australian guy and the French girls chuckle. The Germans look stony-faced, and the American woman is already trying to think of another question to ask.

Greg told me that this job was a great way to meet attractive, young, single women. He failed to mention the annoying, demanding, inquisitive tourists.

As we reach the Cabot Tower, taking a significant detour so we don't walk past my old barber's, it starts to rain. I wonder why anyone would want to walk around the city in this weather. At least they're getting a proper British experience. They all have umbrellas, so it's only me who is getting drenched and at risk of catching pneumonia.

'Giovanni Caboto, or John Cabot as we call him, set sail to find Asia. However, he ended up going the wrong way and found North America instead,' I shout over the sound of the rain clattering against the concrete. 'He called it Newfoundland. Giovanni wasn't the most imaginative guy.'

The rain starts to pelt down, harder and harder. It feels like I'm on a kids' gameshow where I'm being pelted with buckets of water while trying to answer questions. As I'm halfway through the story, I notice Jake walking hand in hand with other Jake past the back of the group.

What are they doing here?

He stops to make silly faces, trying to put me off. Clearly, he has not grown up. I wouldn't be surprised if he's deliberately tracked me down to remind me to revise for the TV quiz, which he's getting over-excited about. Fortunately, he hates getting his hair wet so he doesn't hang around long enough to heckle me. I don't need any more irritating customers today.

As we approach the end of the two-hour tour, I point out one of Banksy's stencil artworks at the bottom of Park Street. As I turn to my group, having to shout to be heard over the noise of cars, a rival tour group emerges on the other side of the street. The guide is dressed as a pirate. Perhaps I should be thankful I've not sunk to that level.

Yet.

'As I said at the start, there is no set fee for the tour, but it would be really great if you could give however much you think the tour was worth. Thank you very much, and enjoy the rest of your time here in Bristol.'

As the small group clap mutedly, and I step back, my clothes soaked through, I wait for the first person to dig into their pockets. I've quickly learned the significance of group mentality. However much the first person gives, everyone else copies.

The American woman, coming from a country where tipping is standard practice, approaches me first.

She hands me 20p.

17

After spending the last twenty-two days giving walking tours around Bristol, I am looking forward to a day off relaxing in front of the TV. Unfortunately, Mum has other ideas.

'Hurry up, I said we'd meet Nan and Pap at eleven at the garden centre.' She unfurls my bedroom curtains, blinding me with the bright summer daylight.

I struggle to see why old people like garden centres so much. What is the attraction?

'Do I have to come?'

'Yes, you haven't seen them for ages. I said we'd see Julie afterwards to drop off her birthday present.'

Julie O'Nion is one of Mum's friends, whom she met at her post-natal group after having me. We used to spend lots of time together with her and her daughter, Elizabeth, when I was a child. Mum always says that their actual surname is Onion, and they added the apostrophe to sound posher. However, they really are the kind of people who talk about polo being a sport rather than a mint.

'Really?'

'Yes, really, come on.'

'I've got to ask the coin first.'

'Go on, then,' she sighs.

'Heads, I get to binge-watch Netflix all day, tails I come with you.'

The garden centre has been transformed since we used to visit when I was a child. Far from selling just plants, it is now described as a 'shopping village', complete with home, fashion and pet departments. At least it means I can buy some food for Jeremy. Pap's back is bad so after walking around for twenty minutes, we decide to sit in the café while Mum and Nan browse the plants.

'So how are you feeling about the quiz?' Pap asks. 'Not long to go now.'

I finish chewing a mouthful of the Danish pastry he has bought me before I speak.

'I know, that's what's worrying. I don't think we're going to do that well.'

'I'm sure you will. You're a very clever lad, and we'll be there to cheer you on.'

'Thank you, but please don't get your hopes up. We should have probably listened to Jake and revised more.' I take another bite of the pastry. 'This Danish is lovely, by the way. Are you sure you don't want any?'

Maybe the café is the real reason old people like garden centres.

'No. I'd better not, thanks, I'll just stick to the tea. How's everything else?'

'The job is OK, although I'm bored of saying the same things over and over again. I've met some interesting people, at least.'

'Anyone special?' He raises his eyebrows.

'No one like that, unfortunately.'

'What about this girl you met in London?' Pap winks.

'How do you know about that?' My voice gets higher as I ask.

'Your mum might have said something.'

'Of course she did. No, I don't know. I didn't get her contact details and don't even know where she lives, so I think there's more chance of us winning the quiz than me finding her, and that's not saying much. Even then, I don't have the money to go and find her.'

Pap takes a big sip of his tea, looking like he's trying to remember something.

'Can you remember when we used to take you to the Bristol Museum when you were young and you'd search for the paintings?'

'Yes, of course I do. I remember it really well. I was telling the girl about that. We actually did the same.'

'So think of this search for her in the same way. It is just a bigger treasure hunt.'

'Just a *little* bit bigger.'

'OK, but do you remember what we used to say to you?'

'Yes, you would always tell me "Don't give up." Although I remember that time we were looking around for hours until we realized the painting was on loan somewhere else.'

'Yes, we were there for ages that day, weren't we?' Pap chuckles. 'But the point is, you really can't give up.

When I was courting your nan, it took me six attempts before she let me take her dancing. If you think this girl is special, don't give up.'

I listen intently as I finish my pastry.

'How did you eventually win her over?' I ask.

'She used to come to the village hall for dance classes, and I played the organ there. Each week while I was playing, I'd watch her dance. At the end of every class I'd ask her if she would dance with me sometime. Finally, she said yes, and I guess we've been dancing together ever since.' He looks up as Nan and Mum head back towards us with a plant.

'How are you both getting on?' Mum asks when she reaches our table.

'Good, thanks. We were just talking about the football.' Pap smiles to me.

'We'd better head off now, as I've got to go to Julie's. Are you leaving too?'

'You go on, I need to pop to the loo again. You know what it's like when you get to my age.' Pap makes a face at me.

We hug them both goodbye, and I pick up the plant to help Mum take it to the car.

'We'll see you at the quiz. If I don't get to talk to you beforehand, best of luck.' Pap shakes my hand and slips a twenty-pound note into my palm. 'That's to go towards the search fund,' he whispers.

We park in Clifton outside the front of the O'Nion's beautiful four-storey Georgian house, complete with a wrought-iron balcony, Mum's Ford Fiesta looking the anomaly in a street full of Jaguars and Bentleys.

'When did you last see Julie?' asks Mum.

'It must be at least ten years, I reckon, but I don't think I've been here to their house since I was a kid.'

Before we get out of the car, Mum pauses and turns to me. 'Did I mention that Elizabeth is here too?'

Now I know why I've been dragged along.

'No, you didn't, Mum, you definitely didn't.'

She knows she didn't.

The last time I saw Elizabeth, we were seven years old, before she was shipped off to a boarding school the other side of the country. Mum still gives me her life updates, and we exchange the annual happy birthday message on Facebook.

'Why didn't you tell me? If you're going to try and set me up with someone, then at least allow me to prepare properly. I look a mess,' I say as we get out of the car.

I remember playing here as a boy, and as I look up at the house and around at the shared private garden behind me, remarkably it is all as big as I remember. Mum locks the car door and walks around the front of the bonnet.

'Firstly, I'm not trying to set you up, and secondly, you look very handsome,' she says as she licks her finger and rubs a Danish pastry crumb off my face.

'Mum, stop it.' I shoo her away. 'You do know it's not going to work, don't you?'

'I remember when you wanted to marry her.'

'I was seven.'

'You two used to get on like a house on fire when

you were younger, and she's doing very well for herself now. And she's from a good family.'

'Sorry, I didn't realize we were living in a Thomas Hardy novel.'

'I know you liked this mystery girl you met in London, but you might never see her again, so it doesn't hurt to consider all the options, right?'

What happened to her belief in synchronicity?

We walk up the steps, decorated with pot plants, towards their large, imposing black front door. I half expect a butler to greet us as the door swings open, but it is Mrs O'Nion. She's aged somewhat since I saw her last. Her blonde hair has turned to grey.

'Oh, hello, you two. It's lovely to see you, Joshua. It's been so long.'

I've not been Joshua since my birth certificate.

Inside the house, the decor is equally beautiful, in keeping with the age of the property. Portraits of noble-looking figures hang from the walls in golden frames.

'Elizabeth, look who it is,' Mrs O'Nion calls out as a tall, thin woman with cropped dark hair strides down the imposing staircase. She looks good.

'Hello, Josh, how lovely to see you.' She kisses me on the cheek when she reaches us. Mum is unable to hide her delight.

'Shall we leave you two to catch up in the living room?' Mum asks, pushing us into the front room.

'Good idea, I'm going to put the kettle on. We'll go and sit in the conservatory, join us whenever you like,' Mrs O'Nion concurs.

If it didn't feel like a set-up before, it definitely does now.

I follow Elizabeth into the front room. It's not like our lounge at home, it feels more like a National Trust property. I'm not sure if I should sit down for fear of damaging the antique furniture.

'It's OK, you can take a seat,' Elizabeth says, beckoning to an armchair. Her voice is even more upper-class than I remember. I feel like I've won a prize to have dinner with a minor Royal.

'So what's new with you?' I ask as I sit opposite her. The room is so large I almost have to shout to be heard.

'You mean in the last, what, twenty years?' She chuckles loudly.

It wasn't that funny.

'Yes, I suppose so.'

'Well, where do I start? I'm sure you remember I went away to boarding school, and that was a hoot, I must say. I had such a wonderful time there, and although I obviously missed home and Mummy, I met the most lovely people, and it gave me such a good grounding for life . . .'

I don't need to know everything you've done in the last two decades.

'I then decided to take a year out to concentrate on my art before going to volunteer in Namibia. What can I say? Such a beautiful country, but the whole experience was so thought-provoking. Mummy then secured me an internship in the Houses of Parliament . . .'

She really is going to tell me absolutely everything.

'After that, I went to Oxford to read Human Sciences.

That was such a remarkable time, and awe-inspiring to learn from such incredible lecturers. Anyway, then, after finishing my undergraduate degree there, I decided I wanted to become a dentist, so I moved to the University of Manchester to study Dentistry . . . I graduated – what was it? – it must be two years ago now – can you believe that? – and I can now proudly say I'm a qualified dentist.'

'Yes, I think I saw. Congratulations,' I say, falling asleep listening to her.

I'm not sure I want her to ask me any questions, given my answers aren't going to compare to hers, but I needn't worry, as she doesn't.

'So do you enjoy it, you know, looking at teeth?' I fill the silence, realizing I've started speaking in a faux posh accent.

'Oh, yes, it is such a marvellous career. I did have this one patient the other day . . .'

Elizabeth is beautiful and intelligent, from a nice family, and with a great career. But even with our childhood history, which should make for the perfect start to an adult romance, there is nothing there. I'd much prefer to be sitting opposite Sunflower Girl. As Elizabeth rambles on and on, I zone out and start thinking about her instead. I wonder if she's going on other dates? Meeting other guys? I wonder if she's forgotten me already?

'Shall we go and have some tea, Josh? . . . Josh?' Having been speaking about herself for the last twenty minutes, she takes me by surprise when she finally asks me a question.

'Oh, yes, sounds like a good idea,' I reply, smiling politely, pleased I don't have to hear any more about her giving someone a filling.

It is ironic that the conversation has been as painful as pulling teeth.

She leads me along their hallway. I forgot just how majestic it was. I feel like I should have picked up an audio guide at the entrance and be appreciating each of these museum pieces on display. Even their conservatory is decorated with plates, paintings and portrait busts.

Mum, sitting on the cushioned settee, looks up expectantly when we walk in, as if we're about to announce our engagement.

'That was quick. How have you two been getting on?'

'Good, thanks,' I exaggerate, taking a seat next to Mum.

Mrs O'Nion is lounging opposite us on a beige chaise-longue, holding a cup of tea in her hand. I glance up and notice the portrait hanging above her head.

It's a portrait of herself.

Naked.

And I mean *completely* naked.

Sitting in exactly the same seat she's on now. In exactly the same position. Legs akimbo.

I desperately try and look anywhere else, but the portrait is right in front of me, and my eyes can't avoid it.

Stop it, Josh.

I stare directly at Mrs O'Nion. The clothed one.

'Do you like the paintings, Joshua? Elizabeth painted them all.'

You've got to be kidding.

'She's very talented, isn't she?'

I start looking around at the rest of the room. I notice the other paintings are all close-ups of intimate body parts and hope they're not all of Mrs O'Nion.

'Um, no, wow, yes, no, I think it . . . you've captured . . . you're very talented . . .'

Where on earth has Mum brought me?

It is then that I decide I can't wait any longer. Pap is right. I need to go and find Sunflower Girl.

18

'Come on, guys, I've got a good feeling about today.'

'You seem to have changed your attitude. I thought you were against going on TV.'

It is the big day. Our TV appearance. Our fifteen minutes of fame. It's 8.30 a.m., and we are in a taxi on the way to the studios, just outside Bristol city centre. Jessie and I are sitting in the back, while Jake, the self-elected team captain for today, rides up front.

'I was never against it,' I lie. 'OK, maybe I wasn't the most keen before, but now I think this might be a good chance to help me find Sunflower Girl.'

'What? You think she's going to be watching this wherever she lives, spot you and get in touch?' Jessie says doubtfully.

'Or she will see us embarrass ourselves and think, "Thank God I avoided that guy who knows nothing about anything!"' Jake turns around and jokes.

We both ignore him.

'No, I was thinking more that I need money to be able to afford to go and find her, and this is the best chance I have of getting enough money.'

'What? Go and try and find her in those cities?' Jessie seems surprised I've listened to her suggestion. 'Do you actually think you'd be able to track her down?'

'I don't know, but I'd like to try.'

'I think that's a great idea,' she smiles.

'Exactly. Just think it's better to say "oops" than "what if",' Jake quotes.

'I didn't realize you were a philosopher now. Where did you read that?'

'I saw it on a sign in a gay club the other night.'

'Of course you did.'

'Have you checked what the coin says? Surely you have to toss it for this?'

I've been hesitant about asking the coin, not wanting it to reject my idea.

'OK, here goes.'

I toss it up in the air, nearly hitting the roof of the taxi. The driver looks in his rear-view mirror, wondering what we're on about.

'The coin says yes,' I am pleased to announce after it lands safely in my palm.

I stare out of the window, picturing my reunion with her.

'Sorry to burst your bubble, Josh, but you do know we actually have to win first in order to get the prize money,' Jessie whispers reluctantly, tapping me on the shoulder.

'When we win,' Jake far too confidently declares, 'at least you will actually be able to pay for her dinner on a date.'

'Yeah, yeah, very funny.'

'He could even pay for his own dinner on a date,' Jessie blurts out. 'Sorry, I had to.' She sympathetically puts her hand on mine.

They are both still ribbing me about that incident.

'What do you think you'd both do with the money if we won?' I ask.

'I've not really thought about it. I need a haircut, though,' Jessie says, with her dark locks almost down to her waist.

I'm not sure that a haircut is the most exciting thing to spend our winnings on, and it strikes me as strange that Jessie wants her hair cut after rather than before her national TV appearance.

'It's got to be a holiday. Me and Jake both want to go to Berlin, so I think we'd go there for a few days.'

The taxi pulls up outside the entrance to the Bottle Yard Studios. The former winery and bottling plant is now home to some of the world's leading TV shows, as the signs tells us, but it still looks like an old industrial estate from the outside.

'Not quite Hollywood, hey,' I say, looking out the window.

'OK, guys, you're going to be the second episode filmed today, so I'm afraid there will be a bit of waiting around. I'll take you through to Wardrobe first, and then to the Green Room, where you can prep for the show,' the runner, a spotty girl of about eighteen, says as she marches us along a maze of corridors armed with a clipboard.

The walls are lined with framed photographs of other programmes filmed in these studios. Jake gets excited that he is following in the footsteps of Michael Sheen, Aidan Turner and Benedict Cumberbatch.

'I'm going to leave you with Sharon here. She's going to help you with your outfits. Can I get you all something to eat? We have bacon sandwiches. Or there are vegetarian options.'

'Bacon sandwiches sound great, thanks.' We all nod in unison.

'I thought you were vegan now?' I turn to Jake.

His face sinks, having become vegan in solidarity with other Jake.

'OK, I'll have the vegan option, I suppose. Thank you.'

Sharon is a woman in her fifties with a dark bob and a questionable sense of style herself.

'Have you all brought a few different plain tops?' she asks. We were each instructed to bring a suitcase of outfits so the stylists can pick what we wear. No branded clothing, no slogans. 'Let's see what you've got.'

She turns to me, making me try on each of my selections, before finally settling on a plain white top.

Sharon then takes one look at Jessie's multicoloured options and recoils in horror.

'Sorry, none of these are going to be suitable. Can you try on this top instead?' She lends Jessie a plain navy top to try on and pushes her into a changing room. 'Make sure you give it back after filming,' she says curtly, as if Jessie has decided to spend a whole day sitting around in an out-of-town TV studios just to steal a Primark T-shirt.

As Jake tries on his options, the runner returns with our bacon butties. I take one bite and ketchup spurts onto my white top. I swing around checking to see if

Sharon saw and frantically dab away the stain before she makes me change again.

We are eventually led into the Green Room with our new outfits. It is a far cry from the mythical Green Rooms of showbiz columns. There are no luxuries – just a few leather sofas and copies of today's papers, which we flick through in case they remarkably help with a question. As Jessie and I sit down, Jake limbers up by practising tongue-twisters while pacing around the small room, 'Irish wrist watch, Swiss wrist watch, Irish wrisht wash, swish wrist rosh.'

As I continue trying to get my ketchup stain out, making it worse in the process, the door swings open again. The runner returns, out of breath. She seems to be justifying her job title.

'Sorry to interrupt. These are your opponents for today's show. Be nice to each other!' she jokes as she leads the other team into the room.

I do a double take as I see them.

It can't be.

Anyone but them.

The Quizlamic Extremists march into the room, as if preparing for battle.

'Hey, guys,' they say in unison, finding the coincidence more hilarious than us.

My plan to find Sunflower Girl is crumbling already.

'Do you know each other?' the runner asks.

'Yes, unfortunately,' I mutter under my breath.

'We actually go to the same pub quiz,' Jessie responds.

'Ah, that's funny. Who usually wins?'

'They do. Every time,' I say, frustrated.

'Well, good luck to both of you. If anyone needs anything, give me a shout.' With that, she turns around, closes the door and leaves us in awkward silence.

At least they acknowledged us for once.

'Where did you hear about this quiz?' I whisper to Jake as they take their seats at the other end of the Green Room, which is no more than a few metres long.

'At the pub.'

'From who?'

'Well, now you mention it, it may well have been from one of their team. I was waiting to get a drink, and Big D was talking to them about their application . . .'

'So when you told us at least we wouldn't be facing the Quizlamic Extremists . . . ?'

'I didn't know we'd end up playing them, did I?'

'Well, we've got no chance now.'

'I don't think we had much of a chance before, to be fair,' Jessie jumps in.

'Don't be like that.' I can feel Jake's Churchillian speech coming on. 'Today is the day when we finally beat them, when we make history, when we topple the Quizlamic Extremists. Yes, we may be the underdogs, but every dog has its day, and today is ours.'

'Jake, you do know they can hear every word you're saying?' Jessie glances over at them still staring at us.

'Well, we need to concentrate on the game, not our opponent. Let's run through some more questions . . .'

Jessie and I look at each other despairingly.

Jake flicks open his trivia book again.

'Oh, I don't think we've done these for a few weeks. What year was the first model of the iPhone released?' Jake asks.

'2008?' I guess.

'No, Josh! That's wrong. It was 2007. What is the Greek word for fire?'

I look at Jessie, nonplussed, and then across the room at the Quizlamic Extremists, who are listening in and clearly know the answer.

'We don't know,' I whisper.

'*Pyro.*'

'Oh yeah, that makes sense,' Jessie nods.

'Which Apollo 11 astronaut did not set foot on the moon?'

Jessie jumps up in excitement.

'I know this one ... it's ... it's ... no, I can't remember.'

'Michael Collins,' Jake sighs.

'Yep, I knew that.'

'Really, what are the chances of these questions coming up in the show?' I say miserably, deflated now that I know our chances of victory have deteriorated.

'You never know, and it's good to get your brain in gear.' Jake's enthusiasm for his moment in the limelight has still not dwindled.

'They're not practising.' I point my head in the direction of the Quizlamic Extremists.

'They don't need any practice,' Jessie says.

The producer interrupts us to quickly explain the

rules and then runs off, shouting into his mouthpiece, before our friends and family stream into the room.

We were each allowed four tickets, so Mum, Dad, Nan and Pap have come to cheer us on, and I'm anxious about how they can most embarrass me in this situation. Mum is dressed up to the nines, Nan is trying to steal Jake away from Jake to dance with him, and Dad is helping himself to free food. The families of the Quiz-lamic Extremists are all dressed smartly, looking equally as serious.

I notice Pap is missing so I slowly back out of the chaos to the doorway and find him sitting on a seat in the hallway.

'Are you OK, Pap?'

'Hello, Josh. Yes, it's just a bit crowded in there. What do you think about it all, then?' He slowly gets to his feet and puts his arm around me.

'If we didn't have much chance of winning before, we've got even less now. That is the team we always lose to at our normal pub quiz.'

'Come on, have some faith. You know we're proud of you whatever happens.'

'Sorry to interrupt, guys, but you're going to be on in ten so you need to come and get your make-up done now,' the runner shouts over the Green Room hubbub and beckons us to the adjoining mirrored room.

'Best of luck, Josh, not that you need it,' Pap says, patting me on the back.

As the make-up artist dabs my face with powder, I expect to be transformed into David Beckham, but I don't notice much difference in my reflection in the mirror. Having been beautified, we are guided through to the studio, which looks smaller than I was expecting. And so too does the presenter. Shorter, fatter, balder. Dressed in a navy suit, I recognize him from the papers as a washed-up soap star who has courted his fair share of romantic controversies over recent years.

'How are we doing, guys? Excited for the show?' he says in the most unexcited tone as he comes and shakes our hands. His acting didn't used to be this bad.

'Good luck to all of you.' You can see the resentment in his eyes that his career has dropped this far.

As I take my seat in between Jake and Jessie, I look around and spot everyone in the front row of the audience. Jake's Jake is told off for trying to take an Instagram story of the set. Mum is tapping her head repeatedly – a technique her therapist taught her to invite good vibes. Nan is trying to get on TV herself, smiling at the camera, unaware that they haven't started recording yet. Pap smiles at me encouragingly.

'Three, two, one . . .'

This is it.

The lights are both boiling and blinding. The nerves have kicked in. I can feel the cameras staring at me. There is a lot more pressure here than at Little D's quiz. I am conscious of every movement I make. I sit up straight, unable to relax.

'Welcome to *Unlock*, the gameshow where knowledge is the *key* to winning.' The presenter has turned on his trademark smile now that the cameras are rolling.

'The game is simple. We will have three head-to-head trivia rounds, and the team which scores the most points will win a key. That key unlocks one of two doors. One of the doors contains the thousand-pound jackpot, the other contains nothing.' He turns to us. 'Got it?' We all nod back.

'But before we start the first round, let's meet the teams.'

When you are sitting at home at 4 o'clock on a Thursday afternoon, flicking through the channels, you don't consider how much time goes into making one of these awful quiz shows. We need to cut every time the host fluffs his lines, or the camera is not at the right angle, or someone coughs in the audience. By the time we eventually reach the final round we are remarkably only trailing 11–9.

'So today's final round is on . . .' The presenter presses a fake button, and the screen, controlled by someone else, flashes up with: 'Disney Movies.'

Jessie jumps up off her seat.

'Oh, I might actually know some of these,' she whispers.

'That's what you always say,' I whisper back.

'No, I actually might this time.'

'Let's play *Unlock* . . .'

Dramatic music and flashing lights soak the studio before the timer starts ticking loudly.

'Who is the only Disney princess who was inspired by an actual person?' the host reads off his card.

Jessie buzzes in.

'Pocahontas.'

'Correct. In *The Little Mermaid*, what are the names of Ursula's two pet eels?'

'Flotsam and Jetsam.' Jessie almost trips over her words in her excitement.

'Correct again.'

The screen flashes up the updated score. 11—all.

'Which short film featured Mickey Mouse's first appearance?'

Me and Jake look expectantly at Jessie, but she shakes her head apologetically.

The Quizlamic Extremists buzz in.

'*Plane Crazy*,' they say confidently.

'That's right. You're back in the lead.'

Crap.

12—11.

'Which real-life actress was the inspiration for Belle?'

'Katharine Hepburn.' Jessie beams with delight.

How does she know all of this?

12—all.

'Who is the only main character in a Disney movie who doesn't talk throughout the entire film?'

I look at both Jake and Jessie, and across at the Quizlamic Extremists. Blank faces all round.

'I'm going to have to hurry you . . . Anyone want to buzz in?' The timer ticks down. Five, four, three . . .

Jessie hits the buzzer just in time.

'Is it Dumbo?'

'Correct!' The buzzer rings. 'And that's it, we're out of time. What a finale!'

The Quizlamic Extremists look shell-shocked and slump back in their seats.

'Congratulations to the All-Jays, who have just edged this encounter, 13–12.'

Surely that didn't happen?

I pinch myself as I look across at Jessie, ecstatic. I can't believe we've won.

'So you have beaten the competition but you have one more challenge before you can take home today's prize money. I'm going to give you this key, and you can unlock one of two doors. One door contains the jackpot, the other contains nothing.'

We are suddenly drenched in red spotlights. The sound effects start to crank up the pressure again.

'Which one shall we go for?' Jake asks.

We all look at each other.

I try to avoid the glares of Jake, Jessie and the glaring lights and catch sight of Pap. As I look closer I can see he is gesturing to me to toss the coin.

Am I allowed to do that on TV?

It feels like déjà vu.

'Shall we flip the coin?' I say, probably too quietly for the microphones to pick up.

'It didn't go very well when we tried it in the pub-quiz tie-breaker.'

'Maybe it might redeem itself today.'

'Chances are it will be right this time.'

I don't think Jake understands probability.

'Sure, let's let the coin decide.'

'Are we allowed to flip a coin?' I ask the presenter hesitantly.

'I've never seen a quiz team flip a coin to decide on an answer.' He looks around, unsure himself.

The producer gives a thumbs-up and looks excited at the added tension as he instructs the camera operator to get a close-up of the coin toss.

'OK, let's say door number one is heads, and door number two is tails. Happy?' I say.

Jake and Jessie both nod.

I flip the coin.

'It's tails!'

'So you're going for door number two?' the presenter asks.

'Yes, please.'

'Are you sure?'

'Yes, we're sure.'

'Final answer?'

'Final answer.'

Get on with it.

'Let's reveal what is behind door number two . . .'

The music keeps beating steadily, as my heart rate soars. I can't bear the tension . . .

'You've won one thousand pounds!'

As soon as the director calls 'Cut', we run over to the audience, where we're submerged into a sea of congratulatory hugs and embraces.

'Congratulations!'

'Well done!'

'You did so well!'

I look back at the set and see the Quizlamic Extremists are still in their seats, engaged in a heated post-match debrief, trying to pinpoint where it went wrong.

'So what are you going to do with the thousand pounds? What's that, £333 each?' Dad asks, probably about to encourage us to invest in one of his new schemes.

'I think Jake wants a holiday, and, well, Jessie, you can have a few haircuts now,' I say as they both join me. She looks at Jake then back at me, smiling.

'Actually, Josh, we have decided that we want you to have the money. You can use it to find your Sunflower Girl.'

'Don't be daft!'

'No, really, Josh, we'd like you to have it.'

'Are you sure? I can't take all the money.'

'Yes, you can, and we're not taking no for an answer.'

'I'm swamped at the moment at work, so me and Jake probably won't be able to get away for a while anyway. I think you need the money more than us,' Jake says.

'And it's more important than me getting a haircut!'

'Thank you so much, that's incredibly kind.' I am almost lost for words. 'Honestly, guys, you are the best. I can't believe I'm going to go and find her.'

I am close to tearing up.

As we all embrace, I catch Pap smiling at me from across the studio.

Autumn

19

We are standing in front of the departures board at Bristol Airport. A seemingly endless procession of holidaymakers passes by us, bundling through the revolving doors, as they trundle in from the airport Flyer bus parked outside in the rain to the check-in desks. People pulling, dragging and carrying large suitcases, rushing and running, last-minute unpacking, repacking and panicking. Holidays never seem to be very relaxing.

'Are you sure I should do this?'

'It's not about whether we're sure, it's about whether *you're* sure? You're the one who is going!'

'I know, but I'm just thinking it's a lot of money to spend on a potential wild goose chase. Do I want to spend all of my money looking for a random girl who I might not even find?'

'Our money, you mean,' Jake butts in. He doesn't do mornings.

'Don't think about the money,' Jessie says more supportively.

'I know, but now the summer is over, I'm jobless again. The prize money could tide me over for a while until I find something else . . .'

'You were so sure that you wanted to do this. What's changed?'

'I don't know ... Honestly, I guess I just started thinking what happens if I get my heart broken again. I'm not sure I can deal with that. Maybe it's better not to know.'

'But you have to go and find her, and find out if there's something. Otherwise you're always going to wonder, and the not knowing will be worse in the long run. You can't even go on a date right now without thinking about her.'

'That's true.'

'And the coin said to go for it, and as you've been banging on all year, you've got to follow the coin's decision.'

I nod. I know all of this, and deep down I want nothing more than to go.

'But equally we don't mind if you get cold feet. We can just hop back on the bus and go back to town if you're not one hundred per cent,' Jessie continues.

'Not at £7.50 each on the bus, we are not. He's going now he's dragged us out here,' Jake interjects. He doesn't do public transport either.

'No, you're right. I really do want to find her. I'm just worried that I'm not going to. Or worse, that I do find her but she's moved on, met someone else, or we just don't click again, or, I don't know, she has forgotten who I am.'

'But equally she may miraculously fall in love with you . . .' Jake pipes up.

I feel *miraculously* is a bit harsh but I don't comment.

'This is the last call for Flight EZY6025 to Barcelona,'

the automated voice says in a firm tone, as if it has been programmed to be angry with latecomers.

'So, is it to be Munich or Amsterdam?' Jake asks, in between yawns, wanting to get back to the comfort of his bed. This is his day off from having to wake up at the crack of dawn. 'I guess you need to flip your coin to decide where you're going first.'

I've ruled out visiting Philadelphia or Tokyo, on the basis I can't afford to go for now, so the two options are there illuminated in front of me:

08.50 BM1841 Munich
09.25 U26161 Amsterdam

I've always wanted to arrive at an airport and randomly decide where to go, but now the pressure is getting to me, and I'm not so sure.

I take the coin out of my pocket and toss it into the air.

'You are absolutely sure that you don't mind me spending your money?'

Jake rolls his eyes.

'No, of course we don't. We just want you to be happy. You deserve this,' Jessie says.

'It's OK. You can pay me back when you discover she's a millionaire.' Jake smiles for the first time this morning. 'Good luck, Tosser, go get her.'

'And Jessie, thanks for looking after Jeremy. Remember he likes kale not carrots.'

'No worries, I'll keep him safe for you.'

Jessie, looking like she's about to cry, gives me a huge hug. Jake jokingly joins in, and before I know it we're having a group hug in the middle of Bristol Airport.

'Thanks, guys, I will see you soon!'

I go to the check-in desks, praying the coin has made the right call.

20

'So are you coming to Germany for holiday?'

I've reached the front of the queue at Passport Control and I'm presenting my passport to Andreas Keppler, as his name tag proudly states. The flight was non-eventful. Apart from fearing I was about to plummet to my death when we hit turbulence. Twice.

Somehow, I've managed to pick the line with the scariest official. Andreas looks like the kind of person who doesn't want anyone entering his country and he's so fed up with his government's immigration stance that he's taken this job to personally prevent people from crossing onto German soil.

He asks the question in a stereotypically strong German accent and fails to make any eye contact with me as he asks it, choosing instead to pay extra close attention to my passport, which was analysed just two hours previously at Bristol Airport, and I'm unsure what could have changed in it during that time.

How should I answer this question?

'Well, actually, I'm trying to find a girl who I think works in an English bookshop in Munich, and who I think I'm in love with.'

Probably not like that.

Andreas's eyes immediately dart up from my passport

to examine me in the flesh. I don't think he likes my response.

I never know if the officers at Passport Control are interrogating you or simply making friendly chit-chat. Does this stern-faced, tattooed German sitting inside a glass box want to know the intricacies of my planned visit to the German city or just that I'm not going to be importing and exporting massive qualities of illegal substances?

'How long will you be in Germany for?' he asks, now in a more serious tone, as if I've triggered an alarm.

'I guess as long as it takes for me to find her, or until my money runs out.'

My ears popped on the flight, so I struggle to hear what he is saying, and I shout my answers back.

'How much money do you have with you?'

Nosy.

'I've got one thousand pounds, which I won – well, actually, I didn't win all of it; my friends gave me some.'

Too much information again, Josh. Too much.

Even if he was at the start, I really don't think he's making polite conversation any more. I knew I should have gone to the electronic gates. They never work, but they would be preferable to this.

A queue is starting to form behind me, and the businessman behind is gesticulating and sighing so loudly that I can hear him over the tannoy announcements. It's not like I'm deliberately holding him up and enjoying a good catch-up with my old mate Andreas.

'Where are you going to be staying?'

'I haven't booked anywhere. I haven't really had time to think about that. Probably just some hostel.'

He shakes his head. I start to panic. Are these the standard questions they ask everyone, or do they suspect me of something? The woman to my left who handed over her passport at the same time has been allowed through already. That can't be a good sign.

Who does he think I am? A drug smuggler, a terrorist, an illegal immigrant, a spy? I remember reading at university that during the Second World War Germans would use the word 'squirrel' to detect spies. I can't pronounce it. And I certainly can't pronounce the German *Eichhörnchen*. If they're still using it as a shibboleth, then I'm in trouble.

'What is your career?'

OK, I've got this one.

'I am a tour guide, I take people on walking tours and show them around the city,' I say clearly and succinctly, hoping that's the last question and he lets me go.

'Where do you do these tours?'

Crap.

'Oh, sorry, well, I did them in Bristol but, well, it was really just for the summer actually.'

'So, you don't have a career now?'

It looks as if Andreas doesn't like liars. Or the unemployed. His face starts to fold up. The lines on his forehead bulge. His grasp on my passport is becoming firmer.

'Well, no, I suppose I don't have a job, if you put it like that.'

It suddenly hits me. What have I done? What am I doing? Have I lost the plot? I've blown all my money on a girl. Again. Have I not learned from Jade?

He looks up at me, and then back down at my passport, and repeats this again on loop. I realize the photo of me taken nine years ago doesn't bear much resemblance to the figure standing in front of him today. I try to pose in the same way, deliberately not smiling. I never understand why everyone has to look so unhappy in their passport photos.

'So, you have no job, nowhere to stay and come to Germany to find a mysterious girl you don't know . . .'

I can feel sweat dripping from my brow, and if I can feel it, he can certainly see it. This makes me sweat even more.

I must look so guilty. He's going to call Security to take me to some back room. I've seen this on those undercover airport reality shows. I look down nervously at my backpack and worry I accidentally packed a knife, or a bomb, or someone has slipped something into it when I wasn't looking. The coin was in a lavish mood on the plane, so I ended up with a newspaper, a winless scratch card and a muffin. What happens if the muffin has got drugs in it?

Here goes . . .

'Well . . . good luck, sir. I hope you find her.'

He hands me back my passport with a grin and a wink. I look back at him, confused.

Did I imagine that?

'Try the English bookstore on Schellingstrasse . . . Words' Worth.'

As I walk past his cubicle, I notice he has a copy of *Jane Eyre* open on his desk.

Andreas is actually an old romantic.

Before I encounter any other official, I make my way quickly through Baggage Reclaim and then out into the German daylight.

Now just the small matter of finding Sunflower Girl in this city of 1.5 million people. At least I have my first destination.

21

'I think they're expecting about six million visitors this year for the festival, so it's going to be very busy everywhere,' the young man sitting next to me on the airport bus explains. He is dressed in a blue check shirt with traditional lederhosen, and until he mentions the festival, I wonder if everyone dresses like this in Germany.

Who knew that Oktoberfest actually takes place in September?

Apparently everyone but me.

It seems like false advertising. Like having Christmas in November.

So my one in 1.5 million chance has already become one in 7.5 million. If I was trying to find a needle in a haystack before, I'm now looking for a needle in a field of haystacks.

After I am dropped off in front of the Hauptbahnhof, thousands more check shirts pass by me, all heading in the same direction, presumably towards the beer. Accompanying them are dozens of women with plaited hair and dressed in traditional dirndls, although some look more like the kind of outfits that you would find in a branch of Ann Summers than an authentic Bavarian store. Everyone seems to be speaking in an English or Australian accent.

I definitely look the odd one out, dressed in jeans and a sweater, but I push on against the crowds and walk towards Andreas' recommended bookshop, Words' Worth. A quick search online tells me there are only two English bookshops in the city, and both are within a few minutes' stroll to the Neue Pinakothek, where *Sunflowers* is on display.

As I get closer, it's clear from the abundance of coffee shops and takeaway food outlets promoting their student discounts that I'm entering the university area. Teenagers tumble out of a vintage clothes store onto the pavement, having just bought a bag full of denim by the kilo. Every time I see a flash of a yellow jacket I get excited, as if that is all Sunflower Girl ever wears. I follow the herd of students towards Munich University's Department of English and American Studies, which is right next door to the bookshop. The copper-coloured sign tells me I've arrived. I walk in through the maroon steel doors of the shop with butterflies in my stomach.

The handful of customers inside don't look like Andreas, they are young, carrying backpacks and presumably study English next door. An oversized black-and-white rug covers the right-hand side wall, with the slogan *Booksellers Words' Worth since 1985* embroidered across it. More than an English bookstore, it seems to be a tribute to English culture. Tea trays and porcelain mugs, royal memorabilia and jars of marmalade, dainty napkins and postcards of Henry VIII and his six wives are all on sale. There is a whole gardening section complete with Alan Titchmarsh books. I didn't realize he was so popular in Germany.

The shop is smaller than I expected and is spaced out over three mezzanine levels. I shuffle around the store, pretending to look at the books, but I'm really keeping an eye out for Sunflower Girl. There don't appear to be any staff around, let alone the one I want to find. I take the few steps up to the first mezzanine level, where there is a DVD section. I browse through the collection, quickly realizing it is made up of the most stereotypical British movies from Harry Potter and James Bond to Monty Python and the entire Carry On collection. Do the Germans think we just watch Mr Bean constantly?

I notice a series of framed letters hanging on the opposite wall. They are all addressed to the book-shop from Clarence House. The first one is from the Queen Mother's secretary, informing the shop that the Queen Mother won't be able to open Words' Worth; the second thanks the shop for their birthday wishes to the Queen Mother; and the third apologizes that the Queen Mother won't be able to attend the shop's anniversary celebrations. I expect the fourth one is from the Queen Mother telling them to get lost and stop bothering her, but before I can read it I notice a pair of legs around the corner. Tucked away on the top level, a fifty-something man is kneeling down on the dark-grey carpeted floor stacking the shelves with new books.

'Excuse me . . .' I startle him slightly as I approach him from behind.

'*Hallo, kann ich Ihnen helfen?*' he says automatically

before realizing he can speak in English. 'Um, sorry, can I help?'

'Well, I hope so. I have a random question, I'm looking for a girl who I think might work here, she's in her twenties and has got dark hair, she's English . . .' I ramble.

The guy looks back at me confused.

'Is there a young English woman who works here with dark hair, by any chance?'

I repeat it much more slowly this time, although I'm not sure if he's confused by the words or the question.

'You mean Clara?' he says as he gets to his feet, towering over me. He must be about six foot three.

'Maybe, I don't actually know her name.'

He looks at me, trying to decipher why I want this information.

'I will go and get her for you.'

Can it be this easy? Maybe fate really is on my side. I've managed to find her on my first attempt. Jake and Jessie aren't going to believe it.

Still looking bewildered, he wanders off and heads through a door at the back of the shop, squeezing between customers and bookshelves.

My heart starts beating more quickly, my hands sweating.

What am I going to tell her?

I didn't expect to find her straightaway. I haven't even thought about what I am going to say. And I didn't envisage having to talk to her in front of a crowded bookstore with the owner standing beside us. How am

I going to explain why I've travelled to Munich to find her? Maybe I should just leave before they come back.

As I pace up and down, contemplating just running out of the door, I notice the man coming back. There doesn't seem to be any sign of a woman with him. Maybe she has spotted me and refused to come out. Maybe he's going to ask me to leave the store before they call the police.

'Sorry, sir, I think Clara left for the day. She studies in the afternoon.'

'OK, can I just check that Clara is definitely English? And she's about this height, with dark hair?' I gesture with my hands.

'Yes, that's right. That's her. She will be working tomorrow morning, or I call her if necessary?'

'No, that's OK, I will come back tomorrow. Thank you very much for your help.' I sense a phone conversation would be even more embarrassing. I want to ask him if he has a photo to confirm it's her, but I can't bring myself to ask. I will just wait until tomorrow to see her in person.

I smile, unable to believe my luck, and head back out into the street, my heart racing.

I am already daydreaming about my reunion tomorrow with Sunflower Girl, or Clara. I didn't envisage her being called Clara. It makes sense that she works in this shop next to the university; I can see her studying English Literature there. I wonder where she is now? I look around at all the students, trying to spot her in the crowd, wondering if she is at a lecture. Or maybe she is at the festival? Perhaps she's dressed in a dirndl and downing beers while dancing on tables?

As it's only around the corner, I decide to check out the other English bookstore, the Munich Readery. It is set away from the hustle and bustle of the university campus and has a more discreet frontage. It's purely a second-hand bookshop, and so just a handful of relatively new books are propped up in the window, with no royal memorabilia adding to the display. Although if you shouldn't judge a book by its cover, you shouldn't judge a bookshop by the outside. By the entrance, there is a stack of blue bric-a-brac crates containing half-price books. I have a quick browse through before I go in, flicking through dog-eared James Patterson novels and out-of-date travel guides.

The inside of the shop is like a private medical-surgery waiting room, with light-wooden laminated flooring, large green IKEA plants in white pots and comfy armchairs. Separating the room is a labyrinth of large floor-to-ceiling black bookshelves which are positioned at different angles. A bald-headed, bespectacled American man, who could be Stanley Tucci's twin, sits behind the counter, discussing his pets on the phone. I can't help but listen in as I linger by the non-fiction section. It takes me a while to realize Dickens is the name of his dog.

'You know what it's like . . . Yes . . . Yes, exactly . . . They take a while to settle in, don't they . . . I remember when we got the two kittens . . . Yes, that's right . . . Now they get along with each other, and with Dickens. Thank God . . .'

'Excuse me, do you know when the new Danielle Steel book will be in stock?' I hear a woman's voice ask him.

'It depends when someone brings it in,' he says, before going back to his phone conversation.

I wait to hear him put the phone down before I walk over to the counter.

'Can I get you an espresso?' he asks as I approach, in a thick New York twang.

I look back at him, confused, thinking I am in a bookshop not a Starbucks, until I see the sign on the counter advertising hot drinks for sale. He is enterprisingly putting the kettle next to his computer to good use.

'No, I'm OK, thanks, I was just wondering if there is an English girl who normally works here? She's in her twenties with dark hair?'

'Sorry, man, I am the only person who works in this shop and I haven't been twenty or had hair for many years.' He laughs at his own joke. I muster a little chuckle back so as not to appear rude.

I am not too despondent as I leave, confident that Clara is indeed Sunflower Girl. I am more concerned about where I am going to stay tonight, given every hotel, hostel and guest house in the city is fully booked, or priced exorbitantly, due to the influx of tourists from around the world. I wander back through the city centre, past the Rathaus-Glockenspiel, where some of these tourists are gathered, waiting to see the figures coming out of the clock.

Having been turned away from four hotels, just as I

am about to find a piece of pavement to settle down on for the night, I spot a hostel near the main train station with a sign 'Rooms Available'. *Thank God*, I think, until the receptionist reveals the price. Even with my knowledge of hotels, I can't haggle the price down much, considering they only have one private room left. I begrudgingly hand over a large portion of my quiz winnings and head upstairs, realizing when the lift takes five minutes to reach the third floor that this isn't going to be the best accommodation in Munich. I turn the key and walk in, but it's difficult to actually fit myself and my bag into the room. If it seems like false advertising to have a festival named Oktoberfest in September, then it certainly is false advertising to describe the cupboard I have paid 150 euros for as a 'premium private room'. Describing a cupboard as a 'room' is pushing it. Describing it as 'private' when it lacks any curtains is a step too far. Especially as the window looks directly out onto a multistorey office block. I would say I can just change in the bathroom, but the 'bathroom' isn't quite how it had been described. There's no bath for a start. There's not even a door. And someone took the unique decision to place the toilet directly underneath the sink, meaning only a contortionist can use it. Most bizarrely of all, the floor is heated. Forget curtains, or a toilet door, underfloor heating is the one luxury you just can't do without.

Still, all that matters is that tomorrow I'm going to be reunited with Clara.

22

I lie in bed waiting for the clock to move. I feel like I'm seven years old, waiting for everyone else to wake up.

I wasn't expecting to be excited about my twenty-ninth birthday. I was dreading it. Another year with nothing to report. In fact, I stopped being excited about birthdays after my twenty-first, when I got food poisoning at a cheap restaurant Dad picked for us. I spent the entire evening throwing up in the toilet.

But today is different. Today is going to be the best birthday ever.

I don't even mind when Jake and Jessie both text with digs about my age. Nor when I open the football-boot card from Mum and Dad that is designed for a five-year-old.

The bookshop doesn't open until 10 a.m., and it's only about a twenty-minute walk. I have plenty of time to scoff down the eggs in the breakfast buffet and pack my stuff, which is easy when everything is within an arm's reach in the box room.

'How was your stay?' the young man in the hostel reception asks as I hand back the key.

Well, I've barely slept, because of nerves and the constant noise of the revellers returning to the hostel, which now means I look awful. It also didn't help that the air-con system was on all night.

Bloodshot eyes, swollen, puffy skin and a blocked nose are not ideal for our big reunion. And for 150 euros, I didn't even get any shower gel.

'It was fine, thanks,' I say, handing back my key and rushing out into the cool Munich morning breeze. Having spent so long on the other side of the desk, I know the receptionist doesn't want to know the truth.

As I make my way back towards the bookshop, I overhear what looks like the Munich Free Walking Tour. The poster advertising the tour was plastered all over the hostel, along with adverts for day trips to nearby Berchtesgaden and Neuschwanstein Castle.

'There is an old tradition that towns try to raid their neighbours' villages to steal their maypole. If successful, the city who loses the maypole is obliged to host a party in honour of the group responsible for outsmarting the city.'

The large group of tourists listen attentively as they are gathered around Munich's maypole. The German woman leading the tour seems to speak English with a Scottish accent, as if she learned by watching episodes of Taggart.

'A few years ago, Munich Airport's maypole was stolen. When the airport staff realized the pole was gone, they called Munich's city police to get their help, but all the airport police heard on the phone was laughing. The city police had actually stolen the maypole and changed the security footage so they wouldn't see. The airport ended up throwing a party for the city in order to get their maypole back!'

The whole group laughs along, and I wonder how many times the guide has told that same story.

As I continue towards the bookstore, I go through my own script in my head and rehearse what I am going to say to Clara.

I know that this, um, is quite random and, well, you probably weren't expecting to see me again, but, well, I guess I really liked you and well, um, I wondered if you maybe felt the same?

I realize as I practise that I sound too much like a Hugh Grant character. It sounded much better when I practised in the mirror last night, even if I did have to contort my whole body to see my reflection.

In my haste, I reach the street a few minutes early. I contemplate that it seems keen to get to the shop for opening, but too keen to be waiting outside before it opens. As such, I opt to hover down the road, watching the entrance from a distance, seeing if I can spot her going in to work. I decide to give Nan and Pap a call to thank them for their birthday message.

'Seven six nine eight two four.'

I never understand why Nan always recites her phone number when she picks up the phone.

'Hello, how are you?' I say.

'Good morning. I'm very well, thank you. And how are you today?' she says very politely in her phone voice.

It usually takes her at least a minute to recognize who I am, so I speed up the process.

'It's Josh, Nan. How are you doing?'

'Oh, Josh, so lovely to hear from you. Happy Birthday! Has someone given you the bumps yet?'

'Not yet.'

'Happy Birthday to you . . .' She sings the entire song as I stand in the chilly street, watching the shop.

'Thank you very much. I just wanted to say thank you for your lovely message.'

'That's OK. We've got a present for you too when you get back.'

'Aw, thanks.'

'Now then, I wanted to ask you if you knew which route you took to get to Germany? It's Germany you're in, right?'

'Yes, that's right, Nan, I'm in Munich.'

I can hear her flicking through her atlas, which was published when the British Commonwealth still ruled the world. Half the countries either don't exist any more, have changed their name or have merged with another country.

'How did you get there?'

'I don't know, I didn't fly the plane,' I say flippantly, concentrating more on the store.

I see the man from yesterday unlocking the door and moving a sign outside.

'Sorry, Nan, I've got to go.'

'Just a minute. Pap just wants to wish you a happy birthday too.'

'Sorry, Nan. Can you tell Pap I will call him back a bit later on? Thanks again. See you both soon.'

I hang up.

As the clocks around the city chime, a sudden rush of students floods onto the street, heading in and out of their classes. As I squeeze through them, my heart is beating rapidly, and I feel like I'm going to throw up. When I'm almost at the door, I stop dead in the middle of the pavement. My legs don't want to move.

Is this it? Is this the moment? Am I actually doing this?

I think of my journey so far this year and all the choices the coin has made that have led me here. I force myself to walk slowly on.

Come on, Josh, you can do it.

I pause, once more, outside the shop and take a deep breath.

Here goes.

I swing open the door, bound into the shop and see Clara immediately.

She is standing behind the counter on the first-floor mezzanine. She is wearing a turquoise-green jumper and dark-rimmed glasses, and her brown hair is tied back in a plait. She looks up from what she is doing and smiles at me as I walk in. '*Guten Morgen,*' she exclaims.

My heart sinks.

She doesn't recognize me.

And I don't recognize her.

Clara is indeed an English girl in her twenties with dark hair, but she's not Sunflower Girl.

I stare at her, trying to hide my disappointment.

'Hello?' she says. 'Can I help you?'

'Um, no, sorry, I'm OK, thanks.' I walk up the steps and read her name badge in disbelief.

How can this be?

I was so sure that this was the shop, that this was the moment we were to be reunited.

I bounded into the store with such enthusiasm that I decide I need to buy something so I don't look too weird. I pick up one of the postcards of Anne Boleyn by the counter and pay, without saying anything. Although, as I leave, I realize someone coming into a shop that excited to buy a postcard of a beheaded Tudor queen looks pretty mental.

I trudge back out into the street, feeling despondent. If anything, I feel further away from finding her than I did before arriving in Germany. I am back to not even knowing her name.

Did I really think it would be that easy?

I am tempted to go straight back to the airport and head to Amsterdam, before wondering if I should give the art gallery a try. The coin tells me to go for it. I spot a bakery on the way and step in to buy myself a small birthday cake to cheer myself up and put it in my bag to eat later.

In the midst of festival fever, the Museum Quarter seems to be the most tranquil part of Munich. The collection of several museums, dedicated to different art periods dating from the Roman times to modern day, are surrounded by lush gardens. I'm looking for the Neue Pinakothek, which focuses on European art from the eighteenth and nineteenth centuries. I do an entire loop of the large brutalist building before I work out how to get inside. There are no signs pointing you in the right direction. Eventually I find the entrance and head in. The old lady at reception greets me and gestures towards the rusty lockers downstairs to store my bag. This isn't quite the Louvre.

I check the plan of the gallery and see that Van Gogh is displayed in the penultimate room, so I speed through the other rooms, bypassing Gainsborough, Reynolds, Goya and Delacroix without giving them a second glance. I am immediately struck by how quiet the gallery is. When I say quiet, it is completely empty. By the time I reach a room full of Greek landscapes, I still haven't seen another person. I presume everyone else in Munich is getting drunk, and the few cultural visitors are probably still circling the gallery trying to find the way in.

Manet, Cezanne . . . I'm getting closer. As I finally reach the lilac-painted room containing Van Gogh's works, I half-expect Sunflower Girl to be there, admiring the painting. But, as in the rest of the gallery, there is no one to be seen. I am alone with three more of Van Gogh's works, a couple of Gauguins, a Sérusier and a sculpture by Rodin. I am alone with my thoughts.

As the humidity machine ticks away in the corner of the room, I sit on the couch in the centre admiring *Sunflowers*. For the first time I truly appreciate the colours, the thick brush strokes and its simple beauty.

I look at *Sunflowers*, wondering if she has sat in this very seat, similarly admiring the painting. If only art could talk.

23

I hear the commotion before I see what is causing it.

And it's fair to say what I see is not what I am expecting.

A short, middle-aged man, clinging on to a long-lensed Nikon camera, is sprinting along the terracotta-paved street, sidestepping through the crowds. Behind him, and running even more quickly, is a six-foot-tall, blonde sex worker wearing black skimpy lingerie. Above her head, she is waving an oversized dildo as if it's a truncheon. The crowd clears considerably more quickly for her.

As she catches up with the man, she prises his camera out of his hands and throws it in the canal before launching into a four-letter tirade. He clearly didn't read the graffitied signs declaring 'No Fucking Photos' which decorate the red-light district. Almost anything goes in the De Wallen neighbourhood, but the one rule is it must not be captured on camera. The man, stunned and confused, stands on the spot, petrified. The woman turns round and walks back to her booth to return to work.

Welcome to Amsterdam.

Even if I had wanted to, I couldn't have afforded to stay in Munich for another night, and once I realized that Sunflower Girl wasn't there I had nothing else to stay for. I headed straight from the gallery to the airport and on to the Dutch capital, having booked a B&B online.

I continue past the neon-lit glass booths dotted alongside the canal, subtly checking my phone for directions to my accommodation, ensuring it doesn't look like I'm taking any photos. A woman adorned with tattoos, piercings and not much else taps on the window and beckons me in. I decide not to pose the question to the coin. I feel strangely flattered that a sex worker wants to have sex with me, and then almost heartbroken thirty seconds later when I hear her also knock on the window for the obese man twenty yards behind me.

A young family are walking alongside me, presumably having taken a wrong turning.

'Daddy, what are all these shops?' the girl, probably no more than seven years old, asks.

I can see his brain whirring, trying to think of an explanation.

'They're barbers, this is where men come to get their hair cut.'

For a second he looks relieved and thinks he has got away with it.

'But why does a man with no hair need to have a haircut?' she replies as a large, bald man disappears into one of the booths.

They avoid walking past the sex club and scuttle off, taking the next turning. I'm almost tempted to go into the club just to get warm for twenty minutes, because the breeze blowing from the canals is making me shiver.

It doesn't help either that all the canals and bridges look exactly the same, meaning it's almost impossible to get your bearings. I end up walking past the same sex worker three times. By mistake, honestly.

I'm not the only one circling the area. As darkness has descended, large groups of over-excited men flood the red-light district. I try to manoeuvre my way through the crowds of gawping blokes, egging each other on.

My mobile data is refusing to work, and I realize there's no point in asking any of the intoxicated stag groups for directions. I can't keep on walking around in the freezing cold, so I approach one of the booths. The woman behind seems a bit more demure than the others, slightly older and wearing a few more items of clothing.

'Hey darling, you want suck and fuck? Fifty euros.'

When I said demure . . .

'Um, no.' I panic.

'Come in,' she says, ignoring my response. She is caked in make-up and fake tan. Her teeth glare bright white in the luminescent lighting.

I step inside, and she shuts the door behind me immediately. She stares at me expectantly, waiting for me to hand over a wad of notes.

'You been busy this evening?' I try to make chit-chat, realizing this line has different connotations to a hooker than to a taxi driver.

'What you want? We go upstairs.'

'Actually, I was just wondering if you knew where this place is?' I point to the name on my phone, not wanting to attempt the Dutch pronunciation.

'Are you taking a piss? Fuck off!'

I check my flies, wondering what she means, until I realize she has just misused her articles. Taking *the* piss.

'Josh?' a voice calls out.

Of all the places you could be recognized, coming out of a brothel is not the best. Especially with your hands on your flies.

'Oh my God, Josh, it's you, right?'

As I stumble onto the street, and the door is slammed behind me, I look up, panicking about who has caught me in the most compromising of positions. How do I explain this one? No one is going to believe I was asking for directions.

Who is it?

Please tell me this isn't the moment when I find Sunflower Girl.

In the darkness, I don't recognize the girl standing in front of me. She's plump, pretty and has short blonde hair. I quickly search my memory for who she is – someone I've worked with? Went to primary school with? A friend of a friend?

This is now even more awkward. Do I pretend to know her?

'Don't worry, you don't know me!' she says. I realize I've stared at her and not spoken for the last thirty seconds.

'Ah, OK, so can I ask how do you know me?' I laugh nervously.

'I've been following your search.'

'What search?'

'You're searching for Sunflower Girl, right?'

I look at her suspiciously.

'How do you know about that?'

'I'm following the search online.'

'Sorry, I'm really confused, how are you following my search online?'

Who is this stalker?

She takes her mobile phone from the front pocket of her navy jeans, types in her passcode and opens up Instagram. After clicking a few times, she shoves the phone in my face.

'Look!'

I'm looking at an Instagram account with pictures of me. But it's not my account.

#FindSunflowerGirl.

I take the phone and click on the first photo to read the caption.

'Josh is now in Amsterdam, can you help him find Sunflower Girl? If you have any information please DM us or email FindSunflowerGirl@hotmail.com. J+J.'

Of course, it's them.

4,327 followers. Wow.

I scroll down through the various posts: photos of me, *Sunflowers*, the marathon, a Photoshopped 'wanted' sign. The first one was uploaded two days ago.

I can't believe Jake and Jessie have done this. I am speechless.

I want to call them immediately but remember my phone has no signal. After I scroll through the rest of the Instagram posts, I hand her phone back.

'Thanks for showing me. I actually didn't know anything about this.' I'm still flabbergasted, and pretty furious.

'It's nice of your friends, no, to try and help?' she says, sensing my reaction.

'That's one way of looking at it.'

'Maybe you need some more help? Do you fancy going for a drink? I'd like to hear more about your search.'

'Well, I was actually hoping to go . . .'

'Might be useful to have a local guide.'

'Yes, but I was . . .'

'Come on!'

She's not going to take no for an answer. It's not even a choice.

She leads me away from the hordes of tourists, and the sex workers, and fortunately doesn't bring up what I was doing exiting a brothel.

24

We walk to the more hipster area of the city, and she gives me an impromptu guided tour as we go. I think we're getting further and further away from my B&B, but I don't object as I gaze through the windows of the stylish open-plan office blocks that line the street. We walk into what looks like a large converted cinema which now operates as a trendy café. The menu reads like a vegan's dream.

'I'll have a decaf Aussie skinny latte, thanks,' she says as she takes a seat.

I order and take our coffees to where she's sitting, counting how many euros I have left.

'I should really ask your name.' I'm learning from my mistakes.

'It's Eva. Nice to meet you, Josh.' She sticks out her hand and shakes mine. She'd get on well with Uncle Peter. 'You're British, right? I was reading an article the other day which said eighty-three per cent of British men who die in Amsterdam are found in the canals, so you better watch out,' she says smiling.

Nice to meet you too.

'Is that how you always start conversations, with facts about death?'

I make a mental note not to stray too close to the water.

'Not always, but it's a good fact, no?'

I laugh at her kookiness.

'So, how did you find out about my search, then?' I ask.

'I just broke up with my girlfriend, or I should say she broke up with me. This was a few weeks ago. And I was having a conversation with one of my best friends about romance being dead . . .'

Is everyone heartbroken these days? I thought I had a patent on it.

I try to console her, but she talks so fast that I can't get a word in.

'So yes, to cut a long story short – isn't that what you guys say? – this friend told me about your page, and, well, I'm kind of hooked now to see what happens. I think it's very romantic. I wish someone would come and look for me. How strange I actually bumped into you. Hang on a second, I just need to message my friend to let her know.'

Before I can object, she shoves her mobile in my face and takes a photo, blinding me with the flash.

'Oops, don't know why the flash was on. Let me take another one.'

Is this what it's like being a celebrity?

'Julia is going to be so jealous. Actually, I should see if she wants to join us now.'

She starts texting her friend.

'So, what was I saying? Ah yes, that's how I found your account after my break-up.'

'I'm sorry to hear that. You doing OK now?'

'We don't want to talk about me. You're the famous one, Josh. So you think this Sunflower Girl is here in Amsterdam, do you?'

'Well, she wasn't in Munich so I'm hoping so. I'm running out of options. I can't afford to go to Tokyo or Philadelphia.'

'You know, if she's not here, there are lots of other good-looking women in Amsterdam. And you don't have to pay either . . .' She winks dramatically.

'Oh no, I wasn't . . .' I nearly choke on my pepper-mint tea.

'It's OK, we're very open-minded here, Josh.'

'Good-looking, open-minded – what other traits do people have here?'

'We're all quite, um, how do you say it, to the point?'

'Yes, to the point. Like blunt?'

'Yes, we're all quite blunt in the Netherlands. We say what we think. The good thing is you don't have to worry whether I'm telling the truth or not. I am always honest. If I don't want to see you, I'll tell you to fuck off. But I won't be blunt with you today, it's your birthday!'

With the excitement of the day, I'd almost forgotten it was my birthday. I presume Jake and Jessie must have notified the world of this fact too.

'Is there anything you don't know about me?'

'I'm not sure. This sounds like a good game. Tell me something that I don't know about you.'

'I've been flipping a coin to make big decisions this year.'

I regret saying it before it even comes out of my mouth, especially as Jake told me to never mention it, but I am tired, and it's the first thing I can think of.

'I did not know that. That's so weird . . . But so cool. Oh, this sounds so much fun. Come on, let's ask the coin something.'

I don't know whether Eva is on something or she's just naturally this manic.

'It's not a toy.'

'Ask it if I should have another drink.'

You can use your own coin.

I flip it to please her. Tails.

'Ask it if I should go out with Julia on Friday.'

We could be doing this all night at this rate.

Heads.

'Ask it if I should start dating again.'

'I think the coin is a bit tired now.'

'So, Josh, what time are we starting the search tomorrow?'

'You're coming with me, are you?'

'Well, you're going to need a local to help you, and you will probably need some help when you actually find this girl. You don't seem a natural with women, may I say.'

Blunt, indeed.

'It will also look better if I ask after her, rather than you. You look a bit like a stalker, to be honest.'

And again.

'Do you not have a job, or something better to do tomorrow?'

'No, I have the day off tomorrow. Perfect, isn't it? So shall we, say, meet at nine by the Van Gogh Museum and we can go from there?'

She picks up her handbag and coat in one movement and rushes off before I can ask for directions to my B&B.

Significantly later than I had expected, after logging into the café's free Wi-Fi – Martin Router King – to seek directions, I stumble into the reception. I crash on the bed as soon as I get to my room. I'm too tired to call Jake and Jessie and I remember I never called Pap back. As I reach down to unzip my bag I realize I forgot all about my birthday cake. I take the now broken and battered cake out of my bag and blow out an imaginary candle.

I wish that I will find her tomorrow.

25

'Hello?'

That is definitely not Jessie's voice. It is deeper, more northern and, well, simply put, a man's voice. I look down at the screen of my iPhone to check I've called the correct number. I have.

'Er, hi, is Jessie there?'

'Sure, will just get her for you. It's a bit early, isn't it, though, mate?' he sighs. His voice is familiar, but I can't pinpoint it.

I look at my watch, which reads 8 a.m. I forget that I'm an hour ahead. As Jessie takes the phone, I go to apologize but then I realize I'm meant to be mad at her.

'Hey, Josh, you OK?' That is Jessie's voice.

'Who was that?'

There is a muffled noise, which sounds like Jessie is moving.

'Hello, sorry, it's nobody.'

Well, it's obviously somebody.

'What do you call this Instagram page?'

'Good morning to you, too, Josh. Yes, I'm very well, and you?'

'What's going on with this page?' I repeat.

'Is this an inquisition? I take it you've seen the page, then?'

'Yes, I've seen it, only because I bumped into someone here who is following it and she recognized me. I'm now going to be spotted as a weirdo everywhere thanks to you guys.'

'I think everyone thought you were a weirdo before this, Josh.'

'This isn't funny. I remember telling you in Pinkman's that I didn't want to do any social media campaign. And then you go and do it behind my back. You had no right to do that.'

'I'm sorry, but we just wanted to help. We were going to fly out and help you but figured this would probably be more productive.'

'Whose idea was it?'

'Well, me and Jake were discussing it, and then Jake's Jake offered to help, and we went with it.'

Of course. No wonder it's got so much traction already with a social media marketer behind it.

'So you're all in on it. Great. Everyone except me. Couldn't you have told me about it at least?'

'OK, we probably should have done. I'm sorry.'

'I'm going to look like a stalker now. This is going to scare her off, if anything.'

'No, I promise it won't. We can close it down if you want. But we've had lots of interest, and it's clearly working if people in Amsterdam have seen it.'

True. Maybe it isn't such an awful idea.

'Have you got any leads?'

'Nothing concrete yet.'

'What does that mean?'

227

'Nothing. I think you're getting close.'

'You're holding something back from me, aren't you? What is it?'

'OK, so we've had a few messages from girls who claim to be Sunflower Girl. But I don't think any of them are her, as they don't live in the right places. One was from Paris, another Melbourne, I think one was from South Korea. There were a few. It's a bit weird how many girls want to be with you.'

'Keep their details just in case,' I joke.

'And, well, we did have an email, which Jake thinks could be real, but I'm not so sure.'

'What did it say?'

'It was from another girl who claims to be Sunflower Girl . . .' She pauses. 'She said to take the campaign down as she already has a boyfriend.'

My heart sinks.

'Why would someone lie about that?' I ask.

'I don't know, but I don't think it's her.'

'Why does Jake think it's real, then?'

'She mentioned what you were wearing that day.'

Now my heart breaks.

'Come on, how else would she know that? It must be her, then. She's met someone else already.'

'I don't know. The message just seemed a bit off, and when I asked for more information, she didn't reply again. Like I feel the girl you described would have sent something nicer, even if she didn't want you to find her.'

I consider Jessie's words.

'Look, I am only telling you so you can keep it in the

back of your mind. I still think she's out there. You're there anyway, so you may as well have a look at the bookshops today and see if you have any luck. We'll keep the page up until the end of the day and see what happens.'

'OK, I will let you know how I get on. You had better get back to Mr Nobody.'

'I've got to go and feed Jeremy, actually. Good luck.'

'Thanks, Jessie, but don't think I'm not cross with you both still.'

I put the phone down, confused about both the message and the mystery man.

26

As soon as I approach the Van Gogh Museum, I spot her. In fact, I can't miss her. While all the holidaymakers are in shorts and T-shirts, she is dressed like Sherlock Holmes. The only thing she is missing is the pipe.

'Why are we going to need a magnifying glass?' I ask her, bemused, as she greets me with an embrace that is over friendly, considering we've known each other for less than twelve hours. As we hug, I accidentally knock her deerstalker hat off her head.

'This is what detectives wear. No wonder you haven't found her yet, wearing those.' She points at my jeans. I am wearing the same black jeans I've worn for the last few days, complete with a hoodie.

'You do know we're just going to go to a few book-shops to see if this girl works there, not trying to solve a murder.'

'Fine, then,' she says, annoyed, putting the magnify-ing glass away in her backpack, simultaneously revealing an array of other detective gear stuffed in her bag. I'm sure I catch sight of a listening device but decide not to mention it. After all, she kept schtum about my brothel faux pas.

'I thought you could maybe put a photo of me on the Instagram page?'

'That's why you've dressed up? Just to have your photo taken? You do know I don't run the page, right?'

'Well, you could send a photo to your friend and ask her to upload it?'

'You really want to be on it that badly?' She nods enthusiastically and retrieves her magnifying glass again, ready to pose.

A stray football bounces past us as I take a photo of her on my phone. One of the kids playing in the large park next to us runs after it, scaring off the dozens of seagulls which have menacingly settled on the grass.

'OK, where are we going first, then?' I ask, now that we've got the photoshoot out of the way.

She unveils her large paper map of Amsterdam, a retro item these days.

'There are four English-language bookstores in the centre of Amsterdam. Each is in close proximity to the Van Gogh Museum, where *Sunflowers* is displayed. I have marked them with a red pen.'

She has certainly done her homework. Four red circles mark our destinations. Could one of them be the shop?

'I figure we go this way, head here and work our way around.' She points to the map and illustrates our planned route with her finger, as if she's a football manager delivering her tactics for the game.

'Great.'

It takes her almost five minutes to fold the map back down again, and in the end she just scrunches it up and shoves it in her bag.

'Any time today. Let's get going,' I joke.

'We're not going anywhere yet. Before we go to any of these shops, we've got to go into the museum. No trip to Amsterdam is complete without seeing *Sunflowers*, especially your trip.'

'Is that really necessary?'

'We need to get into her mindset. We need to channel Sunflower Girl.'

I look at her, bemused.

'Come on, Josh, do you want to find her or not?'

'Don't we have to book tickets or something?'

'It's OK, I booked them last night. You can pay me back later, don't worry.'

Our tickets? Brilliant. I'm meant to be on a tight budget.

'We've just got to go and collect our audio guides first,' she says without giving me a choice.

Oh yippee, even more money.

We eventually head up the escalator to the gallery, although Eva is not happy having to be separated from her detective equipment when we are instructed to leave our bags in the cloakroom.

Despite the throng of people, the gallery is eerily quiet, with everyone walking around listening to their audio guides. The only voice that can be heard is Eva's; she doesn't realize she is shouting.

We skip past Van Gogh's early works to get to the main attraction. It has a wall to itself, positioned centrally in a golden frame on a turquoise wall. Unlike in Munich, it is hard to get a good view of the painting as the crowds swarm around it. They all look down at their multimedia guides, which have close-up pictures and extra information.

'For Van Gogh, yellow was an emblem of happiness. He famously only used three shades of yellow to complete this painting. In Dutch literature, the sunflower was a symbol of devotion and loyalty. In their various stages of decay, these flowers also remind us of the cycle of life and death.'

We head up another flight of stairs.

'This could be something.' I take off my headphones and call out to Eva as I browse the display of original letters written between Van Gogh and his brother Theo. 'She said she'd been reading his letters recently, so maybe she saw them here.'

'Yes, that sounds possible. Let's have a look in the gift shop.' Eva drags me across the room to the shop tucked into the corner. 'And look what we have here,' she says in full-on detective mode.

Alongside every conceivable item of merchandise printed with *Sunflowers* – key rings, pencils, T-shirts – there is a pile of the Penguin Classics edition of *The Letters of Van Gogh*.

'I reckon she came here, saw the letters in the museum and bought the book.'

'It would make sense.' She nods along in agreement with my theory. 'Do you think we should buy a copy to channel her?'

'Actually, I've already read it,' I reply, putting the copy that Eva passes to me back down.

I downloaded the book and read it in a day after

Sunflower Girl mentioned it so we could discuss it, if we ever met again.

As we head down to the ground floor and hand back our audio guides, I don't confess to Eva that the museum was a good idea, but I am now more optimistic about the search.

'Do you feel like we're in the right mindset now to go and find her?' I ask sarcastically as we head back out into the fresh air.

'I think so, but I'm quite hungry after all that. I've not had any breakfast yet, so shall we go and eat first? Do you like omelettes? Good, because I've got the perfect place for you.'

'So, you can have pretty much any type of omelette you want. It's great, isn't it?' she says as she takes a seat at a large booth. Old vintage musical theatre songs are playing through the speakers, competing with the sound of the frying.

'What are you having? I guess you're going to flip the coin? Can I do it as well?'

'Sure.' I hand her the coin.

We are choosing between an omelette or an omelette.

The restaurant has really gone big on the theme: the walls are decorated with artwork depicting flying eggs, and the chef is wearing a red T-shirt saying 'Eggspert' on the back. As I watch him cooking, he lives up to his title as he makes four omelettes simultaneously.

'So, what are you going to say to her when you find her, then?'

'I'm not really sure.'

'What do you mean, you're not sure? You must have thought of something. What if you had found her in Germany? You weren't just going to stand there in silence staring at her, I hope?'

'No, I guess I was just going to tell her . . .'

'Shall we do a role-play?'

'What? Of the conversation?'

'Yes. I'll be Sunflower Girl, and you be you. Pretend you've just seen me in the bookshop.'

'We're not doing this.'

'Yes, you need to practise. You're only going to get one chance. I don't want you to fuck it up.'

'Shall we just eat first?'

I know in my head what I want to say, I just don't want to go through it with Eva.

'Someone's getting a bit hangry, I think. Come on, just until our food comes.'

She's not going to stop.

'Hi there, hopefully you remember me from London? We met in the National Gallery on the day of the marathon?' I say in a silly voice.

'You're starting with 'Hi there'? Really? And it sounds too nervous. It needs to be more bold. More confident. Start again.'

Why did I agree to spend the day with her?

'Hey, we met in London, at the National Gallery, on the day of the marathon, and I really wanted to ask you out on a date but never got your number so I tracked you down.'

'Ugh, ugh, you really sound like a stalker. "Tracked you down"? Don't say that.'

'OK, what should I say?' I try my best not to get angry.

'It's a good thing we're practising, isn't it? What happens if she doesn't remember you? Or she does and she doesn't like you? Or she has a boyfriend?'

'I thought you were meant to be helping me?'

27

As we step out of the restaurant, full of omelette, I'm nearly knocked to the ground by a cyclist who comes out of nowhere. I really don't understand the Amsterdam road system, and what is scarier is neither do any of the locals, apparently. Cyclists, motorbikes, cars and lorries all come from every angle across roads and pavements. Even the trams don't seem to be constrained to the lines.

'OK, this is the first shop.' She points to a tall townhouse that sits alongside the canal. A cute blue sign pokes out discreetly, with white text reading 'Used English Books'. 'Let me do all the talking when we go in. Obviously let me know if you see her, but otherwise I will ask.'

I feel my search has rather been hijacked.

As we walk in, the man standing behind the counter must wonder why a Sherlock Holmes impersonator is coming into his bookshop. It looks like we should be heading to a convention.

'*Hallo*,' he says.

'*Hallo*,' Eva replies.

Even I understand this, but I just nod and head deeper into the store.

The shop is completely silent, bar the noise of the

creaky floorboards, which wail every time we step on them. It feels more like I am browsing this man's house than a bookstore. As Eva browses the ground floor, I venture into the basement, crouching down, careful not to hit my head on the low ceiling. It's deadly silent, and the smell of musty books is overpowering.

I jump when Eva taps me on the shoulder.

'I'm sorry, she's not here. The man is the only person who works in the shop. On to the next one.'

One down.

We head towards the main shopping area in the city, away from the cannabis and sex museums, and on to Waterstones, which is the next circled shop on the map. The front window display is full of quintessential British children's book characters: Harry Potter, Paddington Bear, Peter Rabbit and Alice in Wonderland. Inside, the dark-green patterned carpets and mahogany bookcases are immediately reminiscent of every other Waterstones branch. We split up to cover the four floors, stocked not just with books but also with board games, gifts and notebooks.

'I can't see anyone matching her description, and I asked a couple of the guys who work here, and they didn't think such a girl has worked here recently,' Eva says as she rejoins me.

I'm transfixed by the British food shelves, which separate the books on the second floor. This section is an expat's dream: Tunnock's Tea Cakes, Walkers Short-bread, Yorkshire Tea, Hobnobs, Jammy Dodgers, Lyle's

Golden Syrup, Branston Pickle, Aah Bisto Gravy, Bovril, Marmite . . .

'Did you hear me?' She shakes me.

'Yep, she's not here either. But we still have two more stores to go,' I reply.

'What are Hobnobs?' Eva asks, noticing me staring at them.

'You've never had a Hobnob?'

'Isn't that what you guys call dicks?'

'Knobs?' I laugh out loud. 'No, these are just a type of biscuit. Come on, I'll get a pack so you can try one.'

Despite the heavily inflated price, we need a snack to keep up our energy, and something to cheer me up.

'Not bad, actually,' she says as she crunches her way through half the pack before we've even left the store.

It's only a few hundred feet to our next destination, but we don't spend more than two minutes in the New English Bookstore. The street could be anywhere in the world – with brands such as Superdry, Mango and Levi's – and the shop is equally as generic – a modern bargain-basement store selling cut-price Nicholas Sparks novels, and *Anne Frank's Diary* translated into every language. Two Dutch women, one stocking the shelves and one behind the counter, talk to each other as a local radio station plays in the background. As I browse the mindfulness colouring-in books and wonder who buys a calendar half a year early, I receive a shake of the head from Eva, and we're back out into the street.

'Looks like our last hope is that she works in the

American Book Store, then,' Eva says optimistically. My glass is now definitely less than half full. 'We can take a shortcut. This way.'

We head through a narrow alleyway and by the time we come out the other side, I feel high from the fumes inhaled. Before we go into the shop, Eva pulls me to the side and gives me a pep talk.

'I know this is our last shop, but if she's not here it doesn't mean you won't find her. She is out there somewhere, and if it's meant to be, it will be.'

Despite how annoying she can be, it's really nice to hear this and to have had someone to help with my search.

'Thank you. Let's just hope that she works here. It would make everything a lot easier.'

I immediately catch sight of a poster of *Sunflowers* hanging behind the counter on the right of the entrance. *Could it be?*

That's got to be a good sign. It's a megastore. Multiple floors of opportunity. Eva looks around the ground floor with the large coffee-table books and the magazine section – every title imaginable is on sale, from luxury periodicals to *Marie Claire* and *Hello!*.

I head up the staircase, which has bookshelves built in, showcasing an extensive music section, and which winds round to the first floor. I'm greeted by large, tall shelves of fiction paperbacks and a café selling Ethiopian Fair Trade coffee and a selection of cakes. A couple of people sit and read while having a drink, listening to the jazz music played through the speakers.

I take another flight of stairs and meander through the biography section. This floor is buzzing with customers and staff, but none of them are Sunflower Girl. A good-looking man lounges on a leather seat reading a book as if it's a library rather than a shop. A rope stops customers going up to the top floor. The sign states 'Staff Only'.

Is she up there?

I turn around and see Eva.

'OK, so I have good and bad news,' she says as she approaches me.

'Yes, go on, tell me.'

'Well, which do you want first?'

'Whatever is the most important.'

Get to it.

'So the good news is, I think we've found her. The manager said there was an English girl who worked here who matches the description.'

My face lights up.

'There was a girl? Where is she now?' I ask impatiently, sensing we're near to finding her.

'So yeah, that's the bad news. She quit her job a few weeks ago.'

Why did I leave it so long to come and find her?

My heart sinks, knowing that I was so close. Now she could be anywhere again.

'OK, does he know where she's working now?'

'Um, this is the really bad news. He said she talked about moving to New Zealand.'

New Zealand? I can't afford to fly there to find her. Why couldn't she have moved to Newcastle? Or Newquay?

'And there's something else you should probably know.'

'Yes, what is it?'

Eva looks hesitant. It's the first time I've seen her lost for words.

'Apparently she was moving there with . . .'

She doesn't want to end the sentence.

'She was moving there with . . . her . . . boyfriend.'

'Why didn't you just tell me that first? Clearly that was more important. There's no good news, then, is there?' I vent at Eva, even though it's obviously not her fault.

'Sorry, I . . .'

'So, I guess that means the email Jessie got was from the right girl,' I interrupt her.

'I guess so. I'm sorry it didn't work out for you, Josh. I really wanted to help.'

In the self-help section of an American bookstore, I hug a Dutch girl dressed as Sherlock Holmes whom I met outside a brothel.

28

I sit on the train to Amsterdam Airport Schiphol, feeling like a complete fool.

I've spent most of our winnings on a fruitless search. Of course she was going to have met someone else. Or maybe she secretly had a boyfriend all along?

Rain hammers against the train windows. I look around the carriage at the couples holding onto their luggage and to each other. They are preparing for exciting, romantic foreign getaways. I am heading back alone to the UK, feeling like I've been through this all before.

Is this why British men end up being dredged out of the canals?

As the train arrives at the airport, I check the electronic boards for information about the next departure. I am happy to fly to whichever UK airport is cheapest. It's not like I have anything to rush back for. I'm in the queue at the easyJet counter when my phone rings.

'Hey, Jessie,' I answer, in a downbeat tone.

'Hello, Josh? Are you there?'

'Hello, can you hear me?' I say as I examine my phone to check how many bars of signal I have.

'Yep, just about, where are you right now?'

'I'm at Amsterdam Airport about to come home.'

'I can't hear you. Can you speak up? Are you at the airport?'

The tannoy announcer rudely talks right over me.

'Yes, I'm at the airport, I'm on my way home,' I shout into the phone to try and be heard over the hubbub in the terminal, which is getting busier and busier as people flood in from the incoming trains.

'Why are you coming home? What's happened?'

'It's all over. The last shop we went to, the manager told us there was an English girl working there who has just left to move to New Zealand with her boyfriend. It fits with the message you received,' I summarize solemnly.

She is silent on the other end of the phone.

'OK, I'll admit that does sound disappointing. But we don't know for certain that this girl is her, and, well, the message could have come from anyone.'

'I don't know, I think I should just leave it now. I've given it a go, but I think it's time to come on home.'

'You can't stop now.'

'But Jessie —'

'I've got some news for you. I was calling to say *Sunflowers* isn't currently in Philadelphia. It's on loan to the Musée d'Orsay in Paris and has been for the last six months. The exhibition is ending there this month.'

I don't really know what to say. I think back to that time I searched the Bristol Museum with Nan and Pap for the painting that had been loaned to a gallery elsewhere.

'Did you hear me?' Jessie asks. 'I was telling someone

at work about you, and they'd seen it in Paris a few weeks ago.'

'Yep, thanks for letting me know, but between what we found out today and the message you got, it seems like she was here in Amsterdam.'

'But just think if — just if — that message is wrong, you've already ruled out three of the five paintings now. So there's a fifty-fifty chance she's in Paris. Isn't it worth one last shot?'

'Yeah, but that is only if what she told me in the first place was right, and she's not moved, and a million other possible scenarios. She could be anywhere in the world, to be honest. And she clearly doesn't want to be found, otherwise she'd have responded to your Instagram page.'

'I don't think that's the right attitude. We don't know she's even seen the page. Aren't you meant to flip your coin for decisions like this?'

I'm shocked that Jessie tells me to trust the coin.

What's happened to her?

I don't want to put this decision to chance, or fate, or whatever higher force is controlling my life. I just want to go home. I can't do this any more.

'Come on, do it,' she says, sensing my hesitation.

I reluctantly get the coin out of my pocket and awkwardly try to flip it while holding my phone between my head and my shoulder. It falls onto the floor.

'Sooo?' I can hear Jessie saying.

I bend down to see which side is facing up.

'It says I should go to Paris,' I reply quietly.

29

A woman – short, red-haired and petite, with tattoos covering her arms – taps me on the shoulder, as soon as I end the call to Jessie.

'Sorry, I didn't mean to listen in, but do you need to get to Paris? My friend who just dropped me off is driving to Girona. He will be going via Paris if you need a lift?'

She has been standing behind me all this time in the queue for the easyJet counter, listening in to my love-life ramblings.

'Oh my God, yes. I do. That would be amazing. Thank you so much. That is so kind. I've barely got any money left, so if I can get to Paris for free that would be a massive help.'

'OK, I'll just check he's not left already.'

I put my phone back in my pocket and pause. Is this mad? Am I actually doing this? What would Mum say if she knew I was accepting a lift from a complete stranger? Not just down the road but to another country?

As the woman turns her back to call him, I decide to ask the coin whether I should accept the lift. My head is a mess. One minute I'm going home, now I'm going to Paris.

She talks on the phone in Spanish, complete with lots of vigorous head nodding.

'It's fine, he's still here.'

'Thanks so much, this is incredibly kind,' I repeat as I follow the friendly woman out of the airport terminal. She explains that she is flying to Spain, but her friend has to take their luggage in the car.

'It sounds like you're looking for a girl?'

'Yes, that's right.'

'Well, I hope you find her. I'm happy to help anyone searching for love.'

We head into the short-stay car park, where a brand-new white Audi is waiting. The engine is still running. As we approach, a tall, tanned, dark-haired man in his late thirties jumps out of the driver's seat. He's wearing a Barcelona football shirt and has his long brown hair tied up in a top knot.

'*Holá*, Jesus,' he says, tapping his chest emphatically to indicate that it is his name.

'I'm Josh,' I respond, slightly underwhelmed by my own name. 'Thank you very much for giving me a lift. It's very kind of you.' I shove my bag on the back seat of the car, piling it on top of the large suitcases and folded-down furniture that already occupy the seats.

'Sorry, I no . . . talk much English.'

'It . . . is . . . very . . . nice . . . of . . . you . . . to . . . take . . . me . . . to . . . Paris. Thank . . . you . . . very . . . much,' I repeat as slowly and clearly as I can.

'It is OK.' He smiles.

'Sorry his English isn't the best,' the woman says

apologetically to me as she picks up her small carry-on bag. 'But he will drop you off in the centre of Paris.' I thank her again before jumping into the front seat, accidentally muddying the pristinely clean floor mat with my rain-soaked shoes. She says something to him in Spanish, or perhaps Catalan, and waves us both goodbye.

As we pull out of the airport car park, I have an idea. I get out my mobile and start typing a question into Google Translate.

'*Eres parti . . . partidario del club de fútbol de Barcelona?*' I say in the worst Spanish accent ever.

This confuses him more than my English.

I decide to shove my phone in his face instead so he can read the translation.

'No.' He points to his eyes.

'Um, eyes . . . glasses?' I suggest, as if we're playing a game of charades and I'm guessing the answer.

'*Sí*, no glasses.'

'You like Messi?' I point towards his shirt.

'Messi. Yes. The best.'

And that is the end of our conversation.

I decide I should let him concentrate on driving, especially if his vision isn't the best. I sit back into the seat and look out the window, resigned, hoping there is some nice scenery to keep me company for the next five or so hours. The main thing is I am on my way to Paris. There is still a glimmer of hope, however small, that I might find Sunflower Girl.

As I stare out at the motorway, it strikes me as incredible that a man called Jesus has saved me.

Admittedly, this isn't quite how I envisaged the Second Coming.

Given I have to flip a coin to choose which bottle of water to buy, choosing a faith is beyond my decision-making capability. As a family, we have always been twice-a-year Christians. We celebrate Jesus's birth and his resurrection, and we don't think about him for the rest of the year. Dad typically spends these two services altering the lyrics of the hymns to football chants and was keen that our attendance dropped further after the local council appointed a severely overzealous 'god-damn' parking attendant who started towing away cars parked on the double yellow lines outside the church. I did take confirmation classes when I was younger but was kicked out for asking too many questions, and the vicar, a man who preaches forgiveness, still refuses to give me a chocolate at the end of the Easter service. Yet when you're stuck in need of a miracle at Amsterdam Schiphol Airport and a man called Jesus offers you a lift, you have to wonder.

I can tell he's been trying to think of how to say something for at least twenty miles now. I look across at him, in his modern clothes, thinking it's about time he got a makeover. He must be embarrassed that he is always portrayed in stained-glass windows wearing the same outfit.

'Eeee, Jesus forgive you,' he laughs, pointing to the mess I have made on the floor mat.

'Oh, I'm very sorry,' I say, trying to pick up the mud and throwing it out the window, but he's already turned his eyes away, and we revert to silence again.

I check Google Maps on my phone to see the route we will be taking, and how many more hours the journey will take. We have to go through Utrecht, Antwerp, Ghent and Lille, but before we've even left Amsterdam I am fast asleep.

It's about an hour later when I am swiftly awoken by Jesus shouting.

'Fucker!'

What's happened?

'Jesus. Fucker!' he shouts again. I look around to see if a car has cut him up, but there are no other vehicles nearby.

I don't know where we are or what's going on, but I am not expecting the Son of God to speak like this.

He starts slapping his own face, leaving just one hand on the wheel. I preferred when he didn't speak.

Who have I got in a car with? Maybe I have been too trusting, hitching a ride with a complete stranger.

He continues to speak very quickly in Spanish, and the only words I can make out are 'fuck'.

I suddenly worry that this is aimed at me. I agree it's a bit rude falling asleep in the car, but this seems a bit harsh. I stare straight ahead, not wanting to look at Jesus.

As we approach a service station, he pulls in and parks up. Is this where he is going to kill me, dismember me and dump my body parts? Am I going to be found in a few days' time hidden around the back of the Belgian equivalent of Little Chef?

He smiles and signals that he is going to the café. I hesitantly smile back, completely confused, and decide to give Jake a call so at least someone knows my last location if I go missing.

Clearly Jake's not very busy, as he picks up after just one ring.

'Jake, you will never believe what has happened to me.'

'You've found Sunflower Girl?'

'No, don't be silly.'

'Um, you've decided you're going to repay me the money I gave you?'

'No. I'm with Jesus.'

'Jesus? Oh God, Josh, what have you been smoking in Amsterdam? You didn't go into any of those coffee shops, did you?'

'No, I did not. I was at the airport ready to come home and then Jesus came along and offered me a lift to Paris.'

'What, on his donkey?'

'No, Jake, he has a rental car.'

I suddenly start to feel as if I am Mary Magdalene, justifying to everyone that I have seen Jesus by the tomb.

'Of course he does. So let me get this straight: you're saying you got offered a lift to Paris? By Jesus? What was Jesus doing in Amsterdam? It doesn't strike me as his kind of place.'

'I don't know. That's not the point. Presumably he wouldn't have had the chance to visit Amsterdam all those years ago,' I mutter.

'Good point. Probably just on a trip with the lads. I can imagine Judas would have his stag do in Amsterdam.'

'Anyway, I called you just to let you know I'm somewhere near Antwerp at a service station with Jesus, in case anything happens to me.' I leave out the part about his outburst.

'What is going to happen? Pontius Pilate is going to come after you? You're with the Son of God, you should be pretty safe.' I can almost hear Jake rolling his eyes.

'Hilarious. Anyway, I've got to go, he's coming back from the service station café now.'

'Let me know if he turns his bottle of water into wine.'

I say goodbye to Doubting Thomas, as Jesus gets back in the car with a takeaway cup of coffee.

'Coffee . . . help me to *enfocar*,' he says, pointing at the coffee, smiling.

I look back, nonplussed.

'*Enfocar* . . . I don't know in English.' He's now the one consulting his phone for the translation. 'Focus?' He says, showing me the word.

And then I finally realize what he means. He hasn't been swearing. He hasn't been shouting at me. He is simply tired.

Enfocar *not fucker.*

He was shouting at himself to focus.

That makes more sense.

I hope that the coffee will indeed help him, as we still have a few hours to drive. Rather than being murdered by a lunatic, I now fear I'm going to die in a head-on collision.

He points to the stereo system, presumably hoping

that listening to some music will stop him from drifting off and sending us both to our deaths. He flicks through a selection of foreign radio stations before settling on a CD.

It turns out that Jesus can barely speak one word of English, yet he knows every lyric to Andrew Lloyd Webber's *Phantom of the Opera* by heart, so we spend the remaining journey duetting to the soundtrack. He insists on being the Phantom, so I am Christine Daaé. Jesus has an angelic voice.

As we sing along, I barely notice our approach into the French capital, not until I start seeing the iconic buildings and boulevards. We take our curtain call as he pulls up, in the centre of Paris, outside the Gare du Nord. Darkness has descended upon the City of Lights.

'Thank you so much for your help. It means so much,' I say, shaking his hand as I am halfway out of the door. I finish the movement with a big thumbs-up so that he understands.

'Please . . . I not God. I just Jesus,' he chuckles.

I decide that when I see the vicar at this year's Christmas service I should tell him I'm now ready to be confirmed.

30

I haven't shared a bunk bed since I was a child and I now remember the reason why. I'm lying underneath a man who has a flatulence problem and snores all night. The other bunk in the small room is occupied by two large, intimidating, tattooed men who come and go looking like they're going to kill me at any given time. Unsurprisingly, I don't get much sleep.

I call Jessie as I head out into the Parisian daylight, yawning. Despite the nagging voice in the back of my head which says Sunflower Girl is currently bungee jumping in Queenstown with her seven-foot-tall, male-model boyfriend, I'm feeling fairly buoyant. Third city lucky and all that. Plus, I have new friends in high places.

'I hear from Jake that you had an interesting journey.'

'Yes, what can I say? The Lord works in mysterious ways.'

'Oh God, he was right, you have lost it.'

'Please don't use the Lord's name in vain.'

I am unable to check the directions on my phone while speaking to Jessie and end up taking a much longer route across the city to the Left Bank, where the English bookshops are located. I smile to myself as I pass the impressive Palais Garnier, where Jesus's favourite phantom resided.

'Didn't you say there was a girl from Paris who got in touch? Maybe she's the one.'

'Yes, you're right. There was, I remember she emailed us rather than DM-ing, but I can't find her message any more, and I can't remember what she said her name was.'

'You're as bad as me, not knowing her name.'

'Sorry, I didn't think she was Sunflower Girl. We didn't think she could be living in Paris at that point. I'm sure I have the message somewhere.'

'What was the point in setting up this Instagram page if you're going to lose the messages?' I vent.

'I will find it, don't worry. What's your plan for today?'

'I'm sorry for being short. I'm just tired. I've got a few shops to check out this morning, so keep your fingers crossed for me.'

'I've got my fingers and toes crossed. I really think this could be it. Let me know as soon as you have any news.'

I stroll through the beautiful Jardin des Tuileries, past people resting in green deckchairs mimicking the carved statues lounging on their plinths, before crossing the bridge over the Seine. An entrepreneurial street seller optimistically offers me a love lock.

'I wish I had someone to give it to,' I say to him, apologetically.

He must have a good business model, as the railings of the bridge are adorned with hundreds of padlocks of all different shapes, sizes and colours. Initials are scribbled on in permanent marker, alongside declarations of love and heart symbols. I read that they had to remove the locks from the Pont des Arts further down the river due to the weight, but it doesn't seem to have stopped lovebirds finding a new location to cement their feelings. Rather than throwing the key into the river, maybe they should stick to using a combination lock in case their relationship ends badly.

In front of me I'm greeted by the Musée d'Orsay and a large poster adorned with *Sunflowers*, advertising the Van Gogh exhibition.

You again.

Is this painting the one?

I stop and read the poster. Sponsored by global banks and auditors, I notice the exhibition is only on for another two weeks before the painting will be returned to Philadelphia. Eager tourists, hoping to beat the queues later on, scurry inside. I walk on past the museum, alongside the river, browsing the postcards, pictures and books sold by the *bouquinistes*.

I head away from the river, planning to do a loop around the three bookshops I've earmarked, starting with San Francisco Books. I don't spend more than two minutes inside the tiny store marshalled by one grumpy Frenchman, and all of the other stores in this antique book quarter seem to be closed. The Abbey Bookshop is more welcoming, with a friendly man selling coffee outside from a flask. But it's clear why he's outside as, inside, the books are piled so high and wide that there is no way to squeeze through. She is definitely not hiding anywhere in there.

By the time I reach the yellow façade of the Shake-speare and Company bookstore opposite Notre-Dame, my feet are exhausted from all the walking. There is a hive of activity outside, with people sitting out, eating slices of quiche and cake at the adjoining café. Inside, the shop is packed, with tourists flowing in and out, many flouting the request for no photographs as they upload an artsy picture to Instagram. The shop is indeed extremely photogenic. It's beautiful. From the mosaic floor to the rustic chandelier swinging overhead to the quotes painted on the walls and stairs, the books look happy to be here. There is a warren of narrow passage-ways for customers to navigate, and a traffic jam is forming between the Blue Oyster Tearoom and the Old Smoky Reading Room. I squeeze through, taking the creaky red staircase leading to the first floor, and that's when I see it, painted in black type above the door frame.

'Be not inhospitable to strangers lest they be angels in disguise.'

I have a sudden flashback. Sunflower Girl had a pink badge on her bag with this very quote. Why didn't I remember this before?

This must be the place.

Surely.

With renewed hope, I bound around the first floor, desperately hoping to turn a corner and see her. I walk past someone typing away on a vintage typewriter and listen in to what appears to be a book club with a col-lection of people, all wearing cardigans, pretentiously debating the meaning of *Tristram Shandy*. I step into the dimly lit Piano Room, where a small chandelier with only two of the three bulbs working illuminates the old-fashioned piano in the alcove. A hastily handwritten sign in red felt-tip asks customers not to play after 7 p.m., as it wakes the cat. As I go to make my way back down the stairs, I catch sight of a mirror adorned with notes. People from all around the world have left messages written on scraps of paper, ticket stubs and postcards. I read one that says: 'Icarus didn't think things through, maybe you shouldn't either.'

I make my way through all the customers back to the front desk.

'Hi there.'

The man doesn't look up, engrossed in writing on a piece of A4 lined paper.

'*Bonjour*, hello?' I repeat.

'Yes, how can I help?'

He continues jotting away. I notice a box of identical pin badges to Sunflower Girl's for sale on the counter.

'Is there an English girl who works here? She's in her twenties, dark hair, pretty . . .'

He finally looks up.

'Can I ask who you are?'

I don't want to give this guy my whole story.

'Just a friend.'

'A friend of a mystery girl who may or may not work here, and whose name you don't know?' he says cynically.

'OK, yes, it sounds strange, but is there someone matching that description who works here? Is she here now somewhere?'

'No, she's not here now,' he continues unhelpfully.

'But she does work here, though? Can you please give her this and ask her to contact me?'

I hand him a note I prepared earlier with my number, a message and a quote taken from Van Gogh's letters: 'What would life be if we had no courage to attempt anything?'

He looks suspiciously back at me as he takes the note from my hand. I expect him to put it straight into the bin.

'I'll pass it on to her,' he says begrudgingly.

I thank him for his help and step out of the shop, back into the brightness and bustle. I start to stroll aimlessly across the bridge towards Notre-Dame, when my phone vibrates in my pocket.

'Meet in front of *Sunflowers* at 3 p.m.'

31

That was quick.

Butterflies swarm violently around my stomach as I read the message.

It's Jessie.

Why does Jessie want to meet in front of *Sunflowers*? Why is she coming to Paris? Why didn't she mention that on the phone earlier?

I reply, asking her what she means, but whether she's on the plane or she's ignoring me, I don't get any more information. I kill time sitting in a café, staring at my phone, waiting for a reply from Jessie and hoping for a message from Sunflower Girl. I wonder if the guy in the shop has passed on the note yet. I feel sick with nerves. I'm tempted to return to the shop, but as I look at my watch I realize I should probably head to the gallery. As soon as I approach the Musée d'Orsay, I realize Jessie's idea of meeting in front of *Sunflowers* is a bad one. Especially at 3 p.m. on a Saturday.

She might as well have said let's meet in the middle of Times Square on New Year's Eve. Even outside the peak tourist season, the queue to enter the gallery still stretches, snakes and bends around the building. Those eager tourists this morning were the sensible ones.

When I eventually make my way inside, I am immediately in awe of the impressive building. It is a converted train station with marble flooring and an ornate ceiling, but it is hard to believe that trains used to arrive and depart from here. Signs point me in the direction of the exhibition – *Sunflowers* are everywhere – and the ginormous gold clock above my head ticks down to our meeting time. Twenty minutes to go.

I head into the exhibition, browsing the works and reading the text. I'm soon surrounded by a group of visitors – red lanyards drape from their necks, and audio guides are glued to their ears like mobile phones. They stop and huddle around the same painting, until the voice in their ear instructs them to move on, and, like a herd, they hunt the next painting.

I walk on past the beautiful *Starry Night* and take a seat on the wooden bench parallel to *Sunflowers*, feeling like something of an expert on Van Gogh's works now. After staring at the shades of yellow for almost fifteen minutes, I sense the guard patrolling the room is starting to suspect me of something. I wonder whether I look more like someone who is planning an intricate art heist, or a nutter who is about to destroy an invaluable piece of art history. Probably the latter.

It is 3 p.m.

Where is she? Why is she not picking up her phone or replying to messages?

I tap my foot and fidget with my fingers. I turn around and, instead of her, I see a scrum of tourists forcing their way in, all fighting to get a photo. The exasperated guard's attempts to stop their photography doesn't put them off. It's like being at a concert at Wembley Stadium with all the flashing lights. They should give out an epilepsy warning.

An American man, who has managed to bypass the no-bags rule, shoves into me as he pushes past to take a close-up photo of the artwork on his DSLR camera. He doesn't stop to look, let alone appreciate, the painting for a second before he barges someone else out of the way to get a photo of the next one. Surely he could just download the images from Google? Next, a Scandinavian woman walks past, wearing a red beret, red lipstick and a Breton-striped T-shirt as if that is the official dress code for France. She stops to read the text beside the painting, nodding in agreement with whatever is written. Behind her, there is a large school group of French teenagers who, admittedly like me, appear not to be interested in any of Van Gogh's paintings apart from *Sunflowers*. A couple of the girls decide to pose for a selfie with the painting, sticking their tongues out as they do so. I look around, hoping that Jessie is going to spring out of nowhere and appear on the bench next to me.

Hurry up.

I try calling her again but get no response.

How long should I wait for?

As I stare at the painting of Van Gogh's bedroom, hanging next to *Sunflowers*, I notice that he painted two pillows side-by-side on his single bed. I wonder if he was still hoping to find someone to share his bed with.

I start to feel sorry for him that he never found love and hope that will not be the case for me.

'*Bonjour!*'

A hand pats me on my back. Finally.

I turn around.

It's her.

It's actually her.

At last.

Not Jessie.

But Sunflower Girl.

'*Bonjour,*' I say, unsure why we're speaking in French and completely shocked to see her.

I notice that in her hand she's holding the postcard of *Sunflowers* from the National Gallery.

'I've finally found it!'

And I've found you.

She leans in and gives me a hug.

'Sorry I'm late, the queue to get in was massive. I must say I am very disappointed you are not wearing your unicorn headband today.'

I just laugh. She's wearing the same yellow jacket she had on in London, the one I've hunted across Europe for.

'How? Who? Why?' I hope she can read my mind as I seem to have lost the capacity to speak.

'Your friend Jessie. I emailed her about a week ago after I saw you were looking for me on Instagram, and when I didn't hear back I thought that was it, you know. But she finally replied today and told me to meet you here. The power of the internet, right?'

Of course.

'So you saw the Instagram page?'

'Yes, well, one of my friends back home saw it, actually. I don't have Instagram or Facebook. Do you normally chase women around Europe?' She grins.

'Only from time to time,' I joke, somewhat embarrassed. I'm finally able to speak, although I'm still shaking.

'Van Gogh would be proud, but you do know it would have been a lot easier if you'd just asked for my number in London?'

'I was going to, but you vanished before I could ask!'

'I vanished? You disappeared when we were crossing the road! I thought you'd just had enough of me and run off.'

'No, not at all. I spent ages trying to find you again after we got separated. I walked to the finish line, I went back to Embankment, I went to the gallery, but I couldn't find you anywhere.'

'Same here. We must have just missed each other. I didn't think it would be that hard to find someone with a unicorn horn on their head, but you were nowhere to be seen. There were just so many people.'

'I know, it was crazy. Sorry I lost you.'

'No, don't be sorry. I was actually really surprised when I saw you were trying to find me. Pleasantly surprised.'

'So, you didn't think it was a bit weird?'

'Well, it was a little weird. No, I'm joking, it was very cute.'

'Cute?'

'OK, very romantic. Is that better?'

Our eyes meet. She really does have the most beautiful brown eyes.

'Yes, that's better.'

She looks up at the painting in front of us.

'At least we finally get to see the *Sunflowers* together. Well, kind of. It looks a bit different to the painting in the National.' She compares it to the postcard.

'This version is more like the Munich one, really, and then the painting in Amsterdam is similar to the one in London.'

'Look at you, a proper expert on Van Gogh now. I still can't believe you went to Amsterdam and Munich looking for me.'

'Nah, I just fancied a holiday really,' I joke.

'Of course, I'm not sure you can play it cool any more.' She smiles.

We both stand there, admiring the painting, taking in everything until we are disturbed by another tour group swarming into the dimly lit room.

'Shall we get out of here?' she suggests.

It's been less than ten minutes, but I'm already glad that I didn't give up my search. She is even more beautiful, funny and charismatic than I remember.

We exit the gallery, strolling past the long queue, which still stretches and loops around. I smile, watching an old woman who reminds me of Nan, dressed in a woolly hat and gloves, dancing in the street beside a busker who plays the French horn.

Presumably in France they just call it a horn.

'Do you want the best hot chocolate in the world?'

'That's some claim.'

'Trust me, you will love it. Chocolate is my one and only vice.'

We wander through the streets of the Left Bank, where people are sitting sipping coffee on the side of the road. You wouldn't sit next to the M25 enjoying a drink, but in Paris it looks fashionable.

'Their main store is on the other side of the river close to the Louvre, but it's always really busy, whereas this one you can just walk in. Much easier to get that necessary chocolate fix.'

We step inside Angelina's, a small but perfectly formed bakery selling an array of sweet delights. She orders and chats with the barista in fluent French and gets us two hot chocolates to take away.

'I'll get it,' I offer, reaching for my wallet.

'It's OK. I think you've spent enough coming to find me.'

I sip the warm, thick chocolate up through the black straw. It's delicious.

'Isn't this literally happiness in a cup?'

'It's so nice, I can see why you're addicted. When did you learn French?'

'Well, my mum is French. She was Mademoiselle Auclair before she met my dad in London, and they kind of brought me up as bilingual, although I wasn't really fluent before I moved here.'

I hold the door open for her as we head back out into the street.

'I've just realized I told a stranger my mother's maiden name. That probably wasn't very clever, was it? Please tell me you're not going to steal my fifty pounds of life savings now.'

'It's OK, just don't tell me what street you grew up on or the name of your first pet.'

'I will try my best not to. But yes, anyway, I was saying my French has got a lot better since I started working here. I'm working in the Shakespeare and Company bookshop, if you know it.'

'Yeah, I went there this morning, looking for you, actually. It's a really nice shop.'

'Isn't it? I love it so much. I was only planning on coming to Paris for a month or so after uni, but I found the shop, and I started as a Tumbleweed before they had a permanent job going, so I'm still here.'

'What is a Tumbleweed?'

'Ah, sorry, so basically you can live in the bookshop for free as long as you read a book a day, help out in the shop and write a single-page autobiography when you leave. They call them Tumbleweeds, like a person who blows from place to place, and they've been doing it for decades.'

'Wow, that's cool. So do you still live in the shop?'

'No, I moved out. It's awesome living there, but there's no privacy, so now they pay me I rent a flat near the Sorbonne.'

The streets seem to get narrower and narrower, which makes walking and talking more difficult, as we're separated by oncomers and are forced to walk in single file.

'Do you still have to read a book a day?'

'So I've actually got a confession.' She waits until a small woman walking a big dog navigates past us. 'You can't tell anyone this, but I've never actually finished a book, not even when I was a Tumbleweed.'

'What do you mean, you've never finished a book? How can you work in a bookshop and not have read a whole book?' I say.

'I do read. Lots. Don't get me wrong. I just don't finish them. I know it sounds stupid, and that's why I never tell anyone. I just think, why would I want to know the ending?'

'Why wouldn't you?'

'Do you not think it's sad to know what happens? I like staying with the character, in the universe of the book, and having that open-ended possibility of where it could lead.'

'So you don't know what happens to Romeo and Juliet, or Harry Potter, or Jay Gatsby?'

'Well, they're quite extreme examples, but generally I don't know how most books end, so don't ruin them for me, please.'

'I'm glad I'm no longer the weird one now.'

'You're still the weird one, Josh, don't worry.'

I've never met someone like her before.

A motorbike flashes around the corner, and we have to wait to be heard over the loud exhaust.

'I have to say, whoever was working this morning wasn't very friendly.'

'Oh, really? What did they look like?'

'He had kind of dark scruffy hair, quite short.' I indicate his height with my hand. 'He definitely didn't want to pass on my details to you.'

'OK, yeah, Tom. He's quite overprotective, but he's a really nice guy. He's leaving soon to carry on travelling. He's writing his profile for the Tumbleweed book at the moment so probably was annoyed you disturbed him. There are some amazing biographies and stories in there of people who came to Paris to find themselves, of romances played out in the shop.'

'What did you write for your page?'

'I'll show you sometime, if you'd like?'

'Yes, I'd love that.'

This is going well.

'So are you planning on carrying on working there for a while?'

'I don't know. I don't really have any concrete plans. I studied English at uni, so what does that lead to? I'd like to get a job at a publishing house one day but would love to travel first. What do I sound like?'

She undoes a metallic gate leading into an oasis of greenery with well-kept flowers. The cathedral of Notre-Dame looms in front of us from across the river, and the birds chirp loudly to compete with the car horns and sirens. As I look around I realize this park neighbours the bookshop.

'Well, this is the end of the tour for now, I'm afraid.

Although I can tell you that this is the oldest tree in Paris.' She points to a large locust tree, which is cordoned off and propped up by two concrete crutches.

'How do you know that?'

'There's a sign on the other side which says this is the oldest tree in Paris,' she laughs. 'Sorry our reunion has been a bit rushed, but I have about ten minutes before I start work, if you don't mind sitting with me?'

'Of course not.' We take a seat together on one of the benches, sand and gravel beneath our feet.

'Tell me more about yourself, anyway. I barely know anything about you apart from you being a stalker.' She's not going to drop this in a hurry.

'What would you like to know?'

'Do you know that game, where you have to say two truths and a lie?'

'OK, yes. Give me a second to think of something interesting.'

'Yes, I will be judging you,' she says as she sips her hot chocolate. Mine is long finished.

Three interesting statements about myself?

I flip a coin . . .

I can hear Jake's voice shouting at me to not mention that.

What interesting things have I done?

Nothing.

'OK, so I can play the piano, I came in the top ten students in the country at GCSE History and I have a rabbit called Jeremy.'

'Oh, this is tough. I'm not sure you're a rabbit kind of person. But then I'm not sure you're capable of coming in the top ten at GCSE,' she teases.

'Cheers!'

'I'm going to say that the rabbit is a lie, and if you can play the piano, I'm taking you into the shop right now so you can play for me. I've always thought it would be so romantic if someone could serenade you on the piano. I tried learning on the one in the shop but I only got as far as "Chopsticks".'

'Sorry to disappoint, but the lie was actually playing the piano. My grandad can play the piano really well, and it's always something I've wanted to learn. Even if it was just one impressive song, I don't know, "Hey Jude" maybe, or something by Beethoven, and I'd make sure I'd never play for the same person twice, or ever do encores.'

'Why don't you learn, then?'

'Maybe I will, just to keep you happy. Now it's your turn to give me three statements.'

The bells of Notre-Dame start chiming.

'Looks like I've been saved by the bell. Sorry, I've got to go.' I glance down at my watch. How can ten minutes have gone so quickly? 'But I will think of something for next time, and I want to hear about Jeremy the Rabbit too.'

Next time. Yes.

'When is next time?'

'I've got the day off tomorrow, if you want to hang out? Don't worry if you have other plans, though, or want to see the sights, or just want to do something else now you've seen me again.'

'No, I'd love to see you tomorrow.'

'OK, Sundays are the best day. I'll give you a proper tour around my favourite places. I've got a few things to do in the morning, but shall I meet you at 1 p.m.? And here's my number so we don't get separated again.' She scrawls it on a piece of paper torn from her diary as she speaks.

She gives me a kiss on the cheek as she heads towards the shop.

'Hang on,' I call out to her as she undoes the metal gate. 'I still don't know your name?'

She turns round and smiles.

'It's Lucy.'

32

'So it's not the nicest area, I'll admit, but it's cool, I promise,' Lucy tells me as we meet at the exit of the Porte de Clignancourt Métro station. She looks beautiful, dressed in a white T-shirt and denim dungarees, and I catch a subtle scent of her floral perfume as we hug.

Around us are branches of McDonald's and KFC, houses graffitied with tags and construction workers digging up the main road. It's busy, smelly and loud, and far from the postcard image of Paris that I'd been expecting. Still, I'm happy to be exploring it with her.

We walk along the busy road, past a petrol station, towards masses of makeshift stalls covered with tarpaulins. The stalls are selling clothes of every description. Scarves, hats, hoodies, shoes. In the space of thirty seconds I am offered an iPhone, a bottle of Dior perfume and a pair of Adidas trainers.

'Where are you taking me?' I ask.

We walk on past a game of the three-cup scam played on a cardboard box. I can't believe tourists still fall for this trick, but there are about half a dozen crowded around.

'You'll see in a minute.'

She flicks a strand of hair out of her eyes as she replies. Her hair is pulled back in a ponytail with a couple of loose wavy strands dancing in front of her eyes. Her multiple ear piercings glint in the sunlight.

'Don't worry, you'll like it,' she reassures me.

Just as she finishes her sentence, a group of men sprint past us, carrying large holdalls. Four police officers follow on foot, causing cars to screech to a halt as they run across the road trying to catch up. Presumably the men were selling more than fake Gucci handbags.

Couldn't we have just gone to the Louvre?

'OK, it's just down here. We're nearly there.'

We veer off the main road, away from the police sirens, and head down a narrow passageway. The path quickly opens up into the most wonderful flea market.

In front of us there are hundreds of open garages decorated with red moss and offering an array of goods – from toy cars, to jewellery, to matchboxes, to records, to arcade games.

'I feel like most flea markets now either just sell really touristy items or are always overpriced, but this one is a proper scavenger's paradise. There's always something cool to find. Literally everything in my flat is from here.'

She's right. There are no 'I love Paris' hoodies stocked here. Instead, many sellers seem to have simply emptied the contents of their pockets and bundled them onto a table – earphones entangled around ticket stubs, ripped magazines, single shoes in case you've lost one of your pair. I am not sure of the going price, or the use, for an empty printer cartridge, a broken water gun, or an amputee Barbie doll, but amidst the rubble of Christmas cracker gifts there are some treasures.

I decide to buy a couple of handcrafted Paris souvenirs to thank Jake and Jessie for their support. I haggle the seller down from ten euros to five, walking away as if I have just negotiated a multi-billion-pound company takeover.

Lucy browses a vast selection of china and cutlery, while on the adjoining stall I flick through a dozen or so loose scrapbook pages documenting a woman's travels to Madrid. Black-and-white photographs of her smiling in front of the landmarks, accompanied by travel stubs, hotel tags and handwritten notes. Why is someone selling this?

'These are really cool.' Lucy joins me in browsing the collection of old photos. 'I love things like this. I always want to know more about their lives.'

'Exactly who was she? What was she doing? Who was she visiting?'

'Who was taking the photos? Was it a romantic interest? Did it work out? We should track her down.'

'I think I've done my share of tracking random women down for this year.' We both laugh.

We meander around the maze of garages, stopping to point out items we both like, that we'd have in our imaginary houses, or maybe house, of the future, I think to myself. The antique furniture is an interior designer's dream.

'*Bonjour, chérie, comment vas-tu?*'

Lucy is greeted by a charismatic grey-haired Frenchman, whom she presumably knows, with a hug and kiss. His stall contains everything from buttons, to street numbers, to door handles. I feel slightly jealous as I watch them laughing and joking in French, wishing I could recall my GCSE vocabulary. They point at me, and I smile back, unaware of what is going on. She hands over some money and in exchange he gives her a book, which she swiftly puts in her bag.

'What did you buy?' I ask as Lucy rejoins me.

'I'll show you later. If you've finished looking around here, shall I take you to my other favourite place?'

I follow her as we catch the Métro across the city, laughing and joking as we go. I tell her about my family and friends, she tells me about hers: her parents, who work for the Foreign Office, her best friend, who has just moved to South Africa for six months. The interference of Jake and Jessie. We talk about our childhoods. How she would borrow mannerisms and phrases from obscure books to seem more interesting. We share anecdotes about university, comparing experiences in Cambridge and London. Caesarian Sunday and chunder charts. Her dissertation on 'Jack Kerouac and the Beat Generation', mine on 'The Impact of the Nine Years' War'. We discuss our favourite films, food and music. Whether red sauce or brown sauce. Which *Toy Story* film is the best. Her Kate Bush phase and her newfound love of Ed Sheeran. With every station we pass, I fall for her a bit more.

As we get off at Philippe Auguste station, I spot the Père Lachaise Cemetery ahead of us.

'So, first you nearly get me caught up in a major police raid, and now you're taking me to a cemetery. You really know how to impress, don't you?' I laugh. 'Isn't there quite a famous tower somewhere around here we should be seeing?'

'It was hardly a major police raid! You liked the market in the end, so don't give me that. And I think you'll like it here too. Is it weird that my favourite place to come is a cemetery?'

'I don't think so. OK, maybe it is just a little bit weird,' I say, smiling, echoing her own words to me from yesterday.

We enter the cemetery through a large stone gate, which is bordered by a very well-positioned shop selling headstones. We are joined by a dozen or so tourists all looking at their maps, and I'm surprised by how many other people are choosing to spend their Sunday afternoon browsing graves.

'They're all going to see Jim Morrison, which is ironic, as he may not even be dead.'

'Don't tell me you're into all those conspiracy theories,' I laugh.

'You know there was never an autopsy performed, so who knows? Maybe he is still out there somewhere.'

'Next you'll be saying Elvis is still alive.'

'He is.' She struggles to hold a straight face.

'Very funny. Are there many other famous people buried here?'

'There are loads: Oscar Wilde, Edith Piaf, Chopin, Molière, Proust, Gertrude Stein. I feel sorry for the normal people buried next to them who get trampled on all day. Let's go this way.' Lucy points to her right, as I'm about to follow a British couple. We go in the opposite direction to everyone else as we head off the concrete path. 'Be careful,' she says as I almost trip over a protruding tree root, hidden beneath a layer of leaves.

'It's a bit of a maze here, but I really enjoy just walking around, reading all the epitaphs, imagining what lives these people led. I know it's probably a little morbid, but coming here really does remind me just how short life is and that you have to make the most of it.'

'So you come here every week?'

'Yes, I try to. It's just such a nice escape from the city. There's meant to be over a million people buried here, so I've still got a lot of epitaphs to read. You get some which are really poignant, while others are quite funny. Look at this one, for example.' She points to one written in French, which she translates for me. 'I'm probably just a sucker for love, but I do like the romantic ones.'

I browse the different-shaped tombs, thinking about her words.

'Have you ever been in love?' I ask her, almost hesitantly.

'I was once, but it didn't work out.' She pauses, and I wonder if that is all she's going to say. 'I fell hard for this guy. We were going out for ages, almost two years, but he never wanted to put a label on it. He didn't seem sure he wanted to be with me, or really what he wanted for that matter. In the end, I decided I deserved someone who knew.'

'I'm sorry to hear that,' I say as we continue winding our way through the grounds.

'Aside from that, I've not really been in any long-term relationships, if that even counts. I think I spent too much time in the library at university, and I should probably stop taking guys to cemeteries, right? This is probably where I'm going wrong.'

'No, not at all, I'm pleased you've brought me here. It's really nice.'

'What about you? Have you been in love?'

I pause, deciding whether to tell her the truth about everything.

'Oh, come on. I've opened up to you.'

I decide to drop the bombshell.

'So I actually proposed to my girlfriend on New Year's Eve.'

'Oh, wow, OK.' She glances at my left hand to see if I'm wearing a ring.

'She said no and told me she was seeing someone else, and we were on the London Eye at the time. So, yeah, we were stuck together for the next half an hour, which wasn't ideal.'

Lucy bursts into laughter. It makes a stark contrast to everyone else's sympathy.

'You can't laugh at that.'

'I'm so sorry, I didn't mean to laugh, but come on, it would be quite funny, if it wasn't you.'

'Unfortunately, it was me, but yes, now I think about it, it is quite amusing.' I smile.

'Seriously, though, I'm sorry. It sounds crap. Oh gosh,

and there I was, within five minutes of meeting you, discussing Van Gogh's failed proposals. Why didn't you say anything to me?' she says as she puts her head in her hands.

'Believe it or not, I didn't think discussing my failed proposal was the best flirting technique.'

'But you thought telling me you were going to cut off your ear would work?' She laughs. 'Seriously, though, as they say, isn't it better to have loved and lost than never loved at all?'

'I don't know. I think I was just doing what I thought I should be doing rather than what I really wanted to do.'

Even in four years with Jade, I never felt the way I do right now after a few hours with Lucy.

We climb up the hill and find a bench to sit on. There is one free, its green paint peeling off, and from it we can see the beautiful cityscape of Paris. I now see why this is her favourite place in the city.

'So you asked me what I bought earlier,' Lucy says as she reaches into her handbag and pulls out the book she bought from the market seller.

'Yep. What book is it?'

'It's *Armance* by Stendhal. Have you heard of it?'

'Can't say I have.'

'Each week I buy a different French novel from the market and come here and read it in the afternoon. It's good for me to practise my French, and I'm trying to work my way through all the classics right now.'

'Just not the ending, though, right?'

'You still think that's strange, don't you? The book thing, the cemetery. I should probably just stop telling you all these things.'

'No, don't be silly. I'll admit I've never met anyone else quite like you.' She covers her eyes with her hands. 'But in a good way. I promise. I like that you're different. And I'm very honoured that you've brought me here to your favourite spot.'

'I suppose it's a bit like with all the people buried here. Why do you want to rush to the end? Once it's over, it's over. It's the same with a film, or a roller-coaster, or sex even. The ending may be great, it may be awful, but with all these things, it's the build-up, it's the journey, it's the ups and downs, it's the mystery, it's the unexpected twists, it's the surprises. Where is the fun in knowing how it's all going to play out? Why do you want to turn to the last page and ruin the surprise? I don't know, just ignore me, I'll stop talking now.'

She opens her book and starts reading the first page. 'Maybe you could translate it for me?'

Lucy sits in the sun, reading her new book out loud. Her dark hair swirls and curls down her back.

As the sun begins to set, we head back into the city centre, and I walk her back to her flat, peeking in from the doorway.

'Sorry, it's a bit of a mess. Some people grow plants, or beards. I seem to be growing piles of books. They're taking over,' she says as she looks over her shoulder. There are stacks of books all around the small studio apartment, as if she's playing multiple games of Jenga with paperbacks and preparing to open her own bookshop.

'When was your birthday?' I ask, noticing the line-up of celebratory cards decorating the top of her cupboard in the background.

'It's in May.'

'May? How come you've still got all your cards up? I thought it must have been last week.'

'No, I just always think it's sad to take down cards after a few days so I keep them up all year until my next birthday and then replace them with the new ones.'

My football-boot card from Mum and Dad has already been relegated to the bottom of my bag.

We carry on speaking on her doorstep, most of it nonsensical. I'm really thinking about whether or not I should kiss her.

'I've had such a perfect day,' she smiles.

'Yes, me too. It's been brilliant.'

I so want to kiss her, but I back out and go for a hug. As we let go of each other, we pause, our eyes staring into each other's, before I head into the illuminated Parisian night, kicking myself for not being braver.

33

'What on earth are you doing here?' I say as I open the hostel room door, not expecting to see either of them.

'We've come to get our money back.'

'Stop it, Jake.' Jessie pushes Jake out of the way to give me a hug. 'Sorry, Josh, ignore him. We've come to help you.'

'I can't believe you've come to Paris. Come on in.' I welcome them into the empty room, my dorm mates having left for the day. 'How long are you here for?'

'Don't worry, we're not going to crash your Parisian romance. I've got to be back for school tomorrow and, well, the hotel will probably burn down without Jake there so we're only here for the day. Your trip inspired us to do something crazy and the flights weren't that expensive, so here we are.'

'That's very kind, but you really didn't need to do that.'

'Josh, let's not joke. You need our help. We couldn't let you mess everything up now you've finally found her.'

'Thanks for the faith, guys!'

'Well, it's thanks to us that you found Sunflower Girl after all.'

'Lucy,' I correct Jake.

'Sorry, Lucy.'

'No, I know. Even if you went about it in the most devious of fashions, I'm very grateful for everything you did. I just can't believe you're here.' I worry that the security at this hostel is so bad that two strangers can walk into a dorm.

'I hope we haven't disturbed your plans?' Jessie asks.

'No. Not at all. I'm seeing Lucy tonight so was just going to plan something nice to do with her after she finishes work.'

'Sounds like perfect timing. then. You definitely need our help with planning that. We can make sure you remember your credit card for a start!' Jake teases as he takes his coat off and perches down on the bottom bunk.

How long can they go on about that for?

'Come on, then, what's this special something you're planning with Lucy?' Jessie asks eagerly.

'So I've got a few ideas. Shall we get out of here and go and talk them through?' I say, thinking of all the beautiful places we could be in Paris rather than standing in a dingy hostel room.

'Sounds good. Where shall we go?'

'I don't mind. It's your one day in Paris. You can pick!'

Thirty minutes later, we are sitting on the steps in front of the Sacré-Cœur, alongside hundreds of others, eating crêpes. We watch the stream of tourists flow past along the cobbled street in front, all stopping to get a photo of the impressive church. There is no need for a filter today with the bright blue skies overhead.

'Why don't we come to Paris more often? How nice is this? Just sitting outside, eating food, overlooking the city,' Jessie says in a rare break from interrogating me about Lucy.

'Just think, though. As soon as the quiz airs on TV we won't be able to do things like this any more. We will be constantly swamped with fans,' Jake replies.

''Course, Jake, that's definitely going to be a real problem for us. Savour your normal lifestyle now before you're constantly harassed for autographs and selfies.' Jessie and I laugh to ourselves.

In front of us, at the bottom of the stone steps, an Italian busker, armed with an acoustic guitar and a microphone stand, starts serenading the burgeoning crowd with his rendition of 'Volare'. The crowd laps it up, all swaying along.

'How's Jeremy, by the way? What have you done with him?' I say as the busker reaches the end of the song, and I take the last bite of my crêpe. The poor rabbit is being bundled from home to home.

'I thought you were kidding when you said he was a fussy eater. My God, I thought rabbits ate anything. Not this one. It's OK, Izzi and Bethan are looking after him today.'

Do I trust Jessie's housemates to look after Jeremy?

I lean to the side as a couple of policemen wearing berets and carrying guns attempt to walk up the steps, while a series of spectators head downwards to purchase a copy of the busker's CD. He knows how to work the crowd and seems to be making a fortune. He gets a particularly loud ovation as he alters the lyrics of 'No Woman, No Cry' to 'I remember when we used to sit on the steps of Sacré-Cœur'. Jake can't help himself from singing along.

'I still can't believe how sneaky you were, arranging that meet-up in front of *Sunflowers*. You know I thought I was meeting you?'

'Yes, I was quite proud of that, actually. I wished I'd seen your face when Lucy showed up. So is she as great as you remember?'

'Amazingly, yes. She's just so easy to talk to, and we really get along. I love how she's already done loads of cool things. She was telling me yesterday about swimming in the ocean with dolphins, and she wants to travel and see the world, and what have you.'

'You'd hate that. You can barely stand up in the shallow end of a swimming pool, let alone swim in an ocean.'

'Very funny. You get my point. We just really seem to click.'

'We can tell. Since you've found her you've barely been in touch.'

'I know, sorry. Mum has been calling non-stop today too, and I've not had a chance to call her back either.'

'No, I'm only joking. We are both so pleased you've found her and you're happy again, aren't we?' Jessie says, prodding Jake, who is more interested in his crêpe and the music than us.

'Oh, yeah. So when are we going to meet this mystery woman, then?' He springs to life.

'Soon. Hopefully. Don't even think about crashing my date tonight, though.'

'We promise we won't. You can check our plane tickets, if you don't believe us,' Jessie reassures me.

'When do you think you'll be coming back? Haven't you run out of money by now?'

'So I sold Jade's engagement ring yesterday,' I break the news to them.

'You sold it?'

'Yes, well, I had virtually run out of money after Amsterdam, and I'd brought the ring with me in case I'd need it . . .'

'In case you needed to propose to someone else?'

'Hilarious, Jake, no. If I needed more money urgently. And when I found Lucy, I decided the time was finally right, so I took it to a pawn shop. The cash should keep me going in my luxury hostel for a few more days at least.'

A caricaturist approaches us, asking if we would like a portrait drawn, and whilst Jake is keen, we decide it wouldn't be too flattering, considering we have Nutella smudged around our lips.

'Anyway, that's enough questions about me. I want to hear what you've both been up to over the last week.

Who was that man who answered your phone when I called you the other day? Mr Nobody?'

Jessie looks sheepish.

'Have you not heard? About the personal trainer?' Jake jumps in, excitedly.

'Of course, that's where I remember the voice from.' I have a sudden flashback of Adam standing over me while I struggled to complete one push-up. 'So are you two together, then? When did this happen?'

'I suppose so, yes.'

'Don't be coy. They've been going out since the start of the year.'

'What? Since before I started at the gym?'

'The one time you went to the gym!'

'I wasn't going to go back there after I got knocked out in that class. It was dangerous.'

'You spent more time choosing your workout play-list than actually working out!'

'Stop trying to change the subject. How have you managed to keep this all so quiet? And why didn't you tell me?'

'I guess when we started going out, it was just after you'd broken up with Jade, and I didn't want to make a big deal out of it. Especially with Jake flaunting his new relationship . . .'

'Oi, I wasn't flaunting it.'

'And then I just didn't want to jinx it after that. We're taking things very slow, and it's not really official yet, but yes, it's going well.' I have to lean in to hear her response now the busker has got everyone clapping

288

along to 'La Bamba'. He's performing as if he is head-lining Glastonbury.

'So the marathon? Did you only run it as an excuse to see Adam more often at the gym?'

'Well, I'm not going to lie. It did give me a bit more motivation to train.'

'I thought you were running it to raise money for those poor kids, but it was really just so you could spend more time with some ripped guy. Unbelievable,' I tease her. 'What about you, Jake? When are you pro-posing? I could have sold you my ring!'

'Not quite yet, but everything is so great. We're just really enjoying each other's company, and I don't know, is it crazy if I say I think he might be the one? Oh God, I sound like you now.'

'Look at us, all so happy.' Jessie, sitting in the mid-dle, reaches her arms out and hugs us both as we admire the Paris skyline, and the busker and hundreds of other tourists from across the world all sing along to 'Imagine'.

'It's crazy, isn't it? The things we do for love. I travel around Europe, Jessie runs a marathon, and you go vegan,' I say to Jake as he savours the last mouthful of his crêpe.

'Oh crap, don't tell Jake I had this. What happens in Paris stays in Paris, right?'

34

'Where are we going?'

'It's a surprise. You'll see soon,' I say, leading Lucy through the dark, lamplit streets of Paris. The yellow glow is reflected in the growing puddles on the cobbled stones. The earlier sunshine has been swiftly replaced by rain.

'Don't get too excited, though. I'm not taking you to a cemetery.'

'I'd hope not, now you've made me get so dressed up.'

I didn't think she could look any better, but amazingly she does. She's ditched her jeans for a black long-sleeve dress. Her beautiful dark eyes and full lips are accentuated with a hint of make-up. Elegant silver jewellery wraps around her neck and her wrists. Thankfully Jessie brought me some clean clothes out, so I look semi-presentable.

I protect her from the drizzle, holding an umbrella overhead, and take her hand as she stumbles in her high heels on the cobbles. She looks up at me and smiles as she entwines her jewelled fingers with mine.

'I was thinking this morning, why did your friend send you the Insta page about my search?' It suddenly struck me that this didn't make any sense.

'What do you mean?'

'You said the other day that your friend found the Instagram page. How would she know it was about you? Unless you'd told them about me?'

'Maybe I did. Maybe I wanted to find you too.' She blushes. 'Don't get too big-headed though, all right?'

'No, I'm pleased to hear you felt the same way.'

'The problem is, I didn't have anything to go on. I realized after we got separated that we only talked about me, and art. I don't think you told me anything about yourself, other than that Jessie was running the marathon. I did actually look up names of people who ran the marathon, but I couldn't find a link to you through any of them.'

'It's crazy, isn't it, that even when you know someone's name it's not easy to find them, let alone find someone whose name you don't know.'

'We managed to find each other eventually.' She clinches my hand. Her bracelet rubs against my skin.

It's hard to believe we've only spent a few days together. It feels like we've known each other for years.

My phone vibrates repeatedly in my pocket, but I don't want to be disturbed as we cross over the river to the Right Bank. Despite the rainy weather, the area is swarming with people strolling hand in hand. To our right, the carriages of the large Ferris wheel in the Tuileries Gardens peek out over the trees.

'Did you know that the first Ferris wheel was built for the World Fair in Chicago to try and top the

Eiffel Tower, which Paris had built for the previous World Fair?' This is one fact I do recall from our TV appearance.

'You're not taking me on the Ferris wheel, are you? Don't even think about proposing!' Lucy jokes.

'No, don't worry. I think I've had enough of Ferris wheels for a lifetime.' She massages my hand supportively.

'Come on, tell me where we're going. Or give me a clue at least.'

'You really want to spoil the surprise?'

'Yes! Tell me!'

'So I had a few options, and Jake and Jessie helped me with them.'

'I still can't believe they came to visit you. That's so nice. I wish they'd stayed so I could have met them too, though.'

'I'm sure you will get to meet them soon. So yeah, we whittled it down to two options, and then obviously I flipped the coin . . .'

'You flipped a coin to decide on our date? OK, interesting move.'

Why did I say that?

Maybe I should just tell her anyway? It was only Jake who said not to mention it.

'So yeah, there is something I should probably tell you, actually. It's a bit of a long story.'

'Go on,' she smiles at me as we carry on alongside the river path, behind a sea of umbrellas.

'Basically, since the start of the year, I've been carrying

a coin with me and I flip it to make decisions and I follow what it tells me to do.'

'Are you being serious? I can't tell if you're joking.'

'Yes, it was kind of like a New Year's Resolution. At
the time I just felt like I didn't know where I wanted
to go in my life, I wasn't sure what choices to make, I
wasn't happy with the choices I'd made already, so yeah,
I came up with this idea.'

'OK, so you flip a coin for every decision?'

'Well, it started off as every decision, and I mean literally every decision. I was flipping it to decide what
socks to wear, what to eat, what to watch, but as the
months have gone on, I normally only ask it a few questions each day, for bigger dilemmas.'

'And you've been doing it all year?' Lucy asks
curiously.

'Yes. I started a couple of days into the year, after
everything with Jade. My grandad was flipping a coin,
and the idea came to me. So here we are, however many
months later into my resolution, and I'm still going.'

'You get weirder and weirder, don't you?' she laughs
as we cuddle up underneath the umbrella.

We continue in silence along the riverbank, admiring how beautiful the city looks, even in the rain.

'Can I ask whether you flipped the coin to decide
whether you should come and find me?' she asks after a
while.

'Um, yes, I did. Good thing it said yes, right?' I laugh.

She doesn't say anything back, and I suddenly realize
how that sounded.

'Obviously I wanted to come and find you anyway. It was just my mum wanted to set me up with this girl, who is like an old family friend, and then after that I flipped the coin to see whether I should look for you.'

Lucy takes a moment to process my words. I can feel I'm making the situation worse, not better.

'So you flipped to decide between me and her?' She looks up at me, her tone switching swiftly from frivolous to serious.

'No, I don't mean it like that. That sounds bad.' I laugh nervously now. 'See, my mum always says I wanted to marry Elizabeth when I was a kid, and I went to her house, and she showed me the nude paintings she's done . . . and then after that I realized I liked you, so I flipped the coin . . . I'm not really explaining this very well.'

Stop talking, Josh.

She lets go of my hand.

'All I want to know is whether you would be here if the coin hadn't told you to come?'

'Well, I guess I don't know what I'd have done . . .' I bumble on.

'Josh, is this all just a game to you? Why does this keep happening to me?' she asks, looking up at the sky. I remember what she told me in the cemetery about the guy she loved who didn't know if he wanted to be with her.

'It's not been a game at all. Honestly.' I try to reach out and touch her arm, but she flinches away and moves out from underneath the umbrella. 'You're going to get wet.'

I don't know what to do, what to say. My mind goes blank. She scrunches up her face and shakes her head in disbelief.

'I'm sorry, but I think that maybe this has all been a big mistake. Like, I barely even know you, and we're here walking hand in hand around Paris, like we are destined to be together. Maybe I just got carried away with everything, again.'

'Please, can we just talk about this?'

'No, not right now, Josh. I really don't feel like talking. I'm sorry. Maybe it's not as bad as it sounds, but I just feel like an idiot right now.'

She can no longer look at me but rather blinks to stop her tears. I feel horrendous, and helpless.

'Can you just give me some time?' she asks quietly and turns around to walk off ahead of me, into the rain.

How have I fucked this up?

Josh, you idiot.

'I'm sorry, please come back. It's not like you think,' I shout after her as she side-steps through the crowds that are criss-crossing the river path.

I lower my umbrella and try to chase after her but I'm blocked by people walking side by side.

'Excuse me, *excusez-moi,*' I say, desperately trying to force my way past a family of four.

Masses of umbrellas obscure my path and my view. As I rub the rain from my eyes, I can no longer see Lucy. I veer in and out of people, desperately looking for her. It feels like losing her at the marathon all over again, but this time it's my fault.

As I try to overtake a couple, I don't see the bike coming down the slope onto the river path. And the cyclist doesn't see me either.

The next thing I know the bike crashes into me, and I fall, splayed out across the wet concrete floor. The coin and my phone tumble out of my pocket as I fall over, smashing down onto the ground as hard as me.

Crap.

I yelp out in pain. Thankfully, nothing feels like it's broken. A crowd gathers around to check that I'm OK, and the cyclist keeps apologizing, helping to lift me to my feet.

I reach down slowly to find the coin and then my phone, my ribs aching as I do so. As I pick up my phone I notice the screen is completely cracked.

My heart pauses briefly as I press the button on the phone to check that it's solely superficial damage. The string of messages and missed calls that I've been avoiding appear on the lock screen. They are all from Mum. I read the top text. It's short, and it's blunt. My heart now stops.

'Pap is in hospital. Come home now.'

35

I stagger away from the scene of the accident and return Mum's calls. She warns me that the prospects aren't looking good, and I need to get home as quickly as possible. There is no time to find Lucy, to make amends.

I leave Paris more quickly than the tears can drip from my face.

The journey is a blur. I grab my belongings, check out of the hostel and buy a ticket for the last flight out of Charles de Gaulle Airport. It's meant to be the busiest airport in France but at 10 p.m. it's almost empty. The cleaners are milling around, the shops are shutting. I'm sitting by a family of four, all wearing Mickey Mouse ears, the two young kids half-asleep. I didn't think I'd be following Jake and Jessie home on the next flight. When they asked how much longer I'd be staying for, I hoped it would be longer than a few hours.

'*Mesdames et messieurs . . .*' A muffled announcement is made over the tannoy in French, which I wait to be translated. The groans hint at what's about to come.

'Ladies and gentlemen, passengers on easyJet flight EZY6224 to Bristol, this service has been delayed by approximately forty-five minutes. Please check the monitors for updates on your flight's progress.'

No. No. No. Do they not realize I need to get home now?

I stand and pace up and down the terminal. An employee reaches up to pull down the metal shutters at the last shop open. I catch sight of an advert for duty-free Toblerone, which triggers a thousand memories. It was Pap's favourite chocolate, and he'd always have a supply hidden to the right of his armchair, which he'd secretly share with me, breaking me off a triangle when no one was looking.

My mind, like a VHS player, starts rewinding and replaying more grainy childhood moments. Joking around, playing crazy golf in Weston-super-Mare, inserting penny coins into the slot machines at Clevedon, looking for our lost football in the local park, our trousers stuck to the sweaty plastic seats at the County Cricket Ground, Pap jumping in the stream to rescue my mini fishing rod from floating away. The video pauses repeatedly on a freeze-frame of his face, smiling, laughing. I can't process the thought that I may never see that face again, never talk to him again. What hurts the most is knowing he will never see me make anything of myself.

'Excuse me, sorry, do you speak English?' I rush over to the woman closing up the shop.

'A little bit,' she replies, with the shutters now halfway down.

'I know you're closing, but is there any chance I could buy a Toblerone?'

'Sorry, we are closed,' she says curtly.

'Please? I've got the money here.' I hurriedly dig out a five-euro note from my pocket and shove it into her hands. 'It's for my grandad, he's in hospital, and I would like to give it to him when I go and visit him, that's where I'm flying to now . . .'

'OK, there you go.' I don't think she understands but wants to get on with closing up. She takes the money and passes me a bar.

With the Toblerone in my hand, I walk towards one of the electronic noticeboards, hoping for good news.

An hour delay.

How is it getting longer? Is the plane going backwards?

I take my phone out of my pocket to check if there's any more news from Mum. Nothing.

Is no news good news?

Or bad?

I contemplate ringing her but I don't want to disturb her, and I'm not sure I want to know the answer. Instead, I scroll down the list of recent calls, and click on Lucy's name. I want to apologize, I want to explain to her what's happened, where I've gone. But most of all, I just want to hear her voice. It goes straight to an automated answerphone message. Either she has her phone off or she's blocked my number. Either way, it's clear she doesn't want to speak to me.

Two hours later than scheduled, we eventually board the plane. The flight seems to last an eternity. There is heavy turbulence, and the plane ducks and dives, sending the air stewards flying. As I cling on to the armrests, I struggle to contain my emotions and my tears. The other passengers must think I really hate flying. Fortunately, most are fast asleep. I fidget and think the whole way until we land in Bristol, all of the events of the previous week racing through my head. The excitement in Munich, the despair in Amsterdam, the car journey with Jesus, the joy at finding Lucy, and now Pap.

I sprint from the plane through the long, winding terminal, fortunately having no trouble with Passport Control this time as I make my way out. At this time of night the officials seem more interested in watching the clock than looking at my passport. The woman barely glances at my photo before handing it back and waving me through.

I continue on, barging past the sleepy holidaymakers returning from an assortment of destinations. As I turn around the corner, I see the usual line-up of expectant faces and taxi drivers. I see an old man with grey hair, and although he bears no resemblance facially to Pap, when a little boy runs up to him I struggle to hold back the tears. I look away, to my right, at the other side of the hall, where the departures board stands, where I stood with Jake and Jessie almost a week ago. It seems like I have been gone far longer. So much has changed. Why did I ever think this would be a good idea? Why did I listen to what a coin said?

I exit through the same revolving doors that started all of this, and I walk out into the cool breeze of the starless night. I set my watch back one hour, wishing I could put it back one week.

I spot Mum's car parked up in the express drop-off car park. It's quiet at this time of night, with only a few cars around.

I bundle my backpack into the back seat and open the passenger side door. Mum immediately takes my hand. Her eyes are red and sore.

'I'm sorry, Josh . . .'

I don't really hear the rest.

I remember reading an article that claimed children witness over 12,000 deaths on television by the time they are just twelve years old.

We should be prepared for death when it happens.

Immune, even.

But seeing Bambi's mother die on screen is not the same as experiencing death for real. Not in the slightest.

I don't know what to say. We sit in silence for what seems an age, as the last of the holidaymakers drive off, leaving us completely alone. The car park is now desolate.

I don't cry, I don't know how to feel. I'm just in shock.

'I didn't want to have to text you, but you weren't picking up your phone,' Mum says, almost talking to herself now. 'I've been trying to call you all day.'

'I know, I'm sorry. I had my phone on silent and then I meant to call you back,' I lie. I realize that if there is any form of heaven, and if Pap can look down on us, the first thing he saw was me treating Lucy badly and now he's seeing me lying.

'It just all happened so quickly. Apparently, Pap has been ill . . . sorry, Pap was ill, for some time. Cancer . . . but he kept it to himself and didn't tell anyone,' she stoically explains.

I think back to the last few times when I saw Pap and wish I hadn't been so fixated on my own issues so that I could have seen his. I feel awful that I never called him back when he wanted to wish me a happy birthday. I missed my last chance to talk to him. That's it now. For ever.

'Are you OK, Josh? You're being very quiet. Tell me how you got on. How was your trip?' Mum asks, trying to change the subject and divert our attentions to something more cheerful. She doesn't realize that this is equally as raw.

'Yes, it was good, thanks,' I lie again.

I don't want to discuss everything that happened. I don't want to burden her with anything else, and I don't want to talk through it myself. Certainly not now. Not yet.

I feel guilty that, in spite of Pap dying, Lucy keeps popping into my head. I hate that I can't get her out of my mind when I should be thinking about him. It's as if the memories of her have been recorded over the VHS of Pap.

'Look who it is!' Mum excitedly shouts, interrupting my thoughts.

I'm not sure what I am missing. I can't see anyone.

'Who is it?' I ask, confused.

'It's Pap.'

Oh God. She's lost it.

If I thought I was struggling to cope, then I didn't even think about how she'd be feeling.

'What do you mean, it's Pap? Are you OK?'

'The pigeon, I think . . . I think Pap has come back as a pigeon,' she points at a haggard, fat pigeon hobbling along the tarmac beside the car, confused by the airport lights.

I don't say anything and allow her to continue.

'OK, I know it sounds a bit mad, but when I left the hospital, all of a sudden a pigeon came and landed by my car and just looked up at me. And now here he is again. He's following me.'

'This does sound a little bit mad, Mum,' I say, trying to sound compassionate.

'I phoned Graham when I was waiting for you, and he said that it could well be him. Apparently, you can change into any type of animal,' she replies, almost defending herself.

'If he's come back as a pigeon, does that mean he did something bad in his life? Surely that's a demotion from being a human?' I interrupt.

'Graham says that this may just be a holding animal, and he may transfer again, or a few times, before he finds another body he's comfortable in.' I'm sure Graham must have been thrilled to get a call at this time of the night about pigeons.

'What do you think he'd be?'

'Maybe a panda, or a polar bear?'

We sit in silence again, as Mum stares at this pigeon, and I think of Pap as a polar bear.

'What about you? What would you be?' I ask eventually.

'I'm not really sure, but me and your Nan have agreed

a sign so when either of us dies we'll be able to communicate and know if there's an afterlife or not.'

'What do you mean? Like switching the lights on and off at a certain time?'

'Obviously I can't tell you, silly, it's secret.'

If my knowledge of Christianity is limited to my one confirmation class, then my grasp of reincarnation is even smaller. Pap's not been dead for more than a few hours, and this haggard pigeon looks much older than one day old. I decide to leave it.

As we both stare at the pigeon, waiting for it to give us some mystical sign, or to stop cooing and speak to us, it is joined by a friend. The two swiftly fly onto the metal fence and they begin to do what I can only presume is the pigeon equivalent of making love. If it is indeed Pap, he doesn't seem to have wasted any time in finding a new partner.

'Don't tell Nan,' I say to Mum, holding her hand. 'Shall we go home now?'

She finally steers her gaze away from the pigeons.

'Yes. Can you see if there's a pound coin in the front there?' She points to the glove pocket in front of me.

'How long have you been here for?' I reply, sorting through the collection of CDs and sweet wrappers, looking for some change as she drives towards the electronic barriers.

'I don't know. I was probably waiting for you for about thirty minutes, and how long have we been . . .'

'Mum, did you not see the prices?'

She looks at the blue board next to the barrier, illuminated by a couple of spotlights.

Up to 10 minutes = £1
10-20 minutes = £3
20-40 minutes = £5
40-60 minutes = £20
1 hour-24 hours = £50

She winds down her window and stares at the ticket machine screen, which confirms the fee.

'Surely that must be a mistake,' she says.

'How much does it say?'

'It's fifty pounds! That can't be right!'

She looks at me, completely shocked.

Mum, who has managed to keep herself together while breaking the news of Pap's death to me, finally breaks down into a flood of tears. As I lean over to give her a hug, I start to cry too.

36

It is strange inviting people to the funeral of a person they already thought was dead.

As I call around the neighbourhood, everybody seems more surprised that Pap was still alive a week ago than shocked by the fact he is now no longer. A few people even think they have already attended his funeral. Mrs Biggs, for one, vigorously insists she remembers reading his obituary. So it seems a bit hollow when she follows this up by saying, 'He will be sorely missed.'

To be fair, it must be hard to keep track of whose funeral you've attended when they seem to happen on a weekly basis in the village. With the average age of Cadbury being approximately seventy-four, if there's one thing that Cadbury does well it is funerals. Aside from the WI market held in the parish hall, it is the perfect chance for locals to socialize and get free food. Many bring doggy bags to keep them going until the next one.

In contrast, I've never been to a funeral before. Mum decided I wasn't old enough to go to Uncle Edward's; I wasn't born when Dad's parents died; and we didn't even have a burial ceremony when my fish died. We simply flushed him down the toilet. Dad told me at the time that's what you do with goldfish.

I panic on the morning of the funeral when I realize I don't have a black suit to wear. Since getting back from Paris, everything has been hectic, and I've spent most of my time trying to write something to read at the service, or contact Lucy without success. In the end, Mum decides to pick up one of Pap's black suits when she goes to collect Nan. It feels extremely weird going to a funeral wearing the clothes of the man you are burying. It feels even worse considering Pap was about a foot shorter than me.

'He's not going to need it any more,' Mum says, which I can't argue with.

The black limousine picks us up at 1 p.m. It seems slight overkill, given the church is only a five-minute walk away and we can hear the church bells from our garden, but 'tradition is tradition', as Mum says when Dad argues we could save money and walk. As well as my first funeral, this is also my first time in a limo, but it's not in the circumstances I was hoping for. Dad is shuffling around on the leather seats, trying to get a better signal on his portable radio as he tunes into the BBC Bristol football commentary. He doesn't do earphones, as they 'don't stick in my ears', so we're all listening to it. He's got a tenner on City to win, and they're already trailing 1–0. He's in a bad mood today, caused by the fact that the funeral has clashed with the game and that they bought Pap's Christmas present last week and didn't keep the receipt.

Mum, meanwhile, is staring out of the window, tapping her forehead repeatedly, trying to spot the pigeon flying past. She is presumably expecting Pap to attend his own funeral. I feel if he does, he might be slightly disappointed. It almost seems cruel giving him a church service, considering he hated both the Church and people.

Nan, in complete shock, is dressed up as if she's going to Ascot on a jolly outing. Her hat is touching the roof of the car, and her smile is as wide as the limo. She is trying her best to hide her true emotions. She starts to cough and solves the problem by shoving a Werther's Original toffee in her mouth, which I fear is going to choke her.

I fidget with the printed A4 copy of my speech. My sweaty fingers stain the corners and crease it. As we take a bend, in front of us I catch sight of the hearse with Pap's coffin.

I look away, trying to pretend this isn't really happening.

'Are you OK?' I whisper to Nan.

'Yes, Josh. Aren't the flowers so beautiful? Mary has done a fantastic job . . .' Her voice stutters and shakes, and she quickly wipes away a tear before anyone can notice it.

'I'll just drop you off here, if that's OK, and then will come and collect you afterwards,' the chauffeur interrupts.

The journey really was only two and a half minutes long.

He pulls up outside the church, behind the parked hearse, letting us out before driving on to find somewhere else to park away from the double yellow lines, probably further away than our house. The church is quaint and traditional, and small enough that the congregation can hold hands around its circumference on Mothering Sunday. It's weird to think that two weeks ago I was exploring a cemetery with Lucy, and now here I am at a funeral.

As we undo the latch on the wooden gate and walk through the graveyard towards the church, I notice the fresh mound of earth piled in the corner. His headstone won't be ready for a few weeks, but there is a plot for Pap alongside the graves of other family members I never knew.

I take a deep breath in, and out.

This is the moment everything hits home, seeing the hole in the ground. I reach across and take hold of Nan's hand as we walk on, as much for my own benefit as for hers.

Despite barely knowing Pap, Madeline is positioned on the door, greeting everyone with service sheets. She's not only the self-elected village mayor but also apparently the church warden. A few stragglers are still stumbling in on walking sticks, and there is some commotion caused, unsurprisingly, by Beryl and Desmond.

'We can't get Beryl's wheelchair into the church,' Madeline explains in hushed tones as we watch Desmond repeatedly ram the chair into the stone step, getting more annoyed each time that it doesn't go over, jolting Beryl backwards and forwards.

'Is there no ramp?' Mum asks.

'No one can find it, and Beryl says she can't get out of the chair.' Madeline raises her eyebrows, as we all know there is absolutely nothing wrong with Beryl.

'Gary, go and ask the pall-bearers to help lift the wheelchair,' Mum tells Dad, who scurries off, still listening to the radio.

This is the last thing we need right now. The service is meant to be starting any moment, and I want everything to run smoothly for Mum, who has carefully organized it all, and most of all for Pap.

'How are you feeling, Beryl?' Nan makes the mistake of asking.

'Not good – I think I've got cancer now.'

Really?

Before she can self-diagnose any more, or I get annoyed with her for ruining the day, Dad comes back with all the pall-bearers and the hearse driver, ready to help lift her.

They carry her over the step into the church, and then – due to the old, uneven stone flooring – they decide to continue carrying her down the aisle as if she's in a sedan chair. I know it's the first funeral I've ever been to, but I am guessing they're not all like this.

As we follow behind, the organ recital starts up. Ninety-one-year-old Doris is playing 'Abide With Me'. It's both out of tune and out of time. As an accomplished organ player, Pap would be turning in his grave, if he had been buried already. I half expect Mum to have decorated the church interior with pigeon ephemera, but the only adjustment is a large framed photo of

Pap positioned at the front of the church so the congregation can remember whose funeral they are attending this week. It is one I took of him when we were all gathered in Cheddar Gorge to celebrate Nan and Pap's fiftieth wedding anniversary.

I struggle to hold back the tears.

I walk down the aisle, my trousers riding high above my ankles. I ignore the fact that I can barely move my arms or breathe. Amongst the many people I don't know, I do spot a few familiar faces. There is the ancient relative who gives me an out-of-date diary every Christmas, and another one who always gets my name wrong. Judging by their appearances, either of these two could be being buried this time next week. Geoff is awfully pale and looks almost as bad, presumably already anxious about the reception finger-food. Karen mouths, 'I'm sorry, Joshy,' to me from her seat on the far side of the pews. I'm beginning to think that's all she can say these days. The vicar is standing behind the lectern, checking his reading material, but I swear he turns away as soon as he catches my eye. I thought now that I am friends with Jesus, he might have changed his attitude. Clearly not.

As Nan circulates the church, thanking everyone for coming, I take my seat at the front next to Mum. She ducks her head and quietly says a prayer.

Uncle Peter and the children are sitting in the row behind. They are all wearing sunglasses, inside.

'How are you doing?' Peter asks, shaking my hand.

'Could be better,' I say.

'Tell your dad he owes me my winnings. I put money

on your pap on the sweepstakes at your engagement party thing, couldn't believe it when he died. That's fifty quid for me.'

In the corner of the church, Dad punches the air, presumably meaning City have equalized. He won't be so happy when he realizes he is set to lose his winnings immediately.

Why isn't everyone more upset?

Beryl is still complaining and moaning that her view isn't adequate, so the pall-bearers move her again until she has the best seat in the house and is now blocking my view. The three men from the funeral director's quickly remember why they prefer working with dead people. After a lot of heavy lifting, huffing and puffing, they head back outside to bring the coffin in.

When Doris's unique take on 'Abide With Me' reaches some sort of abrupt conclusion, Mum signals for the music to play. Madeline, done with her greeting duty, is now in charge of the stereo system.

As Nan joins us in the pew, and the hubbub of hushed voices pauses, Nat King Cole's 'Smile' begins to blare out from the stereo system. The vicar gestures for everyone to stand, and I half-expect Beryl to now rise from her wheelchair.

I listen to the lyrics and look at the photo of Pap, picturing his face winking at me. I think, ridiculously, of the Toblerone bar I never got to give to him. I can no longer hold back the tears, and my whole body starts to shake.

This is it. This really is it.

I don't want to say goodbye.

I keep anxiously turning around, waiting to see the coffin being carried in, but by the time we get to the end of the second verse I start to sense there may be something wrong. Everyone is looking around, but there is no movement. The song is only three minutes long. They'd better hurry up.

'Josh, can you go and check what's going on?' Mum turns to me and whispers, her eyes flowing with tears too.

I walk back down the aisle, trying my best to stay composed. As I step outside, back into the brisk, cool air, it takes me a moment to work out what has happened.

The hearse is no longer parked outside.

The pall-bearers are halfway down the road.

Running.

Chasing a tow truck.

A tow truck that has a hearse on the back.

The hearse that still has the coffin inside.

I've heard of brides doing a runner, but this must be the first time a dead man has run away from his own funeral. In the time it took for the funeral directors to assist Beryl, the overzealous clampers decided to tow the hearse parked on the yellow lines.

Amidst the sorrow, I can't help but follow the song's suggestion. I smile through the tears. And then burst out laughing.

Even to the end, Pap is still trying to escape people, social events and the Church.

I wave goodbye to the truck.

And to Pap.

37

'Not a bus but a . . .'

'Coach?'

'Yes! The famous bridge up the road.'

'Um, the Clifton Suspension Bridge?'

'Yeah, just the middle word.'

'Oh, suspension!'

'Yes! Um, oh, OK, this is what Josh is.'

'Old?'

'No, he is that, but how would you describe Josh when he plays games?'

'Competitive?'

'When he doesn't win. Not a good winner, but a something something,' Jake says hurriedly, waving his arms around helplessly, as the last sand grains drop from the egg timer.

'Oh . . . er –'

'Time's up! Stop!' I yell a couple of seconds before it actually is.

'How did you not get that?'

'What was the answer?'

'Bad loser.'

'Ahh, of course.'

'Thanks very much, guys. How many did you get?

Two? Or three?' I go to move their red counter around the board.

'Just two,' Jake says, counting the cards. 'That was rubbish.'

The sports round is not his forte.

The quiz is not on this week, as Little D is on holiday, so we've decided to convene in the pub to play board games instead. The smell of chips being cooked is making me hungry.

'If I'm such a bad loser, it's just as well we're going to win this, then, isn't it?' I say smugly as Jessie and I are running away with victory in Articulate against the two Jakes. Our position is greatly helped by the fact it takes the other Jake the entire duration of his turn to read the card and think of something to say. As much as they look totally loved up, this game could finally signal the end of their honeymoon phase.

'We're going to get another drink, but I have taken a photo of the board so you don't move the counters.'

'You really don't trust me, do you?'

'No,' Jake laughs as the two of them grab their wallets and head to the bar.

'What's the latest with Lucy?' Jessie turns to ask me as soon as we're alone.

'No news, really. I still haven't been able to contact her. She must have blocked my number.'

'I probably still have the email she sent us before, if you want to write to her.'

'I don't know. What am I meant to do if she doesn't

want to talk to me? I feel awful about everything that happened, but as far as she's concerned I only went to find her because of the coin and then I abandoned her when she found out.'

'You left for very valid reasons. When she realizes the truth, I'm sure she will understand.'

'But she said that everything was a mistake.'

'Don't be stupid, Josh. She was upset. Haven't you ever said anything in the heat of the moment you didn't mean? You have to prove to her it wasn't a mistake. You've finally found the girl of your dreams, please don't let her get away now.'

She picks up her glass of wine and sips it. 'What's the worst that can happen? It can't be as bad as what happened on the London Eye.'

This feels worse already.

'Maybe it was a daft idea all along. What am I going to do? Move to Paris with her? I've been offered a job here anyway.'

'Really? What's the job?'

'This was one I applied for a few months ago. They've only just got back now. It's for a recruitment company in the centre. It's a decent job. And I'd get a pension.'

'Congratulations! I'm pleased for you, it's about time someone offered you a job. I'm not sure I can see you sitting behind a desk doing a nine-to-five, though. It's not really very you, is it? Is that what you really want?'

'I guess I'll see. I don't have much other choice right now.'

'How's everything else?' Jessie asks.

'OK overall, thanks, I've just been spending most of my time with Nan, helping her sort through all of Pap's stuff, and making sure she's all right. I feel so sorry for her.'

'Is she doing OK?'

'Well, she says she is fine, but I think she's trying to pretend she's OK. She only gets annoyed that she doesn't have someone to open the jars of pickled onions.'

'I imagine it's just complete shock at this point. It must take ages to come to terms with everything. It's nice of you to help her sort through everything, though.'

'I'm glad I have. Nan was going to get rid of Pap's organ, so I stopped her doing that. And then, when we were going through his wardrobe, we found a suitcase he'd packed for the two of them with two bus tickets to Devon inside. He'd planned a surprise trip away for Nan. I wondered if he'd been inspired by my trip.'

'Josh! Come on, does that not make you wonder what you are waiting for? Look at how short life is. You don't know when it's going to end.'

I know Jessie is right, but I remain quiet.

'What about the coin? Are you still flipping it?'

'Yes. I did stop for a few days after Paris, and Pap, but even if it's just to prove to you and Jake I can actually see something through, I've got to see out the year, now I've got this far doing it.'

'You know, I'd much prefer you to prove it by seeing things through with Lucy, especially after seeing how happy she made you.' Jessie stares at me as I imagine she looks at her naughty school pupils.

I glance away and look up enviously at the two Jakes as they return with their pints, so happy together.

'OK, it's our turn, right? We only need to get four to win. We can do this,' I say.

'Yes, pass me the timer. I don't trust you doing it yourself.' Jake reaches over.

'What are we on?' Jessie asks as she picks up a bunch of cards ready to take her turn describing.

'Working life.'

'Not your specialist subject, Josh,' Jake jokes.

38

'Come on, I promise you'll have fun. And there will be loads of people you know.'

I should have realized immediately that this is the very reason I won't be having fun.

Jake, and the coin, thought it would be a good idea for me to come along to his work Christmas party to take my mind off everything. Yet within five minutes of arriving at Bristol Zoo, I've been asked by seven people what I am currently up to, and my mind instantly zooms back to everything.

Pap, Lucy, my disastrous life.

I really don't feel in the festive spirit.

I'm not sure if this is the exact moment when I realize that coming to the party is a bad idea, but my concerns are certainly confirmed when I almost break my teeth attempting to bite into the stale bread that accompanies the starter.

'God, did they cut this bread on Thursday?' Jake, sitting next to me, tries to rip it and then saw it with a knife and has no luck with either. We eat the chicken liver pâté on its own.

'How much did we pay for this meal? Forty pounds each, wasn't it?'

Despite the cost to hold the event here, you wouldn't

know that we're at the zoo. We don't even get to enter through the main entrance; instead, we make our way in through some side door armed with two hefty bouncers presumably expecting work parties to get out of hand. The only thing that gives it away is the hideous tiger-print carpet. For forty pounds, I was expecting to be served by the orangutans.

'Guess we'll have to go back to the drawing board for next year. I swear these Christmas parties are more trouble than they're worth. Everyone's only here for all the gossip anyway.'

'You better behave tonight then, manager, so they're not talking about you on Monday morning.'

'Don't worry. Jake wants me back by midnight. I am not going to be a party *animal* tonight. You're looking very smart, by the way,' he says, in a tone that conveys what I'm thinking.

I'm severely overdressed.

'The email you forwarded said very smart casual. I didn't know what that meant. Is that very smart? Very casual? How do you do *very* smart casual? Is that smart casual but with a bow tie?'

'I think everyone else just ignored the "very" part.'

I look around the room, and all the other men are dressed in jeans and blazers. One guy is wearing a Hawaiian shirt. There's probably about sixty or seventy people altogether with partners in tow, and I know a handful of faces dotted around the room, either from visits to see Jake or from working with them before they switched hotels.

'Did you hire the dinner suit just for this?'

'No, it's the same tux I wore to Jessie's party actually, albeit I had to have it dry-cleaned. See, you're not the only one who can reuse an outfit. Although judging by everyone else, you could have come in your dog onesie again and wouldn't have looked out of place.'

The DJ is the only other person in a suit. He is an overweight, heavily bearded kid of no more than twenty who looks like he is on day release from the local prison, but at least he's made an effort to scrub up. As he taps his feet along to another cheesy Christmas song, I check his ankle to see if he's wearing an electronic tag. His feet may be enjoying the music, but his face looks like he is as bored as everyone else. I question that DJs must be redundant now, given all he's done is press play on a Spotify playlist and will stand there for the rest of the night alongside a couple of multi coloured disco lights that you can buy from Poundland.

It's far too early for Christmas songs. Both in the evening, and in the year. It's only the start of November. As Jake's hotel and restaurant are always rammed during the festive period, they always celebrate outside of December. Last year, presumably to save money, they held the event in mid-January, but people complained they were well and truly over Christmas by then. This year they've moved it forward, which means that most people here have had two Christmas socials in less than ten months. I've had enough of one after ten minutes.

The waitress looks equally as miserable as she replaces

our uneaten rocks of bread with roast turkey. It's going to be a long few weeks for her. The meat is dry, and the whole plate is so salty that it's like seawater. HR Manager Cathleen makes some comment about it being a shame that so much food is being wasted, and that the kids in Africa could have it. Someone tells Cathleen to shut up.

While we wait for the inevitably disgusting dessert and make the most of the free booze instead, one of those fortune-telling fish that came out of someone's cracker is being passed around. Much more exciting than my set of nail clippers. It tells Jake he is fickle, Cathleen she is passionate, and IT man Harry that he is in love, which inevitably sparks spurious gossip across the table. When it eventually reaches me, it lies motionless in my palm.

'Um, what does it mean when it doesn't move?'

Anna, whom I used to annoy by leaving her to do all the courtesy calls when we worked together, reads off the scrap of paper.

'Apparently that means *the dead one.*'

Pretty fucking intelligent fish.

As the last person finishes their meal, the DJ invites everyone onto the dance floor. It takes a while for everyone to understand this, given he holds the microphone far too close to his lips, so that it sounds more like he's announcing a platform change for the 18.52 train to London Paddington. The mic crackles and fizzes and nearly deafens everyone with its high-pitched shrill. Even when we do realize what he says, we have to physically move all the tables and chairs to the side of the room to create a dance floor, which is littered with pulled crackers, colourful paper hats and dropped food, most likely deliberately discarded.

Forty pounds for this. Really?

He cranks up a playlist that includes Wham!, Dead or Alive, Rick Astley and Foreigner. All the middle-aged attendees sprint onto the dance floor, squashing Brussels sprouts into the carpet, slipping on stray carrots and sending roast potatoes flying. Everyone has had far too much to drink, having smuggled in their own booze wrapped up and disguised as Christmas presents. In the corner, I notice one woman flashing her chest at someone who is definitely not her husband. I wonder why everyone decides to go crazy once a year in front of people they're going to have to see every day.

Jake abandons me to join in with the growing conga line, leaving me to stand awkwardly on the side of the room, resting against the wall. I spot the maintenance man pinching a receptionist's bum as he goes to refill his drink.

Then I see her across the dance floor.

She notices me simultaneously, and our eyes meet. My heart skips a beat. It's the first time I've seen her since that night. I'm not sure whether I should go over to her, but she makes the decision and skips towards me. It's clear before she gets to me that she's had too much to drink. I remember how playful she'd get after a few glasses of wine.

'Hey, baby,' Jade says as she jumps up and leaves a

lingering kiss on my cheek, as if the last year hasn't happened. This is the woman who broke my heart, and the first thing she says to me after eleven months is 'Hey, baby.'

'What are you doing here? I didn't expect to see you,' I say.

I'm glad I wore my tuxedo after all. Show her what she's missing.

'Dad was invited to represent our hotel but couldn't come, so I'm here instead. He only let me know an hour ago, though, so I missed most of the meal.'

She looks amazing for someone who only just found out about the party. She's wearing a fancy red dress that I've not seen before, and her hair, more natural-coloured than last time I saw her, is tied up with a sparkling hair clip. Her lipstick matches her dress.

'Is George not here with you tonight?' I can't help myself.

'No, we broke up. He went back to his wife.'

I'd expect her to announce this sheepishly, but she shouts it over the music.

'I'm sorry,' I say, before realizing that I am apologizing that my ex's relationship with the man she cheated on me with, and subsequently left me for, didn't pan out successfully.

'How about you, anyway? Did you find this girl you were looking for?' She's now brushing her face up against mine to speak over the noise of the Weather Girls. I can smell the red wine on her breath. For someone who missed most of the meal, she's clearly managed to make the most of the free drinks.

'How did you know about that?' I reply, our eyes meeting again. Flashes of memories flood back.

She looks around the room, before eventually answering.

'I can't remember, I think I must have seen Jake's Instagram posts about it.'

'OK. Yes, I found her, but it didn't work out.' I feel embarrassed that I don't have something to provoke a little more jealousy.

'So we're both single, then?'

'I guess we are.'

The music is too loud for us to converse properly. I have to read her lips to understand what she is saying.

'Remember when we came here?' she shouts again.

'To the zoo? Yes, it was a fun day, wasn't it?'

We both look at each other. I think back to that date at the zoo, and the first time we slept together afterwards.

'Do you want to get out of here?' she asks, pointing her head towards the exit.

As Cathleen is lifted into the air and then painfully dropped on the floor in a clumsy recreation of the *Dirty Dancing* lift, I decide I can't endure watching her boogie to cheesy eighties hits any more. The coin tells me it's time to make my exit, so I leave Jake in his element and head outside with Jade, where we can hear each other without shouting.

'So how have you been?' she asks as we walk away from the confines of the zoo, the cool air bracing.

Is this really happening?

'Honestly, I've been better . . . Pap died.'

'I'm sorry, Josh.' She takes my hand. 'I know how close you two were.'

'And I'm not really sure what I'm doing workwise. I've finally been offered a job –'

'That's good, isn't it?'

'Yeah, I suppose so, but I'm not sure it's really what I want to do.'

I realize we're still holding hands.

'And then I thought I'd met someone else . . . but I mucked it up. And they're never going to want to see me again.'

'I'm sorry.'

'It's not your fault.'

A group of drunk students stagger past us.

'I'm sorry, as well, about what happened . . . you know, with us.' She stumbles over her words.

Even if it's just a drunken apology, it's nice to hear her say it.

'Why did you do it?'

'You know what, it sounds stupid now, but I think you were just too nice. Is that weird? I just think there needs to be a balance. Sometimes a girl likes a wanker.'

I've been a wanker for the whole year since you left me.

'So was George less nice, then?'

'He was a right dick,' she shouts as if we were still at the party, and I'm not a few centimetres away. 'I found out he was also sleeping with a receptionist at a hotel in London.'

'Sorry.'

Why do I keep apologizing?

'To be honest, after the excitement went we had nothing in common. I actually missed the stuff that me and you used to do together.'

'Really?'

As much due to routine as desire, we end up strolling back to Jade's flat. As she unlocks the door and I follow behind, I realize I didn't think I'd ever be back here.

'Can you get the bottle of wine from the kitchen? There is one opened,' she says as she kicks her shoes off and collapses onto the sofa.

I still remember where everything is kept, and despite neither of us needing more to drink, I grab two glasses with the bottle of Pinot.

I know Jake told me there would be people I knew at the party, but I didn't envisage my evening going like this.

'There's actually something else,' she says as I take a seat next to her.

She downs her glass and turns to face me.

'So ... I ... I'm sorry as well that I sabotaged your search for that girl. I don't know, I guess I was jealous,' she slurs.

'Wait. What? What do you mean? What did you do?'

She reaches for the wine and, rather than pouring another glass, she takes a swig from the bottle.

'Jade, what did you do?' I say in a serious voice.

'I may have sent a message to Jessie saying I was the girl and I didn't want you to find me. But come on, look how well it worked – you'd much prefer to be here right now with me than with that girl, wouldn't you?'

'You mean the message that said she was moving with her boyfriend? That was you?'

Of course. It all makes sense.

'And you knew what clothes I was wearing as you'd have seen photos of us at the marathon on Facebook.'

'Yes, it was quite clever, wasn't it?'

I look at Jade, unsure whether I should be furious or flattered. For the first time since we broke up, I feel sorry for her rather than for myself.

She takes my hand.

'Why did you do it?'

'Isn't it obvious? I've missed you, Josh.'

She leans over and snogs me, her tongue caressing mine. For thirty seconds, I don't taste the red wine, but rather I'm transported to a parallel universe where everything worked out differently, where different choices were made, where this is right. I run my hands through her hair, and down her back, holding her, intoxicated by her perfume.

That same scent that filled the London Eye.

She starts to unbutton my shirt.

What am I doing?

'Sorry, give me a minute,' I say as I lean away and retreat to the bathroom. I am not prepared for this.

'Sure. Be quick,' she winks.

I lock the bathroom door and stare at my reflection in the mirror. I used to look at this view of myself every day, and I consider whether my portrait has changed since the last time I was here.

Have I changed in the last year?

I slowly take the coin out of my pocket.

The coin I picked up after she broke my heart.

My heart is thumping, my head hurting.

Just say no, Josh, and get out of here.

It spirals up and lands in the palm of my hand.

I turn the coin over onto the back of my hand. Heads, I do this, tails, I don't.

I look down.

It's heads.

This is what I wanted, isn't it?

What about Lucy?

Best of three?

Heads. Again.

Just one night. For old time's sake. I'm never going to see Lucy again anyway.

I can't do this. Not after what Jade did to me.

Best of five?

Heads.

Heads.

Heads.

What are the chances?

I made a vow to abide by the coin. I've got to listen to it.

I pull open the bathroom door and walk through the lounge, where her red dress is now discarded on the floor. I enter the bedroom.

She is lying on the bed, completely naked.

39

My heart is racing. Am I really going to do this?

I hear the shop door opening, and the sound of her footsteps against the tiles as she makes her way across the ground floor below. I start playing as I hear the wooden floorboards of the narrow staircase creak. I have practised enough on Pap's old organ when I have been helping Nan sort through all his possessions, but it is different playing on a piano, especially this old rickety one. It is made even more difficult when my heart is thumping through my chest and my hands are sweaty.

I can't see her from my angle as I sit on the small piano stool tucked into the corner of the room, which is overrun with books piled everywhere. I don't know how she is going to react, or what she is going to say. I look up to see if I can see her approaching but I miss one of the keys and immediately have to look back at the piano again. I want to see her face.

Concentrate, Josh.

I glance over to my left again, and she is suddenly there, sitting on one of the Tumbleweed's makeshift beds. She's smiling and looking like she's doing her best not to cry. I desperately want to get up from the stool and embrace her but I carry on playing until the end of the song. The fairy lights hanging from the ceiling twinkle, the candles flicker, and the antique chandelier gleams, now with all three light bulbs restored.

As I play the final note, she gives me a standing ovation and, jokingly, shouts, 'Encore.'

'No more tonight, I'm afraid. I would, but apparently there's a curfew here at 10.07 p.m. The cat's bedtime, you see,' I say as I check my watch. 'Sorry for some of the notes.'

'That's OK, it was lovely. Really. I can't believe you actually learned to play.'

'I know I said I was going to learn a Beethoven piano concerto, but hopefully Ed Sheeran will do for now.'

'It was perfect.'

'Well, it was meant to be "Perfect",' I joke about the double meaning of the song title.

I didn't think I'd ever get to see her smile again.

I don't know whether to hug her or kiss her, but as I stand up, I stay rooted to the spot, my feet firm on the hexagonal terracotta tiles.

'How did you do all of this? How did you get in here?'

'Let's just say your latest Tumbleweed is a lot more friendly than the last one I spoke to. He's come to Paris himself looking for love, so he understood and helped me out. He's upstairs right now, with the cat. You told me you always lock up every Friday night, so I just hoped you hadn't changed your routine, otherwise I'd have been waiting all night to play this piano.'

'It's all incredibly thoughtful of you. As you can see, I really do appreciate it.' She takes a tissue out of her handbag and dabs her teary eyes.

'Look, I'm so sorry, Lucy, I'm sorry I didn't tell you about the coin, but I promise it's not how it sounds,' I stutter.

I try my best to compose myself. I am struggling to breathe.

'At the start of the year, I had absolutely no faith in my ability to make decisions. I was completely lost in life. I started tossing the coin, hoping it would solve all my problems and give me some direction. The truth is, I still don't know what I want to do with my life, or even where I want to do it, but from the very first moment I saw you, I knew I was certain about one thing. I hoped the coin might help me find myself, and in the process I found you.'

Unlike with Emma, or Olivia, I've not rehearsed anything.

I'd simply realized, as I stood in Jade's bathroom, that I missed Jade's flat more than I missed her. I realized that I'm grateful for the relationship we had, highs and lows, but that it was over. Most of all, I realized Lucy is the only girl I want to be with. I disobeyed the coin's decision for the first time, left Jade's immediately and travelled to Paris.

I pause, trying to think of what to say next.

'I didn't need the coin to tell me to voyage around Europe on a crazy hunt to find you, I did it . . . I did it because I couldn't imagine not seeing you again. I've probably made something like ten million decisions this year, but that was by far the best one. I had an amazing time with you and I only left Paris that night as my grandad was in hospital . . . he died.' I struggle to say it.

'Oh, Josh, I'm so sorry.'

'It's OK, but it made me think, as you said in the cemetery, life really is short. And thinking about the relationship my grandparents had, Pap's life wasn't great because of what he did or didn't do, it was great because he had someone special beside him the whole way. I don't know if we will work out. Maybe this will be something, maybe it will be nothing. But what I realized is, just as you don't need to know the end of books, I don't need to know how this story ends. I just want to spend more time with you and see what happens.'

Even I'm surprised by how that came out.

'So, yeah, that's it really,' I say, running out of steam and finally taking a breath. 'What do you say?' I ask, hopefully.

The shop is completely silent apart from the noise of Parisian traffic outside. It is probably only a few seconds, but it feels like an eternity waiting for Lucy to answer.

'What can I say to that?'

She is the one who now needs to pause to compose herself. She is unable to hold the tears back any longer. I am close to joining her.

'I'm so sorry about your grandad. I wish I'd known so I could have been there for you. I feel awful now about blocking your calls . . .' She takes a deep breath. 'But . . . I have to know – did you use the coin to pick between me and another girl?'

'No, of course not. I'm sorry that's how it sounded, it was never like that . . . since I met you, you're the only girl I've thought about. It was only when Mum –'

'Stop talking, Josh. I believe you. I'm sorry I didn't let you explain it at the time. I guess I was worried about being hurt again, and I just felt stupid for trusting you so quickly, for falling for you and for some idealized crazy romance, and I guess it made me think I didn't know you at all.'

'You do know me. What you've seen really is me. I promise this is all real but I agree, I would love to get to know you more, and for you to get to know me more.'

'I'd like that too,' she smiles.

I smile back, relieved.

As I go to hug her, her smile fades.

'But there's something else, Josh, that you don't know. The thing is, this is actually the last time I'm locking the shop up. I'm actually leaving Paris tomorrow. I'm moving back to London for a few weeks to spend Christmas with my family and then I'm going travelling.'

This can't be. Not after everything.

'Where are you going?' I say despairingly.

'Starting in Europe and seeing how far I get, really. No plan as such. I just want to see as much of the world as I can.'

'Do you know when you're going to be back?'

'Not for a while. I don't know – six months? A year, maybe? Probably whenever my money runs out.'

A year?

My big romantic gesture and hopes of a reunion are going up in flames.

We stand there in silence, contemplating everything.

'I don't really want to have to wait a year to see you again, to see if there's anything between us. I feel like we've already wasted enough time,' I say, boldly.

'What are you suggesting?'

'How would you feel about having a travel companion?'

'But what about your life? You can't just drop everything.'

'I can, and I want to. Pap actually left me a bit of money in his will, and I think he'd approve of me spending it on seeing the world, especially with you.'

I look at her, desperately hoping she will say yes. She looks down at the floor, thinking.

'I think the only fair thing would be to flip the coin – right, Josh? Isn't that how all of this works?' She smirks.

My expectant face morphs into a shocked one. I no longer like the odds of a coin toss. My heart is beating so rapidly it feels like I'm going to explode.

'Are you being serious?'

'Yes, go on, flip the coin. Heads . . . we head off into the sunset together. Tails, we say au revoir for now.'

I rub the coin, for luck, before tossing it into the air. It feels like it's moving in slow motion, somersaulting like an Olympic gymnast, rotating, twisting and taking an eternity to fall back to earth, into my outstretched palm.

I can barely bring myself to look at the verdict.

'Yes! It's heads!'

In a shop where thousands of romances have played out, there, in the middle of the first floor of Shakespeare and Company bookshop on the Left Bank of Paris, I finally kiss the most beautiful girl in the world.

Her soft lips brush delicately against mine, curious and tentative at first, and then suddenly more confident, more determined, more firm. She runs her fingers through my hair as I hold her tightly in my arms, not wanting to ever let her go. We pause for a second, so we can get our breath back. I wipe a warm tear from her cheek, we share a smile, and as the taste of her peppermint chapstick lingers in my mouth, I lean in again for more.

'I should have probably checked it was heads rather than just trusting you,' Lucy jokes in between kisses.

'What would have happened if it had been tails?'

'It was always going to be heads. I knew we were meant to be.'

'Very brave, trusting fate like that.'

'Says the person who has been trusting fate all year.'

'Maybe you should add a postscript to your Tumbleweed bio about your time in this shop now.'

We stand there hugging. Everything seems so natural. So right.

'Is this all a dream or did I just see a rabbit run across the room?' Lucy whispers into my ear.

'Where did he go?' I say as we let go of each other.

'Over in that corner, I think.'

I bend over and reach behind the stack of books she

is pointing to, picking the rabbit up from where he is hiding.

'There's someone I'd like you to meet.'

After leaving him at home for my last European adventure, I thought he deserved to come on this trip with me.

'Lucy, meet Jeremy. Jeremy, meet Lucy.'

'Wow, this is Jeremy. Pleasure to finally meet you. He's so cute,' she says as she strokes him. 'I wonder what he thinks about all this? Actually, maybe it's best we don't know. Imagine if he doesn't like me.' She laughs.

'Who wouldn't like you?'

'You say all the right things, don't you?'

'Not normally, no!' I laugh as she continues to stroke Jeremy. 'OK, that's enough. He's stealing all the attention away from me now. He wasn't the one who just expertly serenaded you on the piano.'

'Expertly? Come here, you.'

I put Jeremy back down on the floor, and she pulls me closer, kissing me again.

'So where are we going first on our travels?' I ask.

'I don't know yet, but we do have a few hours of my last night in Paris to enjoy.'

'Maybe we could go on that date I planned for us last time I was here?'

'Yes, I don't need you to flip a coin to make that decision. Let's go.'

Lucy, Jeremy and I lock up the shop and stroll alongside the illuminated Seine.

Winter

40

'You're much better suited to Lucy. Libra and Gemini are a very good combination,' Mum says as she takes the shop-bought Victoria sandwich out of its packaging. I'm on duty to make sure no one sees the manoeuvre. 'I always knew that Jade wasn't the one, as your stars weren't aligned.'

'It's a shame you didn't tell me that before, really,' I say, rolling my eyes, not that she's looking at me as she lifts off the top layer of the sponge and spoons some extra strawberry jam on, deliberately adding too much so it oozes over the sides.

'Josh, can you put the packaging into the bin?'

'Yep, sure.' I collect it from the kitchen counter and undo the cupboard door where the bin is kept.

'No, not that one. The bin at the back.'

With all the other preparations for today's big TV quiz screening, she managed to forget about baking a cake, so quickly drove to Tesco. I'm surprised she doesn't want me to shred the evidence and then burn it in an incinerator. She picks up a fork, starts bashing the edges of the cake until it looks more suitably home-made, slices it deliberately wonkily and places it on a large plate. Perfectly imperfect.

'I've got some vegan thing for the Jakes, too, in the

cupboard, if they want it. Have you checked if everyone is all right for drinks? We've got more in the utility room.'

As I come back into the kitchen armed with a new bottle of wine, Mum stops me in my tracks.

'Josh, you know we're going to miss you.'

'You mean now you're not going to have someone to help you dispose of cake boxes?'

'No, I'm serious. It's going to be so quiet and empty around the house without you.'

'I thought you'd have been glad to get rid of me again.'

'Of course not. I know you want to get away from here, but this is always your home whenever you want or need to come back. Your bedroom is always here for you.'

'If you stop Dad renting it out?'

'I'll make sure he doesn't,' she smiles.

'I'm sorry if I've been moody and miserable and probably a nuisance for most of the year.'

'Don't worry, we've been through it all before with you! I'm just happy that you seem happier now.'

'Yes, I am, thank you. Anyway, I'd better go and see if anyone wants another glass.'

Before the conversation gets too emotional, I walk into the dining room, where 'All I Want for Christmas' is booming out of the CD player, to see if anyone wants a refill. As ever, Mum has invited half of the village along, and all the women seem to have convened in here – Karen, Madeline, Beryl. Even Mrs O'Nion is here. Fortunately fully-clothed. I decide to quickly head into the lounge.

The bannister is decorated with Blu-Tack-ed Christmas cards, mostly from distant acquaintances who send inadvertently hilarious round-robin letters. I even received a card from Eva, who was delighted to hear I had found Lucy and has found love herself, via Instagram, with a fellow Sherlockian no less. The photo of her dressed up must have worked.

Christmas passed with the usual routine – the over-excitement, the hurried opening of presents, the overcooked turkey, the undercooked pudding, the feeling sick, the Queen's Speech, the snoring, the joke too far, the arguments. The only difference was that a framed photo of Pap took his usual seat at the dinner table. On the plus side, we even got our chocolate at the Christmas service – whether that was due to Jesus having had a word with the vicar, or him feeling sorry for us about the hearse incident.

Despite the cards, it looks more like Easter than Christmas, with a myriad of rabbit-related products dotted around the house. Mum has decided that after his life as a pigeon, and a short transition period as a flamingo, Pap is now a rabbit. And not just any rabbit, but Jeremy. I don't try to understand it. I'm just glad that it means she is happy to look after him while Lucy and I are away.

As I reach the end of the hallway, Geoff and Desmond are there talking about the football results. Geoff is avoiding the food totally this year, even with the protective covering Mum has placed over the sofas. I nearly bump into Dad, who is walking around looking like a bookie trackside at Aintree, trying to fleece everyone despite knowing the outcome of the quiz. He is offering a multitude of markets on the event – who will score the most points, how many points will each team score, who will win.

In the front room, Jake and Jake are canoodling on the floor by the TV, having secured their front-row seats for the viewing. Jessie and Adam are cuddled up on a sofa, and I wait for him to look away before I take a chocolate so he doesn't make me do a press-up to burn off those calories.

'Your nan has just been showing me how to shag,' Lucy says as I sit on the sofa next to her and Nan.

'What?' I exclaim, horrified.

'Yes, see, I've got to dance the man's role at shag dancing now I go with Jean instead of Pap . . .' Nan says.

Oh, shag dancing. Makes more sense.

I try to dismiss the thought of my nan showing my girlfriend how to shag.

'You should ask Jake to show you his Beyoncé dancing.'

'I've not heard of buoyancy dancing before. It sounds interesting,' Nan replies.

I don't correct her or try to explain who Beyoncé is. I'm surprised she's not already up and dancing in front of everyone.

I give Lucy a kiss on the lips. It's so nice to have her here, staying with us for the night before we head off on our travels tomorrow.

'Isn't your dad offering bets on how long you two will last?' Uncle Peter quips from the other side of the room. 'Will I be invited to another engagement party soon?'

I just roll my eyes.

Mum walks in with her faked home-made cake.

'Sorry, I think I overdid it with the jam. It looks a bit messy but hopefully it tastes all right.' I'm slightly scared by how convincing her acting is and feel guilty for colluding with her.

'No, it looks great,' everyone says in unison.

'Everyone, please help yourself to a slice. Has everyone got a drink? Are we all ready?' Mum says in an exasperated tone, as if she's exhausted from a mammoth undertaking.

She places the cake on the coffee table alongside the brand-new copy of my school's alumni magazine, which came through the post a fortnight or so ago, containing a mention of my upcoming TV appearance. They posted it too late if they thought I was going to donate my winnings to them.

'Josh, do you want to go and tell the others in the dining room it's going to be on in a minute? They need to come and get a seat.'

The way this has been built up, you'd think that we're about to watch our performance in a Steven Spielberg movie, not our brief appearance on a TV quiz show that has been sandwiched into the Christmas TV schedule of repeats and reruns.

After giving everyone their two-minute warning, I

collect my mobile from my bedroom. As I push the door open, and it bristles against the carpet beneath, there's a tiny part of me expecting to see Pap sitting inside, hiding from the crowd. I stare at my bed, in my mind playing through the moments we shared here nearly a year ago. It's still hard to comprehend that I won't see him again. He would have loved to watch me on TV.

While it may not be as sprawling or as famous as Père Lachaise, I took Lucy for a walk around the churchyard this morning to see his new headstone and to say goodbye to him before we start our adventure. It is thanks to him that everything panned out as it did. I wonder what he'd think about it all. About the year I've had. About my trip. About Lucy. I hope he'd be happy.

'Josh, are you coming to watch? It's on now.' I almost jump as Lucy surprises me, wrapping her arms around me.

'Yes, sorry, we can't miss my fifteen minutes of fame.'

As it is, the TV glitches just as I'm about to answer my one and only question. Dad worries that this throws his points betting out now and insists that all bets are void due to a technical hitch.

'Brazil, it's Brazil. Oh, come on, how did you not get that?' Uncle Peter yells out.

'It's much harder in the studio,' I reply, trying to concentrate on the TV and not the chitter-chatter of everyone in the room, all shouting out their answers.

'Is that what we actually look like?' Jessie leans across and asks.

'I don't think so.'

'Why do I sound so posh?' Jake says, concerned.

'That's your voice.'

'What was that face you just made?' Jake says back to me, as the camera zooms in for a close-up.

'Look at Jake, he's so relaxed,' Jessie laughs.

'I think I didn't want to come across as nervous, so I overcompensated,' Jake says, as on TV he poses as if he is lounging on a beach.

'Shhh, can we actually watch it?'

'I can't hear anything, put the volume up,' Mum calls out, forcing everyone to frantically search for the remote.

I look around, and Uncle Peter is on his phone, and Desmond is fast asleep.

'Oh God, don't look at Twitter,' Jake whispers across the room.

'Why? Are people tweeting about us?' Jessic asks nervously.

'Yes, there are loads of people tweeting. Oh wow.'

'What are they saying?'

'What kind of person tweets about contestants on a TV quiz show?'

'Umm, RedHead98 for one. He's called me a *speccy hipster twat*.'

'Pretty accurate description, to be honest.'

'This is brutal.'

'Are there any good ones?'

'I quite like this one. *Jake could lock me up anytime*, or there's another one – *Jake has the key to my heart hashtag hottie*.'

'Are they all about you?'

'Sorry, I just searched for Jake Unlock.'

'You're so vain.'

I don't think I want to know what my adoring fans are saying about me.

As the episode ends with a shot of the Quizlamic Extremists looking angry and frustrated, Jessie and I make our way out into the hall, while Jake rewinds the episode to watch his best bits again.

'Congratulations, Josh.'

'What, for getting one question right? You're the one who won it for us.'

'No, for seeing something through. Not going to lie, it's been the most absurd thing to see through, and there have been plenty of times when I wished you hadn't, but you've done it. You've kept your coin resolution for the whole year.'

I had wondered what Jessie was talking about until she mentioned the coin. With everything else, I'd almost forgotten about it. It has become second nature.

'I still have a few more days, but yes, I guess I have. Oh, and I have something else to show you. Wait there a second.'

I reappear from my bedroom, wearing a large coat with a top hat.

'Is this your new style the coin has picked?'

'No. Can you examine the top hat, please? There's nothing inside, is there?'

'No. What are you on about?'

'OK, and now if you look over there . . .' Jessie does

as she's told, 'then suddenly what do we have in the hat now?'

'Jeremy!' she exclaims. 'You've pulled a rabbit from a hat! Well done. You've finally learned a magic trick. How did you do that?'

'And I can play the piano, too. Well, I can play one song.'

'Yes, Lucy told me all about your big performance. She seems lovely. I'm so happy you found her and it worked out in the end.'

'I picked the *perfect table*?' I ask, joking about Jessie's analogy from the café.

Jessie smiles and bites her lip.

'Yes, definitely the perfect table, Josh.'

'And you and Adam, too, you both seem so happy, although I'm not sure how you are going to cope with going to Iceland together.'

'What do you mean? Why not?'

'Jessie, you wear a ski jacket every time I see you. You're going to be freezing there!'

'I will be fine. We're only going for five days. Not like you. How are you feeling about your big trip?'

'I honestly can't wait. I'm so excited to be spending the time with Lucy. I remember you and Pap both telling me at the start of the year that I'd know what I wanted when I found it. I will admit I was sceptical, but you were both right.'

'Like always!' She smiles.

'I'm still waiting to have that same epiphany moment

about my career, but hopefully I will come back with more of an idea of what I want to do.'

'I'm sure you will. Some things take a bit longer to figure out, but you'll get there . . . hopefully before you turn thirty.'

'How did I know that was coming?'

'Sorry, I couldn't resist.'

'To be honest, I've been more like a moody teenager, living back here, than someone nearing their thirties. I actually think Mum and Dad will be happy to have the place to themselves again.'

'I highly doubt that. You know we'll all miss you.'

'I just promised to call Nan every few days and keep her updated so she can follow our trip in her out-of-date atlas. And you know you can follow all my updates on Instagram with all the other thousands of people who for some reason want to keep following the story of me and Sunflower Girl.'

'You influencer! I will be expecting regular calls as well as Instagram updates. I've just realized, though, that this means you're going to miss my annual fancy-dress party.'

'I know. Have you decided what theme you're going with this year?'

'I was thinking maybe of doing a nineties theme.'

'What's Jake going to go as, then? Who's a famous dog from the nineties?'

'Beethoven?' Jake chips in as he joins us in the hall-way, having clearly already dusted off his dog onesie in anticipation. 'You better be back for my wedding.'

'Of course, I wouldn't miss it for the world. Have you decided where you're going to have the reception yet?'

'Maybe the hotel, now that we've moved up to thirty-fourth best in the city. One reviewer even said we were better than average. Can't complain about that.'

'Double congratulations! Seriously, I still can't believe you're getting married, though. This is all so crazy.'

'It is, isn't it?'

'What was it you said to me? That I wasn't old enough to be getting married? So you must be the old one now.'

'Shut it. I don't know, it just felt right, and Christmas seemed a perfect time to pop the question.' Jessie looks at Jake as if he has said the wrong thing.

'No, you're right,' I nod. 'It's perfect, and I'm glad Jake said yes. You're great together. And now we've permanently secured another J for our quiz team.'

Using Pap's inheritance, I paid Jake and Jessie back the money they lent me, so at least he has some cash to put towards the big day.

'Oh yeah, you're not going to be here to come to the quizzes for ages either. What are we going to do without you?'

'I'm sure you will cope,' I say. 'Now we've beaten those Quizlamic Extremists once, I'm sure you can do it every week. And just think about all the worldly knowledge I'll have when I'm back.'

'No, what will happen is there will be a question about somewhere you've visited and you'll remember you've been there but not remember the answer.'

'That's a good point, to be fair.'

'Are you going to join our team too?' Jake says, as Lucy joins us. The four of us are now huddled together.

'If you'll have me, now you're TV quiz champions.'

'We'd love to have you, although we will have to change our team name now our names don't all start with J.'

'Actually, I don't think I've told Josh yet,' she says, looking at me dramatically. 'On my birth certificate Lucy is my middle name. My real first name is Jenny.'

'What? Really?' We all look at each other shocked.

'No, not really. I'm only joking!'

We all stand in the hallway laughing.

41

'Can you believe that Keats was only twenty-five when he died? I'm older than him and I still don't know what I'm doing with my life.'

'But then Van Gogh was twenty-seven before he picked up a paintbrush for the first time, so we all work on different time zones,' Lucy reassures me.

I still don't know what I want to do, but at least I have a better idea of who I want to be.

We are in Rome for just a few days, the first stop on our global adventure. We don't have much of a plan of where we are going, or when, we are just going to see where we end up. Rome is one of the few places Lucy was adamant about visiting – a literary pilgrimage to the city that inspired Henry James, Louisa May Alcott, Charles Dickens and Samuel Taylor Coleridge. First on our to-do list is to compete with the feral cats to pay our respects to John Keats and Percy Bysshe Shelley, whose graves sit amidst the lush gardens of the Protestant Cemetery, before visiting their Memorial House beside the Spanish Steps.

'Did you know 1.5 million euros are collected from the Trevi Fountain every year? Amazing, isn't it?'

By the time night falls, we are sitting perched on the

side of the very same fountain, gelato cones shivering in our hands, underneath the white glare of the looming street lamps. It is biting cold, but when in Rome you have to eat gelato.

'How do you know all these random facts?' Lucy replies, concentrating intently on licking her cornet as a pink trail of ice cream starts to slowly drip and trickle past her turquoise nails.

'I'm just a genius, what can I say?' I joke, deciding not to reveal the truth about the events of that quiz, and of how that question kickstarted a million other choices for the coin. Since she's only seen me in action the once on TV, I'll let her continue to think I actually know some stuff.

She checks her phone, one-handed, to see if I'm correct. She clearly doesn't trust me.

'Yes, you're right, about four thousand euros a night, and apparently it's all given to charity. That's cool. Hmm, it says the fountain is made from the same material as the Colosseum . . . it spills about 2,824,800 cubic feet of water every day . . . and Pannini was the architect who completed it. There you go, some more facts for you to add to your repertoire.'

'I'm guessing it was not the same Panini who invented the toasted sandwich or the sticker book?'

She rolls her eyes, as a couple in the distance can be heard laughing at something else.

'That guy thought it was funny at least,' I say, which finally makes her giggle and her eyes squint.

'You're so stupid.' She playfully pushes me, and I

pretend to fall back into the water, only confirming her statement.

I doubt the area surrounding the Trevi Fountain is ever very quiet, but tonight the plaza is packed with Roman residents and foreign revellers alike, celebrating New Year's Eve. Fairy lights dangling in the sky twinkle exuberantly, knowing their annual run is coming to a close. Joining in the illuminated performance are the green neon signs of the United Colors of Benetton shop opposite, the blue siren of the police car monitoring proceedings, the white lights of mobile screens and the yellow camera flashbulbs.

With our backs to the majestic sculptured fountain, I take in the panorama. I look at the grand church opposite. It stands there rooted to the spot like a jealous, forgotten lover who used to be the attractive one until the fountain showed up. I gaze up at the flats that surround us − a Christmas tree peeps out of the window, trying to see what is going on. I imagine waking up to this view every morning but then think of having to contend with the constant noise and busyness.

I look across at the crowds, at the people bobbing up and down, making their way closer to the fountain through the sea of scarves and selfie sticks, ducking out of the way of other people's photos. A blonde woman in a pink wool jumper has no concerns about hogging the best position as she poses for pictures, firmly instructing her boyfriend on the exact camera angle. Two thirty-something Italian women, sitting with their Christmas sale shopping bags, celebrate with a bottle of Peroni and a cigarette. The smell of the tobacco wafts through the crowds, competing with the burning smell coming from the roast-chestnut stand. Of all the various accents and languages contributing to the hubbub, a middle-aged British couple loudly discuss the directions back to their hotel, drowning out the sound of the cascading water, as they look intently at their fold-up map, reminding me of Eva in Amsterdam. Everyone checks their watches as midnight looms closer.

I struggle to believe twelve months have passed since I was stuck in the London Eye capsule with Jade. What a difference a year can make.

'Do you know, I think it's been the best year of my life?' I say half to myself, and half to Lucy.

'What, having a proposal rejected, losing your job, moving back with your parents, your grandad dying – yeah, sounds a really fantastic year, I'm not sure how next year can possibly compete,' Lucy says, completely deadpan, with only the glint in her eye revealing her sarcasm.

I nearly spit out my pistachio-flavoured ice cream as I burst into laughter. I realize I should have sent out my own round-robin Christmas card with all these stories.

'And don't forget about me being knocked over by a cyclist, knocked out by a middle-aged woman and having to endure New Year's Eve in Rome with the most sarcastic person in the world,' I reply. 'No, seriously, even despite all those lows, I wouldn't change anything. I've learned so much about myself, and with the help of the coin I've ended it here in one of the best cities in the world with definitely the best girl in the world.' I wrap my arm around her and kiss her cheek.

More intrepid tourists pour out of the gelato, crêpe and pizza shops that surround the square, and which must be making a fortune this evening. The walls of the pizzeria are adorned with football flags and an oversized poster of Francesco Totti. Meanwhile, the man serving inside the gelateria gesticulates wildly with his hands as if he is an Italian caricature, pointing to the array of flavours ranging from limoncello, kiwi and peach to Bounty, KitKat and Snickers.

The boy sitting next to me, who has been allowed to stay up past his usual bedtime, is singing 'Johnny B. Goode', as if he is from a different generation, while his parents teach his sister how to toss the coin properly over her shoulder. It seems that lots of the other tourists need lessons, as coins fly from every direction and distance. It's almost dangerous to be sitting down here.

'So, are you going to throw a coin in, then?' I prompt Lucy, as a stray coin nearly lands on my head.

She fumbles through the change we got from the ice-cream seller, making sure not to contribute too much to the 4,000-euro-per-night fund.

'So, if we throw a coin in, it means we'll come back to Rome, right?'

'Apparently so, Sunflower.' The nickname seemed only natural.

'I'd love to come back here with you.' She smiles. 'But we've got lots of other places to explore first.'

'Of course.' We've both decided, wherever else we

go, we want to reach Tokyo to see the final *Sunflowers* painting in Van Gogh's collection. I may not, yet, be a globally famous, multi-millionaire entrepreneur who drives a Lamborghini, but at least I am ticking off one of my goals of travelling the world.

'Shall we do it together? Have you got a coin to throw in?' She offers me a rusty twenty-cent coin, but I've already got a coin out of my pocket.

'Yes, on the count of three. One, two, three.' I swing my right arm over my left shoulder. Just as I've watched my coin spiral up in the air countless times over the past year, it twists and twirls in the sky, only this time it lands behind me rather than back in my hand. As the coin dives into the basin of the fountain, joining thousands of others, which shimmer like swimming fish under the translucent water, I wrap my arms around Lucy and kiss her strawberry-gelato-flavoured lips. Our embrace is caught in the background of a hundred photographs.

'Hang on, was that *the* coin?' she asks, trying to spot it in the water, before looking at me, surprised, her dark eyes peeking out from underneath her green woolly hat.

I nod. She just smiles. As a pigeon flies past, we stand up and stroll away, hand in hand, leaving behind us the hordes of tourists, and the memories of the past year.

Fireworks explode above our heads, decorating the night's sky with myriad colours. At street level, two narrow, maze-like, gas-lit roads greet us.

'Let's go this way,' I say, confidently.

Acknowledgements

Writing a novel doesn't happen overnight, and there are plenty of people who have supported me throughout. I would like to say a massive thank you to you all. Special mentions to:

My family. Mum, who is always my first proofreader. Dad, who thinks he came up with most of the plot ideas. Nan, who believed in me from the very start. Pap, who really would slip me a tenner and a piece of Toblerone when no one was looking. Rebecca, who was my earliest writing collaborator. Tim, whom I can always count on for an honest opinion. Nana and Gramps, who told me to get a proper job 'with a pension and a paper tray' and inadvertently motivated me the most.

My friends. Jack Chesher and Josie Stay, for their inspiration, humour and real-life friendship. All the members, regular or fleeting, of 'The B Team' and 'Wolf Star' pub-quiz teams. Lisa Shvartc, for being there for all the highs and the lows. Josh Oware, whom everyone will think the main character is named after.

My English teachers at school, whose passion for their subject greatly influenced me. Mr and Mrs Conquest, Mr Earp, Mr Harris, Mr Lewis-Barned, Mrs Waite-Taylor, and, especially, Mr Plowden, who still owes me the Year 8 English Prize.

The team at Curtis Brown Creative for helping me

on my way. Chris Wakling, for his expert tuition. Simon Wroe, for his guidance. My fellow course mates, whose critiques, suggestions and encouragement truly shaped this book. Look out for much better novels from Tim Adler, Daniel Baker, Bella Dunnett, Brenda Eisenberg, Michael Goldberg, Sadiq Jaffery, Sarah Masarachia, Sophie O'Mahony, Michele Sagan, Chris Steer, Hilary Tailor, Claire Tulloh, Alex Wall and Margot Wilson.

Hardman & Swainson. My amazing agent Hannah Ferguson, for her belief, passion and support. She has guided me through the entire journey and turned my dream into a reality. Thérèse Coen, for bringing my novel to readers across the world. Nicole Etherington, for sending me lots of boring forms to fill out.

My editors. Rebecca Hilsdon in the UK and Tessa Woodward in the US, for having faith in the novel and for bringing their expertise to the editing stages and improving my writing. My thanks also to all their colleagues at Michael Joseph and William Morrow for their hard work behind the scenes. And likewise to all the other publishers around the world. It is amazing to think that these words will be read in different languages.

And finally, Lucas Moura, for *that* game against Ajax.